The
Messiah Caravan

Rick Hughes

Cover design by: John Bowen

Here lies the tale

HOMEFIRES BURNING

Plum was sat in the oak tree on the border of
Martha's cornfield when she first saw the devil. She
had been talking to her dead friend, Bo, telling him
she missed him and some other stuff as well. The devil was
walking the long grey road out of the city of New Sodom.
He carried with him no bags, no supplies, which was
suicide considering it was the dog days of summer, and his
vermillion suit was stained with sweat and piss. In the
stillness of the afternoon, Plum could hear the diabolical
hymn he was whistling a full mile away. She raised the
blunderbuss from her lap, drew a bead on him. He was a
big man.

'Bang,' she said.

She lowered the weapon and hung it from a branch by
its strap. As she charted his progression, she built a
cigarette, lit it, and returned the rusted tobacco tin
containing her makings to the pocket of her denim
dungarees. She blew a thin stream of smoke downwards
and tapped away the excess ash, which settled on her
boots like nuclear snow.

'Keep walking,' she said. 'Just keep walking.'

When he reached the point in the road intersecting

1

with the mud driveway of Martha's farm, he stopped, hesitated. Then he flapped his hands above his head as though pursued by something winged and immaterial.

'Just keep walking,' she said.

In that moment a black crow of ill omen broke through the canopy of the oak tree in a daredevil crash land and fled squawking upon finding Plum there. Her heart pounding in her ears, she turned back toward the scene to find the devil halfway up the approach to Martha's farmhouse. Martha, who was smoking a cigar on her porch swing, rose and hailed the visitor. Plum watched their subsequent muted interaction, watched as Martha gestured over the cornfields, watched as the devil turned and disappeared into the serried towers of green and gold.

Crushing her cigarette against the oak tree, she slung the blunderbuss over her shoulder, pulled the aviator goggles down over her eyes, and dismounted. At the foot of the tree lay a bindle sack tied to a ramrod, which she collected before setting off at a run through the cornfield, the golden crowns of the maize flashing above her in the sunlight.

She broke out of the cornfield into a clearing where an old-world Yankee school bus, the black and yellow kind, sat wheel-less on a set of cinder blocks. Basking on a big grey rock before it was her father, Cherry Blossom, naked as the day, his white skin whiter with the application of coconut milk, which sweetened the air around. He was gleaming ethereally in the sunlight, his arms thrown wide to the world like some porcelain Jesus, and in one hand he pinched a plastic margarita glass, the salted rim glittering in the sun.

'What is it, Plum?' he said.

'A guest, papa.'

He sat up. Plum raised a hand against the glare cast by his china skin.

'There's nothing scheduled.'

'No, papa.'

2

'Fetch me my robe.'

Plum fetched her father's silk dressing gown from inside the bus.

'Is that thing loaded?' he said, nodding to the blunderbuss hanging from her shoulder.

'Always.'

'Good girl.'

He threw back the last of his margarita and slung the glass to the red earth. Knotting his robe, he turned to face the cornfield. The snapping of grain heralded the devil's approach. Cherry took a deep breath and threw out his arms in greeting. When the devil cleared the cornfield— crazy-eyed and grunting like a hog—Cherry performed a low and elaborate bow. Rising, he fixed the devil with his watery, baby blues.

'Welcome, amour,' he said. 'How may I be of service?'

The devil's walrus moustache was twitching but he did not speak. He fidgeted on the spot from foot to foot and he had a hand down the front of his vermillion trousers. Cherry brushed off the discourtesy by swinging his long auburn hair away from his face in a flamboyant arc.

'And how will you be paying?'

Still the devil did not speak.

'Amour, the fruits of paradise are seldom free.'

The devil removed a thick yellow ring inset with a rock of obsidian from his right middle finger and tossed it to the dusty earth at Cherry's feet. Cherry retrieved it with a graceful sweep and held it up to catch the sunlight.

'My word, what a fine piece. Payment accepted. This way.'

Cherry gestured to the school bus and the devil approached but stopped at the entrance and waited for Cherry to enter first. The silk robe danced about his white feet as he ascended the steps. Cherry placed the ring on the dashboard and whistled, signalling to Plum its location with a finger. He then led the devil down the aisle of the bus to where the back seats had been removed and a mattress installed.

Plum hung around kicking the dirt awhile before entering the school bus and taking the driver's seat. She angled the rear-view mirror so that in it she could see her face, the purple birthmark staining her right ear like damson jam. In the background, she could see the white of the devil's ass, the tensing of the gluteus maximus as it drove home the phallus.

She shut her mind to her father's weeping and drew her feet up under her. Sitting with the blunderbuss across her lap, she removed her makings and rolled a cigarette. Her fingers were shaking. When she was done, she let the cigarette dangle from the corner of her mouth, the spittle drying it to her bottom lip. She left it unlit, picking up the blunderbuss instead and thumbing back the flintlock.

The devil started snorting like a wild horse. Cherry was silent now, the anguish locked behind his lips. The devil quickened his movements, his breath, then with his last almighty thrust gave an exorcismal roar and, bringing his ham fist down on the back of Cherry's skull, hollered once more.

The devil turned away as though inebriate, clutching the bus seats to brace himself. Cherry remained slumped ass-up on the mattress. Plum levelled the blunderbuss and anticipated the devil's approach in the rear-view mirror, saw the cocktail of jism and blood anointing his relaxing muscle as he fumbled with his breeches. The devil passed by without a look and snatched the ring off the dash as he alighted from the school bus.

'Hey!' said Plum.

The devil did not turn. Plum leapt from her seat and followed him out into the golden afternoon.

'That ring is ours now,' she called after him.

The devil stumbled on in his carnal stupor toward the sanctuary of the cornfield. Plum did not hesitate. She closed the gap between them. As he turned to face her, she shut her eyes and squeezed the trigger.

The muzzle flare burnt the inside of her eyelids scarlet and she felt the barrel explode on that calamity machine and blind she felt her whole body lift from the ground and oscillate through the air until finally the ground rose up to punch her in the back and steal the air from her lungs.

Sucking at the air, she scrabbled from the dusty earth. The kickback from the blunderbuss had launched her a clean ten feet from where she had stood and fired and yonder she could see the dismantled devil lying with his legs detached, his red blood pooling unto the vampiric earth.

Everything out of kilter, she took a single step before falling to her knees and upchucking a crude bile. Raising herself up once more, a long cord of yellow mucus suspended from her chin, she noticed the green eyes of the devil upon her. She turned and scrambled back to the school bus. Inside, she pulled the lever that drew the flimsy bi-folding doors to a close. The devil was clawing at the red earth, wrenching himself after the child, two lanes of blood smeared across the land in his wake.

Plum fumbled with her bindle, her hands shaking as she unknotted the sack. From within she unwrapped a gunpowder horn, which she decanted into the muzzleloader. Then, tearing a patch of cloth from her undershirt, she drove it home with the ramrod. Lastly, she took a handful of shot and dropped it into the barrel.

The devil was at the door. With a single strike, he put through a pane of glass and reached in, moaning like a zombie. Plum steadied herself against the floor of the bus, thumbed back the flintlock and fired. The blunderbuss gave its second terrible report. This time, however, with nowhere for her to go, the buttstock punched Plum hard in the gut. As she desperately tried to sip the air, black spots pocked her vision and she slipped from the waking world to one perfectly dark and silent.

*

Plum awoke to Martha clambering through the hole

blown out of the bi-folding doors. She kicked away the devil's disembodied arm and knelt next to Plum. Plum's head swam from the petroleum reek of the bazooka whiskey Martha manufactured and of which she perpetually smelt.

'Are you okay, child?' she said.

Plum nodded and Martha helped her to her feet. Martha looked her over, snapped open the clasps of her dungarees and raised her undershirt. A black and purple bruise was spreading up her side like storm clouds. Martha delicately pressed her cool fingers to her ribs. Plum winced and tears escaped from the corners of her eyes but she uttered no such cry.

'No breaks,' said Martha.

She wiped the tears from Plum's cheeks and kissed her face and helped her dungarees back on. That is when she spotted Cherry, bowed over on the mattress like a postulant.

'Run along,' said Martha, patting Plum on the rump.

Plum obliged and hobbled out into the slanting sunlight of evening. The headless torso of the devil blocked her path like some bloody boulder and she stepped over it, the weight of her foot drawing blood from the enormous shot holes. The cigarette still hung from her mouth and she fished a match from her pocket and brought it to life. It had dried to her lip so that it peeled off with a film of skin. Sitting cross-legged on the floor, she smoked and cried silently into her hand.

Sometime later, Martha led her father from the school bus. He was unsure on his feet and groped the air about him. Slipping from the final step, he stacked it on top of the devil's remains and rolled about thrashing and screaming among the blood and splintered bone. Martha knelt beside him.

'Hush now,' she said, placing her hand on his face.

Cherry stopped screaming and started to weep, still lying in the font of his infernal baptism.

'Why, Martha? Why is this happening?' he said.

'Why does anything happen,' said Martha, shaking her head.

Then, looking up at Plum, Martha said:

'He is blind. He cannot see.'

*

Martha returned after dark loaded up like a packhorse. She carried a rucksack in one hand and a jerry can in the other and strapped across her back was what appeared to be a bundle of Halloween decorations. The rucksack she tossed to Plum's feet.

'Food,' she said.

Plum was stroking her daddy's hair, who lay with his head in her lap, staring blindly at the sky.

'What's that?' she said, pointing to bundle.

Martha sought counsel with the dark horizon.

'The man you killed,' she said, 'he's the devil. He and his brother run New Sodom. When his brother Lucien learns of his death, he will not stop. He will crucify you both. I have exhumed my husband and son in the hope they mistake their charred bones for the bones of you and yours.'

Plum burst into tears.

'I'm sorry,' she said. 'I'm real sorry.'

Martha shook her head and, kneeling in the dirt, cupped Plum's chin in her palm, the decrepit bodies of her loved ones stretching outwards across her back like the rotten wings of some fallen angel.

'None of this is your fault, child,' she said.

Rummaging in her pocket, Martha retrieved a knife and cut the bodies down off her back. She then parcelled out a piece of the strapping and cut it and tied one end to Cherry's wrist and handed the other end to the child.

'Take the old canal,' she said. 'It will lead you to New Gomorrah. This devil has no influence there.'

'What are you going to do?' said Plum.

'I'll figure something out.'

Martha pulled Plum to her feet and patted the red earth from her clothes and handed her the rucksack. Plum swung it on her back and then bent to collect her blunderbuss and bindle.

'I'm afraid they have to stay,' said Martha.

Plum complied without a word. She stood up straight and looked Martha in her cool, grey eyes. Martha shook her head and pulled her into a long embrace.

'Good luck, little one,' she said. 'Go now.'

Martha let go of her and, hoisting up the corpses, ascended into the school bus. Plum watched her go and then tugged on her daddy's leash for him to follow. Weeping, he loped after her into the warm night. Something glinted in the moonlight and Plum knelt to receive from the earth what just so happened to be the devil's ring with its obsidian centrepiece.

They scrambled the two of them through the bush and rolled down a rise and came to a rest by the old canal. Plum was quick to her feet and gave her father no time to sit with his despair. She yanked the tether and he complied, hobbling behind her.

After a while, a concert of fire could be heard through the trees and she looked back to see the tongue of a great bonfire lashing above the canopy.

'What's happening?' said her father.

'Martha's burning our house down,' she said.

'I see,' he said. 'I see,' he said again, breaking into deranged laughter.

A huge explosion startled her father into silence. Plum turned and watched the dark cloud mushrooming above the treeline, signalling the final destruction of her childhood home. Flaming rubber and metal burned through the air, falling like industrial hail, extinguishing in the black water.

'Let's go,' said Plum.

With that, they tramped on together, the canal stretching out before them, duplicating the night sky.

MARTHA TELLS A STORY

Martha dropped the part-decomposed bodies of her husband and son in the aisle of the school bus. She attributed them no ceremony; this was no new goodbye. Outside, she gathered the smaller pieces of the devil and laid them on top of his truncated torso. Her face was set; her hands not shy of the remains. It was as though she was engaged in nothing more than putting together a jigsaw. Back at the house, her hounds bayed for the meat as she worked by lantern light, by moonlight, stacking hunks of miscellaneous gore, forming a bizarre human pyramid whereby the man became his own monument. She combed the earth outwards from the bus towards the cornfield until the size of the offal diminished to morsels and then to nothing at all. She then transposed the accumulation into the bus along with the instruments that wrought his destruction. She alighted once more and collected the jerry can. Twisting off the cap, she hoisted it to her lips and took several sips of the clear fluid before sloshing a trail up to the bus, making sure to cover the devil's bloody tracks. She then doused the interior, leaving the jerry can sat in a puddle of its contents. Palming her lighter, she stepped out of her clothes, which by now were covered in blood and reeked of the alcoholic contents of the jerry can, and alighted the school bus a final time, her naked body flashing like volcano glass in the light of the silver moon. The wind was on the rise and the cornfield sang as she kindled the lighter and touched it to the pool of alcohol. An innocuous blue flame raced along the red earth towards the yellow school bus and the bus was afire in an instant. Martha slipped into the cornfield, the light of the fire dissecting its way through the crops and imprinting a motley of moving shapes on her back. The light diminished with distance. Before long, she was navigating the familiar field by instinct, by heart. When the petrol tank blew, it threw her forwards, but she managed to keep her footing. Looking up, flaming wreckage drew tracers across the sky and reminded her of the day as a child when she had witnessed the satellites of the old world falling from the heavens. In her reverie, she did not see the huge section of school bus roof that squared out the stars and walloped down like a huge wobble board not a metre from her, flattening the maize and sending out a rush of air that blew her feet out from under her. She was but a moment on her hands and knees before clambering to her feet and loping on.

Back at the house, she heated pans of water on the stove and drew a bath. She did not even half-fill the galvanized bathtub; however, muscular as she was, when she lowered herself into it, it still overflowed. The steaming water bubbled up sanguine as she scrubbed herself all over with the soap and the hounds sniffed around, licking up the water, the mud, the blood. She emerged dripping from the tub and massaged her white afro with a towel. Cleansed, she retired to the bedroom and returned dressed in jeans and a flannel shirt. The bath was drained and it too cleaned. The floors were mopped.

When the devil's brother arrived in his Rolls Royce, Martha was sat on her porch swing smoking a cigar by lantern light, a jam jar of crystal-clear moonshine on the table beside her. The Rolls was an old English white with a gaudy golden grill. Martha raised a hand against the glare of the headlights. The car stopped and two figures emerged from the front seats. The passenger hastened to open the rear door, but before he could, the door swung open and out stepped the devil's brother. He was the devil's duplicate, though a to-scale model, as though he had shrunk in the wash, and his face was softer, pudgier, his lip hair too thin to warrant the moustache. He approached the house and Martha rose.

'Hello, Martha,' he said.

'Lucien.'

'I'm looking for my brother. I hear he come by this way.'

'Yeah. I seen him.'

She nodded at the column of white smoke in the distance. Lucien turned, hesitated. Then, as though in a trance, he wandered off in the direction of the smouldering ruins. The driver, a rakish woman in a black suit and stetson, rounded the car and indicated Martha to the lackey who had failed to get the car door.

'Watch her,' she said.

'Yes ma'am,' said the lackey.

The driver disappeared into the cornfield. Martha turned to the lackey and fixed him with her cold, grey eyes. His eyes—soft and blue—betrayed his innocence, undid the cutthroat image he had so carefully constructed with his shaved head and tattooed face. Under Martha's stare, he could not help but turn away.

'You heard her. Look at me,' she said.

But he was unable to and instead regarded her from his periphery. Martha leant on the pine balustrade of her porch and smoked, the structure creaking beneath the enormity of her. The limitless night rotated above them. Then all of a sudden, across the cornfield, Lucien keened banshee-like, turning the head of the lackey. When he looked back, Martha was gone and the door to the house ajar. He ran up the steps but Martha's hounds started barking and he hesitated. Lucien appeared with the driver in tow.

'Where is she?' shouted the driver.

'Inside,' said the lackey.

Lucien stamped up the boards, drawing his revolver.

'Careful, sir,' he said. 'She's holed up with her dogs.'

Lucien placed the barrel of his revolver to the feeble flesh above the heart of the lackey. A look of comprehension, of terror, and then a cone of destruction ran through him, exploding the lackey's heart. He dropped to the boards. Lucien did not hesitate. He pushed through the door, his revolver raised. Martha was there to greet him, sitting at the kitchen table, moonshine in one hand, cigar in the other. The lantern before her cast fiendish shadows on the wall behind. The dogs barked from the next room, scraping their claws down the closed door.

'Quiet down!' yelled Martha, and the hounds fell back whimpering.

Lucien was seething. The gun shook in his hand. Martha held his eye. Neither blinked. Then he slammed his revolver on the table and drew out the chair facing Martha. He breathed heavily through his nose and his eyes bulged in their sockets.

'Table your guns,' he said.

Martha raised her hands in a show of peace, of surrender. Lucien half turned to his driver and nodded his head in Martha's direction and the driver rounded the table and patted her down. Unconvinced, she passed her hand under the table and then checked the cupboards and drawers immediately behind her. She nodded to Lucien and he told her to leave. She tipped the front of her stetson and slipped out into the night.

'Talk,' he said.

Through the window, the smoke that bore the devil skyward obscured the moon, creating a silver haze.

'My guess,' she said, 'your brother tried to take without

paying. That little girl would nary stand for it. She fires that blunderbuss of hers, hits the fuel tank...'

She shrugged and opened her clenched fist, splaying her fingers.

'Bang.'

'Is that so? Then tell me, Martha, why would a bus with no wheels have a tank full of gas?'

'Same reason I keep my money in my mattress. Cherry was a rich man, Lucien.'

Lucien leaned back in his chair and regarded Martha. He drummed his fingers on the table.

'I ought to kill you,' he said.

Martha shrugged. Lucien continued to drum his fingers.

'How do you think this will reflect on me, huh? He was my brother. Someone needs to pay for this.'

Still nothing.

'Fuck it. I need a drink,' he said, rising from his chair.

'There's shine in that cupboard there. Some rye too if you want something altogether more agreeable.'

He returned with a jar of what Martha was drinking. He took a sip, fought the burn of it, coughed through his nose.

'Killed by a little girl for fucking her daddy.'

He raised the jar, saluting the deceased, and drank a toast. Martha did not move.

'What the fuck do I do now?' he said.

Martha sipped her moonshine.

'I said, *What the fuck do I do now?*'

Martha took another sip and set her jar down in her own time. After clearing her throat against her fist, she said:

'That's up to you.'

'Up to me? Hell it is. No one pulls the strings on their own life, Martha. Not gods, not devils. Not since the new world was born.'

'That's not so. Way I see it, the man who was pulling

your strings is dead. You're the puppet master now.'

'Is that right?'

He stood up and paced the kitchen.

'I'm hungry. You got any food?' he said.

'There's jerky in the pantry.'

He returned chewing the dried cow-meat. His face turned to disgust and he spat a bolus of it on the floor. Martha looked on apathetically.

'That's one tough bastard. You slaughter this here cow?'

Martha nodded.

'If you ask me you're lucky the cows aren't eating Martha jerky right now.'

He laughed, sort of.

'You hear me?' he said.

'Yes,' said Martha. 'That's funny.'

'Yeah,' he said, tossing another piece of jerky in to his mouth absentmindedly and instantly spitting it out again. 'Funny.'

Lucien started pacing the floor, muttering to himself. He took down knickknacks from the shelves, assessed them, turned them over in his hands, and then put them down in new locations, shaking his head all the while. A pig with a body of clay, pins for eyes and a curling tail of green felt. A harmonica with several defunct reeds that channelled his breath silently before bursting into honking life when he switched notes. A charcoal sketch of a young boy in profile. This he held up to Martha as a holy man holds up the gospel, as irrefutable evidence. Martha looked on, she drank, she smoked.

'How am I to save my brother if you can't even save your son? Your husband, he was a man; he should've been able to look after himself. But little Bo… How do you live with yourself?'

Martha was silent, indifferent, almost bored.

'I asked you a question,' he said.

'That's not a question,' she said.

'Well what would you call it?'

'A provocation. You are looking for something... something for which to apply your efforts.'

'I guess you'd know.'

Martha shrugged. Lucien paced.

'What did you do... to those Gomorrhean black hats that murdered your boy?'

'Found them. Killed them.'

'You know that's not what I meant. How'd you do it,' he said, returning to his seat.

Martha took out the cigar she had been chewing and turned it over in her fingers.

'It's a long story,' she said.

'I'm sorry, am I keeping you?' growled Lucien.

Martha sighed.

'I tracked them for weeks. They collared me early on stalking them over the flat ground where there was no cover. Three of them there was. Don't know why they didn't make a stand. Must have thought my farm hands were in tow getting ready to mob them. The red earth turned to grassland. Then the grassland gave way and we found ourselves in that radioactive wasteland to the north. The one they call Santa Muerte. Still I tracked them no big as ticks over that sterile plain. They made for the White Mountains thinking I would not follow. There the lobos lope deranged and balden, the flesh sliding off their bones as though pursued by some phantom predator.'

'Bullshit!' interrupted Lucien. 'Nobody returns from Santa Muerte.'

Martha considered Lucien's accusation. Then, cigar in mouth, squinting against the rising smoke, she undid the buttons of her shirt halfway and pulled away the material, exposing her chest. There, out of the dark skin that covered her heart, grew a darker heart, an exo-heart, a bunch of grapes black as tar growing atop each other in a tumorous mound.

'I suppose you're right,' she said.

15

'Christ,' said Lucien.

'We all went mad out there,' she said as she buttoned her shirt back up. 'Their horses died one by one and then so did mine. I saw them squabbling amongst themselves, brandishing their pistols and clubs at each other. I began to find their clothes. Blood in the sand. At long last I came upon them sleeping on a ledge beneath a waterfall of black water.'

Lucien was rubbing his thighs.

'I bet you gutted the bastards,' he said.

'Naw. I hadn't the energy for it. None of us did. When I walked beneath the curtain of water, one of them watched me approach through hollowed-out eyes. I can still see him now. Young kid. Sort of pretty-looking. He didn't even say anything. Not sure he could. We were all less than alive at that point. I fired three shots and fell down expecting to die right there with them. But I guess I didn't.'

They were both silent for a time and then Lucien spoke.

'What a waste,' he said, rising.

Martha shrugged and chomped down on her cigar. Lucien holstered his revolver and stood looking out the window at the white smoke rising before the moon wherein the particles of his brother danced dizzily up, up and further up.

'What now?' he said.

'Like I said, that's entirely up to you,' said Martha.

'I think I'll go home.'

He turned for the door and stopped when Martha addressed him.

'How does this affect our business?' she said.

'It doesn't,' he said.

Martha stood and watched him go as though she a regular host and he a regular guest. When the driver appeared in the doorway, Lucien regarded her vacantly. But as the driver spoke, low and quickly, Martha noticed his unfocused eyes grow keen and the colour flush back into his face.

'Martha,' he said, turning and drawing his revolver, only to be faced with a wave-like conflagration; for in the moment immediately preceding his action, Martha had dashed her jar of shine off the lantern. The improvised molotov burst into flames, and when the fire touched the jar Lucien had left behind that too exploded, peppering Lucien and the driver with broken glass. Screaming, Lucien unloaded his revolver through the fire, unaware that his clothes too were aflame, and it took the driver to pull him from the burning house. She threw him down the porch steps and Lucien rolled in the dusty driveway as the driver thwacked him with her suit jacket to put out the flames. The kitchen windows burnt orange and red and the fire began to spread rapidly through the wooden house. The dogs howled within and glass shattered in the heat.

'Get after her!' roared Lucien.

She obeyed without hesitation. In a single fluid motion, the driver was hightailing it around the house whilst simultaneously donning her scorched jacket. She easily identified the point of entry into the cornfield for the cane was snapped and bowed backwards and as she approached she could hear her quarry clattering onwards somewhere in the distance. She did not enter for something else took her attention. Blood on the leaves. Blood on the ground. She knelt to inspect further and it was at that point the fire must have found the store of moonshine for a huge explosion blew out the kitchen wall. The driver raced back round to the front of the house. A flaming cavern now occupied where the kitchen once was and out of it came running the hounds wearing pelts of fire. Two ran howling into the cornfield but a third fell short and burnt up right there in the driveway. The windows of the Rolls had smashed in the explosion and a stake of charred timber jutted out through the passenger side door. She scanned for Lucien but could not see him. For the first time that night, she seemed visibly concerned; her body was tense, her fists clenched. But as she rounded the car and saw Lucien sat with his back against the driver's side wheel, she regained her cool. He was not in a good way. Glass glistened in his face and his skin had bubbled up red and blistered where the fire had eaten through his clothes.

'Can you drive?' she said.

'Yes.'

She tossed the keys into his lap.

'She's wounded,' she said. 'She'll make for the doctor over at Salvation. Get yourself fixed up. I'll meet you there.'

'I want her alive.'

'I can't promise that.'

She helped Lucien to his feet and swept the glass from the car seat with a single swipe of her arm. Taking her hand, he lowered himself in and started the engine. The movement had agitated the burnt skin and trails of fresh blood welled up and ran down from the wounds. The driver shut the door and regarded Lucien through the empty windowpane.

'I want her alive,' he said.

She stepped back and he pulled off. She watched the car up the driveway, watched as the single working taillight danced over the uneven ground, watched the white cones of the headlights carve out the features of that solitary landscape. Only once the car was out of sight down the road to New Sodom did she relinquish the orange glow of the housefire and in so doing give herself over to the darkness.

THE STIGMATA OF CHERRY BLOSSOM

They walked the long black night, the long black morning, the stolen stars glittering on the winding waterway. Bound by the tether, Cherry stumbled after Plum like he was her prisoner. His robe had come undone and the white silk trailed behind him like some ghostly nimbus. His white skin glowed in spite of the darkness, as though endowed with bioluminescence. He was wild on the leash, like an unbroken animal, and he veered from path to brush and back again, thrashing at the invisible world. Once, he drifted a razor's breadth away from the canal water and Plum wound the strapping about her arm and pulled on it to straighten his gait.

'If you fall you'll drown us both, papa,' she said.

After that, he was less reckless and hobbled along in whatever direction Plum pulled him.

Another dark hour passed in silence, save for the crunching of her boots and the slapping of his sandals, and then the dawn broke golden through the trees. Plum yawned, a trellis of daylight upon her face, hollowing her eyes.

'What is it?' said Cherry.

'Morning.'

'Can we stop?'

Plum looked backwards along the towpath. All was still as a picture.

'Yes,' she said, eventually.

They sat in the grass by the side of the towpath and Plum set about scrutinising the food Martha had bestowed on them: corn and more corn, the loose husks lining the interior of the rucksack; a couple of green apples; potatoes bound by chrysalises of mud; and a single tin can that had lost its labelling long ago. Plum had never eaten anything from a can before and she turned to her father expectantly but he was slouched over in slumber. She laid him out flat and rolled him on his side. Then she ate an apple, core and all, spitting the seeds into the cut. Then too she slept.

*

She dreamt of Bo. Dreamt they were playing sardines round his house. She found him hiding in the kitchen cupboards. *There you are!* she said. *Shhh!* he said, his finger to his lips. He waved her in and she crawled in beside him and closed the door. It was cramped in there, dark. His cool skin pressed on hers. He smelled of jasmine. He started snickering, which made her start snickering, and they both put their hands over their mouths. Martha was looking for them. It was back when Martha was happy. They could hear her calling, *Come out, come out, wherever you are!* But then something switched. Martha's voice was replaced by a man's. A snarling, lecherous voice. And it was saying, *Come out, come out, wherever you are!* And the man was cackling. And they were both of them terrified. They were not laughing anymore. They held each other and prayed it would go away. Then the cupboard doors were pulled open in a blaze of terrible redness. Then she woke up.

*

When she woke, the sun was flaring off her eyelids, but it was not that which woke her. Voices. Far away, but approaching. Also, sobbing. Sobbing close at hand. She scrambled to her feet and sought her father through her post-dream delirium.

'Papa,' she said, 'Oh my god, papa! What have you done?'

He was sat cross-legged like a pious man and blood was streaming from his skull, running into his mouth, running into his blind eyes. His beauteous auburn hair lay about the floor and draped over his shoulders having been cut away in strips and some strands retained the bloody scalp. In his hands he clutched the instrument of his surgery, a hooked piece of green glass, the remnant of an old-world beer bottle. Fresh blood dripped from between Cherry's clasped hands and Plum approached and whispered fiercely for him to stop it and when he wouldn't she slapped his face and he dropped the glass. Sobbing, he held up his hands, baring his lacerated palms, as if in surrender to the wretched world. Plum kicked the glass into the brush and grabbed up the tether.

'We need to go,' she said. 'Someone's coming.'

She pulled on the tether but her father would not move. There was no way through the perfect seal of his despair. Seeing this, Plum changed tack and scanned the earth for a weapon.

*

A dragonfly of glittering azure zigzagged drunkenly across the canal, touching the black water like a skipping stone, before disappearing into the lush ferns on the far side.

'Blessed is the day, Brother Hiroshi.'

'It truly is, Brother Peter.'

Hiroshi stopped to adjust his vestments, running a finger around the seal of his scarlet codpiece whilst Peter held his ceremonial spear for him. Looking up, Hiroshi caught his companion's wondering eye. Peter smiled, lecherously. Hiroshi turned away, his cheeks aflame.

Having righted himself, Hiroshi received his spear from his companion without looking at him. With that, they trundled on, Peter eyeing his companion with slanting, sympathetic eyebrows. After a time, he attempted to hook his arm with Hiroshi's but his companion let his arm fall limp by his side so that Peter's arm appeared to be imposing, like a worm sticking out of an apple.

'Hiroshi, you dishonour me!' he said. 'It is customary for Brothers of The Messiah Caravan to link arms on their pilgrimages. It is an acknowledgement of comradeship, of… of load sharing. Hiroshi, for the love of god, look at me!'

Hiroshi, whose gaze had been downcast throughout his companion's inquisition, raked his gaze from the floor and faced his Brother, his eyes red as his vestments.

'Look, I'm sorry for what I did,' said Peter. 'If I've said it once I've said it a thousand times!'

'It's fine. Just drop it.'

'Come on. Don't be so pathetic!'

'Please just leave me alone.'

'How do you think I feel, huh? I know how you and the other Brothers indulge in the city. The women. The boys. I only did what I did because I was jealous!'

'I can't listen to this,' said Hiroshi, turning and walking away up the towpath.

'Hiroshi, Brother, you must.'

'No. It's too hard.'

Hiroshi stopped ahead and Peter ran to his side.

'Hiroshi, I love you, can't you see that?'

But Hiroshi did not hear him. He was looking straight ahead, his raw eyes forgetful of their sorrow.

'Hiroshi, what is it?'

Peter followed Hiroshi's gaze and then he saw her. How did he miss her? The ragged child with the purple birthmark on her ear, the sun reflecting off her aviator goggles so that her eyes became themselves two lesser suns. In her hand, she clutched a rock and she stood poised to throw it.

'Back,' said Plum. 'Back you devils!'

Hiroshi raised his spear with a spiralling flourish and adopted a battle stance that saw his feet set apart and knees bent as though he straddled some invisible donkey. He glared fiercely at the child who reciprocated his animosity. Stepping between them, Peter laid a hand on the blade of his companion's spear. Disarmed by the gentleness of this action, Hiroshi lowered his weapon.

'Little one, we are not devils,' said Peter. 'We are Brothers of The Messiah Caravan and we oppose Beelzebub in all his incarnations. By your courageous words, I believe we are allied in our ends. I respectfully ask that you lower your weapon so that we may engage in council.'

'I respectfully ask that you about-face and scurry whence you came,' said Plum.

'Child, we are Brothers of The Messiah Caravan,' said Peter once more, as though the name alone would vouch for their virtue. Plum cut him off.

'I know exactly who you are. There's no mistaking those ridiculous clothes. And let me tell you something my papa told me: there's no trusting a person who welches on a debt to a courtesan.'

'What do you mean, child?'

'Ask your friend there.'

'What does she mean, Brother Hiroshi?'

'She's Cherry Blossom's kid,' he whispered. 'Martha's whore.'

'My papa is nobody's whore but his own. We tenant a parcel of Martha's land and have never missed a payment. It is an honourable transaction. Something you would know nothing about.'

'What's your name, child?' asked Peter, but the question met with frosty silence. He glanced back at his colleague, whose eyes were downcast, his cheeks blotchy and red. Peter continued, 'Child, on behalf of my Brothers, please accept my apologies. There is a sickness in our ranks.'

'I'll be damned,' said Plum, stunned, her weapon lowering a degree.

'What is it?'

'I ain't never heard a man in uniform admit to wrongdoing by him or his own before.'

'I'm sorry but that does seem to be the world we live in.'

The apology he offered on behalf of the world entire hung in the air between them for Plum to scrutinise. She turned it over, looking for some imperfection that might render it false, insincere. Satisfied, she lowered her weapon and raised her aviator goggles onto her forehead. This simple act, the revealing of the eyes, it was like a medieval knight raising the visor on his helmet. She hid behind those goggles like the sun hides behind the earth and the unveiling was as beautiful and honest as a sunrise.

'My name's Plum.'

'My name is Brother Peter,' he said with a bow dramatic enough to rival her father's theatricality. 'And this is my companion, Brother Hiroshi. But if I understand correctly, you've already met.'

Plum glanced from Peter to Hiroshi and then looked behind her, back up the towpath.

'You say that you oppose the devil.'

'That's correct.'

'Whatever form he takes.'

'Each and every one.'

'Then perhaps you would help us?'

'Us… Child, who else is with you?'

Plum grimaced, as though perhaps she really should not have said anything, but she shrugged it off and waved them forwards. She threw the rock she held into the cut, it hitting the water with a dumb-sounding plop. Behind a protrusion of emerald shrub, there sat Cherry in his horrorshow transfiguration. He had quit his weeping and seemed altogether composed. Although the tracks of his tears had washed a bizarre tribal pattern through the blood so that his sorrow remained tattooed upon his face. As they rounded the shrub, first Plum, then the Brothers of The Messiah Caravan, it seemed as though perhaps he saw them, sharp and piercing blue as were his eyes, and being that they were trained in their direction. However, as they moved past, it was apparent no miracle had been wrought, for he continued to stare at the same wash of blue sky behind them.

'My lord!' said Peter.

Peter was dumbfounded. He removed the red leather skullcap that topped his perfectly bald head and massaged his sweating scalp. Stretching the cap back over the dome of his head, he stepped forth and knelt at Cherry's side, craning his neck so as to explore every angle of the image before him. He reached and took Cherry's hand in his own and eyed the lacerations on the palm before kissing the fingers and laying it back in the grass exactly as he had found it. Plum and Hiroshi shared a look of confusion as Peter sidled around Cherry, analysing him, gently pressing the puckered scalp from which the blood still slowly seeped, yet opting not to treat the gashes. Indeed, he was careful not to alter them in any way. He turned to Hiroshi, his eyes sparkling.

'Brother, don't you see?' said Peter,

Hiroshi had his tongue in his cheek. His arms were folded and his eyebrows sat high up on his forehead. He shrugged.

'He wears the crown of love!'

A look of horror began to spread over Hiroshi's face as he began to understand what his companion was insinuating.

'As did Jesus before him!'

'He's a whore, Brother.'

'So?'

'You think he… *he* is the messiah?'

'Was not Jesus low-born?'

'Jesus was no whore!'

'If you ask me, Brother Hiroshi, what more pertinent a profession could the messiah of our time have. God knows which son to send and when. They have been highly as kings and lowly as carpenters, as is illustrated in *The Messiah Caravan*. Yes. Yes. A whore would be the saviour in such base times.'

'You're mad. The Fathers will not stand for it.'

'No. You are right. They will kneel.'

Hiroshi was shaking his head. He made as though to speak but did not, could not, so he turned his back on the scene and crossed his arms in protest. Plum looked from Hiroshi to Peter and then to her father who was still gazing at the same patch of pale sky. She wondered if he had heard what was said. He had not moved throughout but her daddy had always been a good poker player. One time he had fleeced a sucker so bad that, when he went to draw his guns in outrage, he found his holster empty, having gambled away his guns earlier that night. Yes, something told her that inside his synapses must be firing, for there was a whizz of electricity in the air, like a tingling cloud of static. She was sure he must be savvying how to turn this situation to their benefit.

'We need to get to New Gomorrah.' said Plum.

Peter, who had returned to his observations, looked up from where he was charting the slow descent of a blood droplet.

'Oh no,' he said. 'We must get him to the Red Basilica.'

'You said you would help us.'

'And we will. But first we must consult the Fathers of The Messiah Caravan.'

'You don't understand. We're being hunted.'

'Is that so? Who hunts you child?'

'The devil of New Sodom. Or rather his brother.'

Peter gave Hiroshi a smug look, as though Plum's words validated his claim that Cherry was indeed the messiah. Hiroshi shook his head.

'What would Lucien want with you two?' said Hiroshi.

'He aims to kill us.'

'And why is that?'

'For it's a-cause of us the devil of New Sodom is dead, his body burnt to ash.'

'Ludicrous! You expect us to bel—' began Hiroshi, but he stopped short when the child produced the devil's ring. Its massive black stone seemed to swallow the light of the sun entire. Hiroshi made to snatch it but Plum was too quick. He turned to Peter.

'Hellfire! We need to go, Brother. Let him alone. He'll bring ruin to our church!'

'Courage, Brother Hiroshi. You were not always such a coward.'

Hiroshi rolled his eyes and made a pass with his hand as though swatting a fly.

'Whatever,' he said.

Peter eyed his companion with disgust and then turned to Plum, saying softly:

'Child, you mean to tell me that this man here vanquished the devil of New Sodom?'

'No, I—.'

'That is the gospel truth!' boomed her father in his best thespian, the gigantic words echoing down the towpath only to be shouted back by the mouths of old bridges. 'And we will go with you to the Red Basilica so that we might consult with the Fathers of your church. I think they should like to hear what I have to say.'

With this, he seemed to grow larger before their eyes. His chest swelled, his shoulders broadened. It seemed like he might go on expanding until all was crushed beneath him.

At this, Peter flung himself to his knees before Cherry and smushed his face into the earth. He reared up, tears in his eyes, grass and dirt staining his face.

'O heavenly father,' he cried. 'O thank you, thank you!'

Hiroshi looked on with a face full of holy horror, his hand clasped over his mouth. Plum turned away, grinning.

'Help me up for this world is dark to me and the way is long and winding.'

'Yes. Yes. Fear not, O lord, I am here. Rest assured the road to the Red Basilica is none too far nor treacherous.'

'I was not referring to the journey immediate, my disciple. The Messiah Caravan does not stop at the doors of the Red Basilica. Now take my arm.'

MARTHA MAKES A RUN FOR IT

Martha shoulder barged through the back door of her home and out into the night. In the next moment, the projectiles from Lucien's hand-cannon split the wood walls in a shower of splinters and went whizzing past Martha before zipping off through the cornfield. The last bullet however did not skim harmless on into the night. There was that self-same buzzing, like a hornet's, but it stopped with a thwack. A sting. Martha gasped. Arched. Her hand went to her back. Her legs buckled and she hit the dirt but she was quick to clamber back up and she made onwards and pushed her way with bloody hand into the cornfield.

She went clattering through the cane, her guard raised like a boxer. The crowns of corn jiggled above her, signalling her position. Her breath was short. Sharp. Like a piston. And that callous surgeon, anxiety, had transplanted her heart into her head so that she was deaf to all but its cardiac hammering.

She burst out of a parenthesis of maize and on, on she ran. Before her, a barbwire fence scribbled blacker lines across the black horizon. Beyond that was a little cabin, a lantern burning in its window. She made the fence and grabbed it for support and the second she took hold of it her house exploded behind, as though this was the trigger for such an event. Turning, the rising fireball was captured in each bead of sweat that dotted her face so that for a moment she was speckled with gold.

She raised the upper line and lowered herself to slip through the wires but in the bending she felt the metal lodged within her turn against the muscle. The pain of it stole her breath away and forced her down onto all fours. Snorting like a hog, she crawled to where the gap between the earth and the wire was biggest and she bellied it through, the wire scoring down the back of her shirt and tearing out the lining along with a little of her own skin for good measure, as though there was a toll to be paid for such crossings.

Through, she hoisted herself up and loped onwards. The door went on the little cabin and one of her farmhands emerged holding an oil lantern above his head. He was a young man, fourteen or fifteen, with a smiling face, as though the world was one great comedy, and he wore his work shorts and nothing more for the night was sultry.

'Whoa Nelly!' he said, seeing the flames in the distance. 'We're in for it tonight, my dove,' he called over his shoulder. Then, registering Martha's approach, he called, 'Who's there? You. I see you. Stop. Stop right there. Well let's have at it you motherfuckinsonofabitch. Shit. Martha, is that you?'

'Yes,' she said.

She leant on the little cabin and spat, each breath swallowed down with great effort.

'What's going on?'

'It's over. We're done.'

'You mean to say we've fallen out of favour with the devil?'

Martha nodded. The young man smirked and clicked his tongue against the roof of his mouth as if he was only too aware of the transience of such relationships and that he knew this day was as inevitable as tomorrow is and having been proved right it was all just so funny.

'Shit,' he said. 'I'll round up the others.'

Martha nodded. Her face was scrunched in pain.

'Come with us,' he said.

Martha looked him in his warm, black eyes. She shook her head.

'Can't,' she said.

The farmhand nodded like he already knew this too.

'I need a gun,' she said.

'Shit, Martha. You know I don't carry. None of us do.'

The farmhand's wife appeared in the doorway. She was pale, waif-like, not much more than a child herself, with big black hammocks under her eyes. In her arms she cradled a bundle of rags out of which poked a little brown wrinkled face.

'Old Man Malarkey's got a rifle above his bed. For show like. Says there's but one bullet in it though. Says he's saving it.'

Martha nodded and limped off. Behind, she heard the farmhand's wife say, 'I'm scared, Joey.' And the young man replied. 'It'll be alright, my dove. Just like we practiced. Come on. The others are counting on us. So's this little one.' Something in these words set Martha weeping. A stone cast into the lake of memories until now so long so still.

Beyond Joey's cabin, other little homes grew out of the night. Her farmhands and their families were milling about, some with lanterns, some without, like a procession of the dead that had lost their way in the long, dark night. They called out to her but she had not the energy to respond. When she pushed her way into Old Man Malarkey's, the old man was face down on his cot in nought but his stained underwear, unconscious. The room reeked of booze and human waste. Flies crawled over bowls of congealed oatmeal, over the old man himself. On

the floor was a bottle of moonshine and Old Man
Malarkey's arm dangled off the cot, seemingly reaching for
the bottle even in his sleep. On a rudimentary desk—made
from an upturned crate and a piece of plywood—burned a
candle. Beside it were the old man's letters to god, which
were writ in charcoal and read the likes of *Why don't you
talk to me no more?* and *Why now when I need you more than ever?*
On the wall above his bed hung the rifle. It was an M1
Garand service rifle. A relic from some long-forgotten war.
Martha took it down and left.

As she shut the door, Joey was approaching, his stride
bouncing, enormous. Now fully clothed, he had a potato
sack slung over his shoulder that contained within supplies
for the journey ahead.

'Happy hunting,' he said.

Martha just nodded. But when Joey made for Old Man
Malarkey's door she said, 'He ain't in there,' nothing in her
voice to betray that she was lying.

'No?' said Joey. 'He's probably off chasing dragons.
Heh, heh. Safest place to be right now anyhow.'

Martha nodded, turned and set off at a lope. Joey
watched her go. Then he went into the cabin regardless
and emerged with potato sack over one shoulder and Old
Man Malarkey over the other. As darkness enveloped her,
she could hear he was singing of all things.

> *O lordy, lordy, can't you see?*
> *There's a big red devil coming for me!*

His childish laughter died away and she was utterly
alone. Silence without, a hurricane of blood within. The
pain in her back oscillating between a dull expansive
throbbing and excruciating pinpoint sharpness whenever
the bullet lodged there disagreed with the way she moved.
She crossed the canal by an arch bridge of crumbling
stone, the water black and still below, like a mirror, like
another dimension. The land hereon was a hardpan of

fissured red earth but she had no mind left to pay it. The toe of her boot caught in a crag and she went down. Hard. She raised herself onto her hands and knees, the breath roaring in and out of her so that she seemed to swell to twice her size then shrink to half of it. She stared at the ground. Blood was piddling from her face somewheres. She pressed her palm to her forehead but still it went *pat, pat, pat*. The thirsty earth drank it and asked for more. Then she herself tasted it and realised it was running upwards into her mouth and that she had split her chin good and proper.

She leant back on her knees and surveyed the landscape, the blood running warmly down her neck. As if to challenge the land's austerity, trumpet trees grew here, their flowers shimmering silver-pink in the moonlight, like they were themselves the ghosts of trees. It is true she had forgotten them entire. But they were here now to greet her like old friends, like guides to the land of the dead. She could hear a child's laughter when the wind played through their flowers.

'Bo?' she said.

In the distance, a gunshot. Screaming. Another gunshot. The screaming stopped. Martha whirled round and the pain shot through her body. Cursing, she clambered to her feet and continued on.

She languished away the remains of the night, falling, rising. Delirious. Her vision fogged over and she knew a raging thirst. Still death would not come. As if from the reaper, the night concealed. The flatland began to incline and the way was even harder. Then up reared a bluff of red rock. She kneeled up onto a table of sandstone and lobbed the rifle over. From there she managed to claw herself over the rim. As she rolled over, she noticed the sky had paled, the stars extinguished. A thin golden bead drew across the hardpan ahead. The sun was coming over the horizon and it brought with it a prairie schooner raising a storm of dust, four horses driving it.

She looked back and in the new light she could make out her huntress scrabbling up the incline at a determined, steady pace. Martha dragged herself up and began to hobble in the direction of the schooner. She stopped.

'Dammit, Martha, you'll not get this chance again,' she said.

She returned to the crest of the bluff and gingerly lowered herself onto her belly. Bringing the rifle forward, she drew a bead on her pursuer. She was about a quarter mile out. Martha blinked hard. When she opened her eyes, there was a split second of clarity before the figure blotched outwards into a kind of amoeba shape.

'Damn your eyes, Martha,' she said.

The pursuer was tracking Martha's blood and was making straight for the point where Martha lay. So far, she had not clocked the rifle poking over the lip of the bluff. Martha steadied her breathing. Blinked. Again, the pursuer blurred outwards like ink dropped on paper. Eighth of a mile out. She pinched the bridge of her nose and scrunched up her eyes. Opened. A flash of an image. The pursuer with her stetson pushed back on her head, staring straight at her. Confusion. Disbelief. Martha's eyes fogged over and she fired. The en-bloc clip flew into the air with a *ching* and the barrel exploded. Backfire. A piece of the barrel scored a line down her skull. Another winged her cheek. Her hands rang with the force of it. She let go the rifle and it slipped off the bluff and fell clattering onto the sandstone table below. Laughter. She could hear laughter.

'Gun trouble, Arty?' called the huntress.

But Martha was already up and hightailing it across the hardpan with everything she had left. The schooner was big now but it was following a dirt road that was banking away. Martha made herself as big as she could, waving her hands above her head. They were still numb from the backfire. The little figure holding the reins was looking straight ahead. They had not seen her; or were pretending not to. How could they not have heard the backfire?

Calling out, the words were like sand in her throat, miniscule, abrasive, so she put finger and thumb in her mouth and blew. The whistle carried over the pan with pristine clarity. The driver of the schooner turned their head, turned back, continued straight. Martha dropped to her knees, her mouth hanging open in muted moan. Her face was a death mask, her black skin paled to grey and powdered with the dust, the dry blood crusting and flaking away like old paint. She pressed her head to the ground as though in worship. She could feel the horses pounding over the hardpan, the wheels rollicking off that unforgiving earth, and found serenity in this pose, a knowledge that they were all of them connected. Everything connected through her. In through her forehead and out through her toes, her fingers. She was the conduit. All must pass through her. In this way, she willed them to her, speaking directly to the horses, the driver. Not with words but with illiterate desire.

When she raised her head, the horses were turning, turning and riding back through the swathes of red dust that they had invoked. As Martha rose, in unison so did her pursuer come over the lip of the bluff. Martha was now closer to the schooner than her pursuer was to she, so the pursuer stood with feet apart and unloaded her revolver. The bullets went careening over the hardpan. One hit the ground at Martha's feet and spat up the compacted soil. One passed through a thin dust devil turning out there in the near distance and it evanesced as though she had shot out its phantom heart. The schooner came side on and the man driving pulled hard on the reins, the horses stamping, snorting. He stood and hailed her.

'Get in,' he called. 'Hurry. Hurry!'

The pursuer moved forward as she reloaded. Then, once again, she braced herself and fired off every round in steady succession. The bullets went keening for Martha but with the distance strayed offwards and outwards. At the same time:

'Help her in, Lily-Jane,' called the schooner-driver.

Martha rounded the schooner and a girl in a white dress made red by the road appeared from under the awning. She was about Plum's age, twelve, thirteen, perhaps younger, and slight, but still she held out her little arm to this injured giant and when Martha took it she marvelled at her tenacity. The girl Lily-Jane gripped a loop of leather nailed to the wagon interior and in this way Martha climbed up her and in and collapsed face-down on the floor, bleeding over their livelihood, sacks of flour, sacks of yeast.

'She in?' called the driver.

'She's in,' called Lily-Jane.

'Atta girl. Hold tight,' he called, sitting and taking up the reins.

Lily-Jane flinched as a bullet passed through the awning by her face, bringing with it the new sun, a tube of pale light that irradiated the gyrating motes of dust. Then she heard it. Martha heard it too. The wind unzipping straight and true. The driver grunted, exhaled. The breath out long and pained, a terminal puncture. The wood creaked as he shifted in his seat. The schooner remained put.

'Daddy,' said Lily-Jane, stepping on Martha to get up to the front of the wagon. She climbed up out from under the awning and onto the driver's seat. Her father was slumped over, a terrible red flower growing out of his breast pocket. She rocked his shoulders. As she tilted his head back so that she might see his face his eyes rolled over white in his head. His breath was shallow. There was dust on his lips.

'Hold on, daddy,' she said, taking the reins from him and bringing them cracking down upon the backs of the horses. The schooner lurched forwards and her father sagged backwards like a puppet, his mouth lolling, welcoming the dust. His eyes were open, still seeing, but seeing both this world and the next. She brought the horses round expertly, one hand hooked beneath her daddy's braces to save him from flopping off the side. She righted the schooner and set a course back the way they had come, back into the sun. She then turned her attention to her father. He was slouched back on the awning in undignified death and gazing skyward where turned darkly a vulture up there against the deepening blue.

'Daddy,' she said.

He looked at her as though he was coming out of a daydream.

'Atta girl,' he said. Then he died.

In the wagon, Martha lay in her blood listening to the little girl sobbing and begging her daddy to come back from where there was no coming back from.

Behind them, Martha's pursuer shook the empty casings from the chamber. Like metal rain, they tinkled against the hardpan. She thumbed home a fresh set of rounds and holstered her revolver. She took a deep breath, squinting against the rising sun. Then she set off after them.

THE CRUCIFIXION OF CHERRY BLOSSOM

'They'll kill him y'know,' said Hiroshi.

Plum looked over her shoulder. Her father and Peter were lagging behind on the canal towpath, dawdling arm in arm, their heads bowed together, her father giving out some spiel on the latent goodness of man and Peter eating up every word. Drawing on her cigarette, she turned away.

'You think I could take a breath of that?' said Hiroshi.

Plum hesitated. Then, rolling her eyes, she offered out the cigarette. Hiroshi pinched it from between her fingers. Licking his lips until they glistened, he puckered up like a duck's beak and sucked out a mouthful of smoke that he blew out instantly with a little satisfied gasp, as though it were a refreshing drink. He repeated the sodden action a few times over, watching Plum out of the corner of his eye. Sated, he made to return the cigarette, along with a strand of his own saliva, but Plum waved it away. Hiroshi grinned sheepishly and continued to smoke it in his own novel way. He even removed his hot leather skullcap to better enjoy the experience. After seeing Peter, bald as a

38

stone, Plum was surprised to see that Hiroshi had himself a shock of bronze hair under there. He had seemed older with his cap on, an adult. Without it, it was apparent that he was just a tall, grey-faced boy no more than two summer's her senior. She having seen thirteen summers herself.

'What do you mean, they'll kill him?'

'I mean they'll kill him. Peter doesn't get it. The Fathers, the leaders of our church, they're not going to roll over and let your daddy be leader. A whore. A whore who half the Brothers have fucked. But that don't matter anyway, the whore stuff. Even if he was the bona fide son of god—I'm talking halo, cherubs, heavenly choir; the whole shebang—they would still tell us to kill him, and we would, and then they'd say carry on as you were, and we would.'

Hiroshi sucked on the cigarette but nothing happened. The cherry did not flare like last time. Instead, it continued to burn its dim orange-black.

'I don't get it. It's not out is it?'

'You probably stuck the paper together. It's easy enough to do on an unfiltered one.'

'Do you have one with a filter I could have?'

'Do I look like a rich man?'

Hiroshi shrugged.

'What should I do with this?'

Plum gestured for the cigarette and Hiroshi returned it. She stopped and douted out the cherry on the bottom of her boot and then split the paper with her thumbs like she were breaking open a petrified runner bean and returned the unburnt baccy to her tin, the tin to her pocket. They walked on and Hiroshi was quiet now, his cheeks and ears a ruddy red. Seeing this, Plum extended an olive branch.

'What's the deal with you and Peter?'

'What do you mean?'

'I overheard him singing his love for you.'

Hiroshi turned beetroot purple; but at the same time,

paradoxically, he also seemed to relax. With Plum's intrigue, he became puckish, giggly. He glanced over his shoulder to make sure that they could not be heard.

'I know. It's weird. He's really got it bad for me.'

'Do you like him?'

'I dunno. I mean he's sort of attractive. But he's old. He jokes about being twice my age. Not that age is everything. But to be honest, he gives me the creeps.'

Plum was nodding. Hiroshi saw this and smiled appreciatively at her before continuing.

'Yeah. He's been bugging me for over a year now. My friends say that he used to bug them too. But they told him where to go.'

'And what did you tell him?'

Hiroshi had started chewing the nail of his little finger. He gave another look over his shoulder. Plum could see he was scared.

'Don't worry,' she said. 'It's safe.'

'I'm so fucking stupid,' he said. His hand shook as he gnawed it. He was so full of anger. Like how only a thin cord keeps the screaming heat inside the steam whistle's tragic mouth. 'I was only thirteen summers when he started talking to me. Telling me that I was beautiful and brave and strong and that he loved me. He said I was special. Kept saying it. Kept saying it… until I believed him. It went on. Then being a senior Brother he insisted on taking me on pilgrimage. I'd initially been going with another Brother, but Peter changed that somehow. Then this one time we were camped out on a meadow miles away from nowhere and he started acting all strange. He said he wanted me but he needed me to want him back. When I said I didn't want him, he got angry. Started saying I didn't love him, or the Brotherhood. He said that I was a snake, an agent provocateur. Then he hit me. Then he said he wanted me again. Then *hiss, hiss*. Snake. Snake. Snake!'

The boy's whole body was shaking and tears fell freely from his eyes. Plum looked back. Her papa and Peter were still conspiring like thieves.

'Hey,' she said. 'Let's go up here.'

She took him by the hand and together they climbed up the embankment away from the towpath and came out of the rich foliage typical of the canal onto the red, mineral waste of the hardpan. Hiroshi emerged gasping like a drowning man who by some miracle had washed ashore. He palmed away the tears. Thick cords of spittle hung between his lips and it looked as though in the heat of his rage his lips had melted part together. Plum produced her makings and set to rolling a cigarette. She tore a corner from the old-world scratch card she kept, which promised someone long dead ten thousand units of a dead currency, and rolled it to a roach between her middle finger and thumb. This she inserted into the cigarette before licking it shut and handing it to Hiroshi.

'That'll keep the end from sticking together,' she said.

'Thanks,' he said, and leant forward to receive the match Plum had struck for him. His face looked swollen as he cupped the fire between his hands. He looked like he had been boxed in the face. He blew out his lips and a fat cloud of smoke gambolled out.

'Oh man,' he said, wiping his eyes. 'I'm sorry about that.'

'Don't be,' she said.

She put a hand on his arm and Hiroshi smiled gratefully at her. She then set about making herself a cigarette.

'Why did I tell you that?'

'Guess it needed telling.'

'Yeah, I guess… Can I tell you something else?'

Plum nodded as she dabbed her tongue across the cigarette paper.

'I've got a sweetheart in New Sodom.'

'Yeah?'

'Yeah. He's a barman there. He says if I leave the Brotherhood we can run away together. We'll find a nice piece of land somewhere, by a river, and we'll catch salmon by day and cuddle up together at night in big fur coats, like we were bears, and no one'll bother us ever again.'

'That sounds nice.'

'It's too good to be true.'

'Right now, maybe. Tomorrow, maybe not.'

'I hope you're right.'

'Me too. What's his name?'

'Machiavelli.'

'Sounds like one romantic bastard.'

'He is.'

Hiroshi's swollen face was beginning to deflate and by shades return to its ashen grey and though his eyes were still raw there was a tranquil smile upon his lips as he remembered those halcyon days yet to be.

'Come on,' said Plum. 'We best be getting back.'

*

Their arrival at the Red Basilica sparked a furore. Peter led the way, pushing through the assemblage of his peers. All wore identical vestments—red leather caps, vests and codpieces—and each carried with them the same ceremonial spear with the red ribbon knotted around the neck of the weapon like a scarf. Hiroshi was bringing up the rear, silently jostling Plum and Cherry forwards. A boy of similar age drew alongside him and whispered for what was going on but Hiroshi just shrugged and pushed them on.

For Plum, the uniforms towered over her on all sides and made it as though she were looking out from the bottom of a fleshy cave, one that responded to your movements in kind, making escape an impossibility. Through this cave mouth she saw, before the brilliant blue desert sky, the Red Basilica grow and cast over them its leaden shadow. And she remembered that she had once thought tombstones grew out the ground, out of some stone seedling deep in the guts of people, like the fallen fruit turns into a tree. She had thought that right up until the day Martha buried Bo. Right up until Martha took a spade and spanked home a column of sandstone at the head of where her dead friend lay.

The Red Basilica was an old-world university building, a great hall, built of red brick and topped with a grey, bosom-shaped dome. Over the door stood seven stone men from a time gone by, their names erased from their pedestals by the abrasive desert wind, their faces scoured to smooth, anonymous, peach-coloured ovals. Besides the Red Basilica, the rest of the university was destroyed. On quiet nights, you could hear the stomach of that ravenous desert as it digested that once green and pleasant land. Buildings reduced to nought but their foundations abounded and looked like archaeological dig sites. The detached corners of cuboid structures rose out the red earth like modernist pyramids. And the four faces of a felled clock tower stuck out of the ground, smashed and jagged, their massive time-telling hands strewn about and pointing here and there, as though they last saw time fleeing every which way across the desert.

Peter led them up the stone steps of the basilica and under the arches of red brick. They entered into a distinguished foyer area with marble floors and a circular reception desk of dark panelled wood at its centre. A team of receptionists gawped at the massive assembly as it broke around the desk as a river breaks around a rock. Looking up, Plum saw distinguished members of the Brotherhood dressed in black robes leaning on the balustrades of the walkways overhead. They looked down on the commotion with silent, sardonic bemusement.

Plum and Cherry were bustled through the foyer and into the great hall. At the far end, a gargantuan stained-glass window took precedence. However, it had fallen into disrepair, and though the steel mullions and lead cames tattooed the slanting afternoon sunlight with saintly sketches, there was little glass left for it to colour, just a scattering lit up like rubies, sapphires, emeralds. They were muscled down the long aisle like brides at a shotgun wedding and the great many pews began to fill as though perhaps there was in fact some ceremony about to begin. Plum looked to her father but he was lost in his blindness, chin up, gazing towards the big window, and she thought perhaps at the very least he could still sort light from dark. As though he had sensed her eyes upon him, she felt him squeeze her hand tightly and the corner of his mouth curled up into a secret smile. As they stepped from shadow into sunlight, he let go of her hand. He then closed his eyes and the sun washed over him, colouring him gold.

They were taken to the front and Peter stood her father front and centre. Cherry drew himself up to his full height and in the light of the sun he appeared ennobled by his wounds. Peter stood a little apart from him, his shoulders hunched, the perspective lending Cherry extra height. Plum wondered if her father had choreographed this. Then another thought occurred to her: perhaps all messiahs were just good actors who knew how to make themselves look bigger than they actually were.

'Come with me,' whispered Hiroshi.

Placing a hand on her back, he walked her to the far shadows of the hall.

'What happens now?' said Plum as they shuffled off, heads-bowed.

'The Fathers decide that,' he said.

Plum looked back and saw that beneath the big window sat ten men and women in a line looking down on her father from atop a stage. They were each of them dressed in a black robe, like death, and all wore gold jewellery inset with precious jewels. Before them stretched a table festooned with ornate silverware bearing fresh fruit and meats and wine and at either end of the table was a drooling waif, their eyes mad with hunger, wafting massive wicker-woven fans to keep the flies at bay. The Fathers were all of them obese and sweating and a couple of them had servants holding parasols over them whereas the others seemed to revel in their perspiration like slugs in slime.

The last of the Brothers took their seats in the pews and a profound silence descended over the hall, like the stillness at the eye of a hurricane. The Fathers were waiting for Cherry to speak, to explain, to plead for his life; but Cherry was silent. He stood still as a statue before them and the hallowed light from the big window rendered him his own golden idol. The Fathers exchanged amused glances. They were whispering to one another, coaxing, goading. At long last the Father on the far left, the one with the pox-ridden mouth, sighed and spoke.

'And who might you be,' he said.

He forced a grotesque chuckle from between his stretched and blistered lips and the assembly reciprocated his derision.

'*Hul-lo*. Are you deaf?' he continued. Then, turning to Peter, he said, 'Well, Peter, what a fine specimen you have brought us today! My word, son, what do you have to say for yourself?'

Peter remained silent. He did not take his eyes from the floor. The Brothers now teetered on the verge of frenzy. They started to whoop and howl, calling for the death of their Brother, of Cherry, by hanging, by stoning, by spear. The Fathers indulged too, laughing heartily and banging their fists down on the dinner table. Spurred on by the Fathers, the Brothers totally lost it. The pews screeched against the floor as they rocked on them like animals on a cage. And as the Brothers of The Messiah Caravan reached fever pitch, when it seemed mere moments from them rushing forwards and tearing him apart, Cherry spoke. His voice was supermassive, effortless.

'Children. Children. I expected you better prepared for my arrival.'

The excitement went out like a cigarette screwed underfoot.

'Oh, it speaks,' said the poxy Father with a wry guffaw that died in his own syphilitic mouth. Cherry looked in the direction of the noise and his blind, icy blue eyes seemed to penetrate the Father, making him cough and fidget in his seat.

'I suppose this is why I am sent,' he said. 'To prepare you. For him.' At this he pointed a slender finger at the ceiling. 'For it is apparent that you are all so... unready.'

'You will die for this heresy,' hissed one of the Fathers, an elderly woman with sagging, bloodhound chops.

'Heresy? Heresy? Before the eyes of the lord, you ten will stand naked and heretic. For you have led your fellow man astray for your own ends. And as to the matter of my death. Well. I suppose I will die for my cause. For my cause is life. And all those who pursue life, when they catch it, inevitably catch their death also. But in doing so these people come to own both. They become proprietor of both their life and their death. This is what I am here to give you.'

He turned to face the assembly of Brothers.

'My fellow children,' he said. '*This* is what I am here to give *you*. I am here to return to you both your lives and your deaths. Too long have they jangled like gold in the pockets of those you serve. This line of fools here. Fathers. Fathers my toe! There is but one Father. And he struts no earthly stage. The Father walks the boards of heaven. And I am his son and servant. As you all have chance to be. For I am here to return you to him.'

'Enough. Enough. Enough!' cried a Father with plump cheeks scribbled with purple spider veins. With each word, he banged his fist down on the table, rattling the cutlery.

'Yes. Enough. Enough,' imitated Cherry. 'Enough of the hierarchies of men. Enough of the ziggurat of human woe. Let us raise it to the ground. Enough of Fathers and of Sons. Let us be children. Children every one of us. Long live the children! Long live the children! Long live the children!'

Plum looked out from the shadows at the assembly of Brothers. They seemed utterly confused, divided. Some were unconsciously nodding their agreement; Cherry's outpouring having revived their hibernating dissatisfaction. However, none dared join in with Cherry's chant of *long live the children*. Others shook their heads in disbelief. The more militant Brothers tore at their hair in outrage and beat their fists against their temples. Among the undecided, there was whispering, nervous glances. This was all so unprecedented. What were they supposed to do?

Plum thought her father must have misjudged the crowd after none rallied behind his cries. Perhaps Peter had sold him a lie as to the disposition of his fellow Brother. His revolutionary fist hovered impotently above his head, having punched the air in his passion. By degrees, it returned to his side. In the electric hum that followed Cherry's monologue, the poxy Father stood and rounded the table, his hands raised like a wizard begging silence for his next trick.

'Sons o' mine—' he began, but Cherry cut him off once more. For the first time, Plum thought her father looked desperate.

'And another thing. And here I speak to my sisters. Those forced against their will to take the title of Brother. My sisters, I am here to tell you that the heavenly father is also too a mother.'

'Oh no,' muttered Hiroshi. 'This won't fly.'

But with these words, Plum noticed the women of the assembly had switched on. They were leant forwards with stunned, eager faces. The men only scoffed and raised their eyebrows at each other. Plum overheard one man nearby say, 'Ha! He almost had me there.' Even Peter looked concerned by Cherry's segue and was beginning to sidle away from him.

'That's right,' Cherry continued. 'All are equal beneath the almighty parent for it has no favourite. We are each created in its likeness for it is both man and woman combined. Sisters, I promise you, one day you will see the hermaphroditic splendour of our lord. Until then, know your power. Tear away the codpiece and indulge the strength of your birth organ. But be ready. For the male organ cannot do what yours does and because of this it fears it. It is not strong like yours. The codpiece is weakness posing as strength. Like how in the wrong light a worm can cast a snake's shadow. You have a labyrinth of life within you...'

But with the analogy of the worm, the men gave uproar and even Cherry's best thespian was drowned beneath the cries of the emasculated hoards. The male Brothers were on their feet now and they were yelling *Charlatan! Heathen!* and the like and calling for his murder. Even the Fathers, fat as they were, were all standing now. They were seething. Spit flew from between their clenched teeth as they each clutched the table to keep themselves from falling down. The women remained in their seats. But as they were consigned to the back pews, the men did not notice their silent dissent behind.

Plum did not see who started the chant, but a single word began to spread throughout the congregation like a virus until it was all that was spoken. *Cru-ci-fy! Cru-ci-fy! Cru-ci-fy!* They stomped out the syllables on the basilica floor. Then the poxy Father stepped front and centre and, pointing a fat, incriminating finger at Cherry, he cried, 'Crucify him!' The assembly gave an almighty roar and descended upon her father. He did not even flinch. His face was expressionless, composed. He let them grab him, bruise him, tear at his robe, manipulate him as though he were but water breaking over their hands. Peter had tried to run but he was caught in an instant. He screamed as they bent his arms up behind his back; but then one of his fellow Brothers cracked him across the cheekbone with his fist and he went silent. His head rolled on his shoulders, his face split and leaking claret. The Brother who had thrown the punch raised his bloody fist to the assembly and they howled with delight. Then Cherry and Peter were dragged up the aisle, past the women, and out of the hall. The men filed out after them. Although a group loitering at the back of the assembly were whispering and nodding in Plum's direction.

'Come on,' said Hiroshi. 'Let's get out of here.'

They backed deeper into the shadows of the basilica and disappeared behind a tall, moth-ravaged curtain. From there, Hiroshi led her out via a concealed side exit. They scurried through a near pitch-black room, an old-world kitchen, the little light afforded glinting off the stainless-steel surfaces. The room stank of rotten meat and she could hear the whining of bluebottles. At the far end, Hiroshi pushed the bar of an old-world fire escape and they stepped out through a rectangle of red light.

Hiroshi leant against the outer wall of the basilica, his hand over his heart, hyperventilating. He took a double take and realised Plum was running away along the perimeter of the basilica.

'Wait,' he said, but she did not stop. He ran after her, casting around a wary glance should he be seen conspiring with the charlatan's daughter.

At the furthest end, she stopped and poked her head around the corner of the basilica. The men were milling around the front of the hall. There was laughing and games while they waited for the execution to begin. Some heaved their ceremonial spears as javelins over the hardpan. Others fought bare-knuckle and their fellow Brothers cheered as they whaled on each other. Others danced. Some performing heavy-footed quicksteps as couples. Others jigging on the spot by themselves. All out of time with each other, for there was no music.

Aside from this, a cross had been lowered onto its back. It still retained its prior victim, a sorry wretch of a man with blistered skin stretched taut across his bones and grey frazzled hair atop his head. Though to Plum he did not seem to be alive, he must have been, for one of the

Brothers stepped forth and drove his spear through the man's chest and the crucified man turned his head to one side and died. Another man then stepped forward and prized the nails from his wrists and feet using a claw hammer and they dragged him from the cross. Two more crosses remained erect over this scene and the Brothers made crass gestures at the women nailed to them and some threw handfuls of stones.

Her father and Peter were then brought forward. Both were being handled by an unnecessary amount of men for her father was not resisting and Peter was still dazed from the sucker punch across his face. The Brothers tore off their clothes. Then one man held Peter's arms behind his back as the others struck his face, stomach and genitals. One man stepped forwards and squeezed her father's buttocks and began undoing the ties on his codpiece but one of his fellows slapped him around the face and gestured for him to move on. The offended man then kneed her father in the groin and her father doubled over into the dust. Then Peter was grabbed by the face and forced to watch as Cherry was stretched out and the first nail positioned just above the wrist between the forearm bones. The nail the same six-inch wrought iron monstrosity prized from the prior victim and still slick with his blood. Then the hammer was brought down. That sharp chink of metal on metal cut clear across the hardpan. And this was followed by Peter lowing like a demented cow as he watched helplessly on. Cherry did not make a sound.

Plum turned away and wiped her eyes on her sleeve. She paced back and forth beating her head with her fists and telling herself to *think, think*. In the distance, the second nail was driven home and Peter howled anew on her father's behalf. The crowd cheered. Hiroshi watched Plum. He was biting his nails and the blood had drained from his face which before had seemed to flush so easily. She stopped dead and faced him.

'Where's your armoury?' she said.

'What do you mean?'

'Where do you keep your weapons?'

'No. No. I'm not allowed up there,' he said, shaking his head.

'Look, you motherfucker,' said Plum, pushing him against the basilica wall. She came at him again and he tried to parry but she ducked and tripped his legs from under him. He fell to the earth in a swell of red dust and she knelt on him and grabbed a nearby rock. 'Look, it's a-cause of you my papa's up there. Now you show me.' She waved the rock in his face. 'You show me or I'll brain you.'

*

The armoury was on the upper floor of the basilica, which Plum thought impractical. She queried this with Hiroshi.

'I don't know,' he said. 'Only the Fathers are allowed up here.'

'I see.'

'What do you mean, *you see*?'

'Nothing. Doesn't matter.'

She looked out the armoury window at the scene below. Her father's cross was now raised front and centre and the Brothers crowded it. Their jeers a most hateful, hateful song. A hail of stones and other debris peppered the poor souls who were all bound naked to the crosses. The Fathers in their black robes looked on from the side, their servants fanning them and filling their cups of wine. Then Plum noticed the women of the Brotherhood emerging from the Red Basilica. They seemed uncertain. They hesitated, standing apart from the torture. One of Fathers saw this and approached them and gesticulated for them to get involved. Still they did not move. The Father brushed this insubordination off with a wave of his hand and returned to his peers and to his wine.

'What are these?' said Hiroshi.

Plum turned to face him. Using a crowbar, he had

prized the lid off a wooden crate stamped with hieroglyphs that to an old-world English-speaker would have read *DYNAMITE* but to he and Plum were gibberish. He was holding up one of the reddish-brown cylinders for her to see.

'Those are boomsticks,' said Plum, grinning like a rascal. Despite their earlier altercation, Hiroshi found himself grinning back.

'What do they do?' he said.

'My neighbour used them to break the rocks on her farm.'

Hiroshi looked utterly confused. He weighed the dynamite in the palm of his hand. Then he held it like a hammer and feigned hitting an imaginary rock with it.

'How?' he said.

'You'll see,' said Plum.

The two of them looked the rest of the armoury over. There were no ceremonial spears here but instead machine guns, shotguns, rifles, pistols. Crates on crates of ammunition. Little green eggs with pins sticking out of them that Plum had never seen before and figured best left alone. All this was stacked around a lopsided howitzer cannon with only one wheel. While Hiroshi was playing with a machine gun, spraying an imaginary enfilade and rolling his tongue, she pilfered two little snub nose .38's and dropped them in her rucksack along with a few boxes of shells. Then she said, 'Right,' and Hiroshi dropped the machine gun and came to heel like a good dog.

'You want to see something cool?' said Plum.

Hiroshi grinned but gave no answer. He did not seem to know what to do with his hands so he put them on his slender hips. Plum struck a match.

'Pass me that there boomstick,' she said.

Hiroshi obliged. Plum lit the fuse of that innocuous cylinder and tossed it out the window as though it were nothing more than a finished cigarette.

'Now what?' he said.

'*Shhh*,' said Plum, and cupped her ear to the window. 'Listen.'

Hiroshi responded in kind and Plum could not help but grin at his naivety.

The explosion throttled the building's foundation and Plum and Hiroshi were thrown to the floor. She clawed herself to her feet. Hiroshi remained sat, his mouth open and his eyes wide like a halfwit.

'What have you done?' he said.

But she did not hear him. His mouth opened and closed as silently as a fish's, for her eardrums were singing that tinny song her blunderbuss had so often sang. She ran to the window, and as she did, the song evanesced into the sound of people screaming.

Below, pandemonium. The Brothers jostled each other, fought each other, pushed each other down like desperate drowning men. A right pecking party. The Fathers were stood aside and calling for calm, but themselves calling in rattled, frightened voices. They wafted their robed arms as though beating back a fire. The dynamite had blown an evil-looking smile out of the basilica wall, like that of a jack-o-lantern, and it sneered silently at the commotion it had caused. The women composed themselves first. They braced each other with locked arms, like they were a single unit, a lattice of covalent bonds, a diamond.

'Forgive them, lord! They know not what they've done, what they do.'

Silence. Stillness. All waited on her father's word.

'Do not punish them, lord!'

Plum about-turned and made for the box of dynamite. As she knelt by the box, Hiroshi crawled to her and grabbed her shoulder but she shoved him in the chest and he sat back, shaking his head. She scratched a match into life and lit another fuse. This time she counted out the time it took to blow. *One, two.* She stood and ran from the room. *Three, four.* She chucked the dynamite over the balustrade and down into the foyer of the basilica. *Five, six.*

It landed in the centre of the circular reception desk and rolled to a stop against the panelling. *Seven. Eight.* Plum jumped to the floor and put her hands over her ears. *Nine.* She shut her eyes. *Ten.* The fireball flared off her eyelids as the reception desk exploded in a shower of splintered wood.

The screaming started up again. She was back at the window in time for her father's next address.

'O lord, I beg you, leave them be. They may still listen. O lord, if you must punish someone, punish the Fathers. It is they who have led your children so far astray.'

The women conspired amongst themselves and then with spears raised and with almighty battle cry they ran forwards to seize the Fathers. The servants dropped their fans and jugs and scarpered. The wine spilled over the earth like blood. The Fathers waddled after them but were quickly caught by the women who trod on the backs of their legs so that they would kneel and held spear blade to the quivering flesh of each throat. The Fathers called to the men to help them but it was now the men's turn for indecision. They looked from the Fathers to Cherry up on his cross and then to each other.

'O lord, if they let me live, I will teach them. I will teach them your merciful ways,' cried Cherry.

'Help us,' screamed the Fathers. 'Help us.'

A breakaway of men came to the Fathers' aid. The women dared them, heckled them. With their readied spears and fierce faces, they looked like a regiment of Amazons. The breakaways stalled, looked back over their shoulders, hesitated, and then shuffled back to re-join the other men.

'Traitors,' screamed the Fathers. 'Traitors. You will burn for this.'

The men clustered closer together. Some wrung their hands. Some bowed their heads in shame.

Plum returned to the box and retrieved one last stick of dynamite. She then grabbed Hiroshi by the hand and led him from the armoury. Out in the concourse, she took the dazed Hiroshi by the shoulders and said:

'You need to run, Hiroshi. You hear me?' His eyes were unfocused so she slapped his chops. 'You. Need. To. Run. Get as far away from the basilica as you can. Do you understand?'

He nodded his head.

'And don't tell anybody about this,' she said. 'Or else.'

He started to cry and Plum released his shoulders and he set off at an unsteady jog. He took the spiral staircase down, hugging the banister. Plum leant on the balustrade and watched as below he navigated his way around the crater in the centre of the foyer. At the door, he stopped and looked over his shoulder at her. There were tears on his cheeks. She waved him on and he disappeared from view. She waited a moment, drumming her fingers on the balustrade. Then she lit the fuse of the dynamite and heaved it cartwheeling through the air into the armoury.

'Shit. Shit. Shit,' she said as she hightailed it, taking the stairs three, four at a time. 'Shit. Shit. Shit.' On the ground floor, she leapt over the debris of the foyer's dismantled grandeur. 'Shit. Shit. Shit.' Outside, she saw Hiroshi shambling aimlessly over the hardpan. 'Shit.'

*

The universe restarted, such was the cataclysm.

A stovetop kettle was whistling somewhere and all was a terrible whiteness. So white it hurt her eyes. More lustrous even than her daddy's mother-of-pearl skin. Black waves started to break over that whiteness and for this she was thankful. Then she realised that she was looking at the sun and those black waves were the wind-blown corn. She was lying on her back and the earth was soft, a little damp. Martha's farmhands must have watered it. It whiffed of mulch, motor oil, dead fishies; it being the canal water they used to irrigate. She could feel someone's cheek on hers and it was so soft. So soft she started to cry. They were lying like north and south on a compass and their heads were the place where the needles met.

'My mama must be brewing some nettle tea,' said Bo. 'Shall we get us some?'

They sat up. Plum hid her face between her knees and wiped her eyes and nose on her filthy sleeve.

'Uh huh,' she said.

'Why you crying, P?'

Bo put his hand on her shoulder.

'I don't know. It's just…' She turned and took in all of his heart-shaped face, his cheeks high and dimpled, his skin black like the universe is black. 'It's good to see you.'

'I been here the whole time,' he laughed. 'You fall asleep or summat?'

She laughed and sniffed and smeared wet boogers across her face.

'Guess so.'

'Come here,' he said, and with one sweep he palmed the boogers off her face. '*Ewww*,' he said as he wiped them on his shorts.

'Shut up,' laughed Plum.

He stood and pulled Plum to her feet. He looked at her, marvelled at her, his black eyes glittering, as though maybe she had been gone a long time.

'What?' said Plum.

'Nothing,' he said.

He wrapped his thin arms around her and drew her close. She let her head fall onto his bony shoulder.

'It's good to see you too,' he said.

*

She awoke entombed. Above her, those anonymous stone idols that once stood above the basilica entrance now lay horizontal in a latticework that bore the weight of the toppled brick and mortar. The debris amounted on each side forming a cupola and a pale shaft of red light fell sideways through the skylight overhead where the debris did not meet. The dust motes were fat and many as a swarm of flies and when she breathed she coughed. She coughed and she thought she might not stop. Maybe cough herself clean to death. But through sheer force of will she caught the tickle in her throat. Held it there until it died.

Then, tranquillity.

It was so quiet. Yes, there was the noise of the world, the screaming, the shouting, but it seemed so far away and unimportant. She watched the evening clouds pass by through her sepulchral skylight. They were wispy, flamingo-pink creations. Transient. Beautiful.

'Plum. Plum. You there? Plum. Where are you?'

It was Hiroshi. His voice drew closer, closer, and then began to fade away. She let him go.

Who cares? she thought. *Nothing matters anymore. That's not true, don't say that. But it's true. No, it's not. Okay, maybe it's not, but I don't want things to matter anymore. Fine, just give up then!*

She sighed and wormed her way out from under the debris. Up, up she climbed, clambering on the backs of the fallen idols. She reached the skylight and pulled herself out and over onto a stretch of wall that leaned diagonally over where she had been buried. She lay across it, resting her head on her arm. She was cut to ribbons, her wounds cauterised with dust. She watched Hiroshi walk away still whispering her name at the piles of rubble. In the distance, her father and the other crucifixions were being lowered. The nails were prized from their wrists and feet.

Then, as the Brothers of The Messiah Caravan carried her father away on their shoulders, she heard him calling, 'Where... Where is my child? Where is my little Plum Blossom?' To which the Brothers cried back in chorus, 'O lord! I am here! I am here! I am here!'

HIGHDRAW, LOWDRAW

Martha awoke to exquisite pain.

'Steady now,' said a smoke-cured voice above her.

Martha grit her teeth and stared off to the side where a set of shelves housed vials of ointments and potions, all of them vivacious, promising health, life, a vital rainbow. To the side of these stood larger jars of murky piss-green formaldehyde in which were suspended rattlesnakes, chameleons, toads. A homunculus leaned its bulbous forehead to the gloomy glass of its timeless prison and looked out at Martha with sad, innocent eyes, its outsized hands crossed over its bone-thin legs in a manner of great repose.

The doctor's tweezers pinched the steel splinter in her back. As he began the slow pull, her body gave revolt, as though it now considered the bullet a part of itself. She gripped the table so hard her knuckles showed up white. Her breath broke hissing around her locked teeth. In. Out. In. Out. The doctor was nearly clear but she began to rise as he retreated, unconsciously, the pain driving the action, so that it looked as if he would pick her off the table with nought but his tweezers. Then something changed. The agony rolled back in waves, diminishing each time it broke over her. The bullet was out. It tinkled against glass. Then a shadow darkened her vision and the doctor knelt down so she could see him. He was old and lean with silver-black dreadlocks a good metre long and course as shipping rope. Naked from the waist up, his chest glistened with sweat. A fire was crackling in the hearth despite the heat of the day. He smelled of B.O., marijuana and coconut and his breath was hot and sour on her face. He presented her with a conical flask in which the bullet was submerged in clear fluid, her blood throwing out pink ribbons.

'Forty-four special,' he said. 'Ricochet.'

He gave a wide, gold-toothed smile.

'Thanks, Banjo,' croaked Martha.

The doctor's face snapped back to straight.

'Please don't call me that,' he said through gritted teeth. 'My name is Doctor Walters Onabanjo. You may call me doctor. As old acquaintances, I'd even stretch to Walt. Just not that. Not from you.'

'Okay, Banjo, don't get upset,' said Martha.

He rose flapping his hands in the air like a graceless bird.

'Always with this shit,' he continued. 'How many times? How many times have I fixed her up? Still she ridicules me. Banjo. Banjo. You are a sonofabitch, Martha.'

She wanted to laugh but her throat was dust-dry and she broke into a barking cough. When she opened her eyes, he was crouched down, inches from her face, scowling.

'Enough of this nonsense. Are you ready?'

She nodded.

'Very well.'

He walked off and she could hear him raking the fire with the poker. A trio of dried out witch heads hung from their hair like a wind chime sneered wickedly at her with their snub, leather faces, as though they saw what was coming and liked it. She heard the grating of iron on stone as Doctor Onabanjo drew the poker out of the fire.

'Wait,' said Martha. 'How about a little something for the pain?'

He set the poker back in the fire.

'Pain relief is a very pretty penny indeed.'

'Shirt pocket. My poke. Have your choice of coin.'

'Ah. I need to talk to you about that.'

Martha was silent. Doctor Onabanjo continued.

'You came to my table with debts that needed settling. The poke went to the girl Lily-Jane, for her ruined stock, and,' Doctor Onabanjo rounded the table and held up a mirror before Martha, 'for that.'

Therein reflected was the little girl's pappy. Like Martha, he lay on a table; but he lay on his back, naked, still, white as alabaster. Two coins topped his eyes. Martha sighed. She surveyed him as though there might be life there still. Then her eyes flicked from the dead man back to Doctor Onabanjo.

'Give me some poppy water and I'll let you keep his gold glasses,' said Martha.

'They're not for you and I to parley over. They're the boatman's now.'

'Don't give me that hogwash, Banjo. I know you've no respect for the dead.'

'I suppose. Respect for the living though, that I have in spades. The dead man looks out upon his daughter's faith and I'll not betray something so pure. The conscience is the root of every curse, jinx and malediction. Know that, Martha. Know that well,' he said, tapping his temple.

Martha sighed.

'Damn you, Banjo. Close me up.'

Doctor Onabanjo dragged the poker from the hearth in a swirl of ash and ember and touched its red tongue into the hole in Martha's back. She screamed. Her eyes rolled over in her head and the world strobed. The witch heads were cackling. The homunculus moaned with her, as though it felt her pain. She wondered what would give first, her mind or her heart. Then her mind whited over and she thought and felt no more.

*

The one who hunted her stopped to read a lonesome road sign pointing the way the schooner tracks run. It was but two planks of wood nailed into a cross standing no more than four feet off the ground, the townward end sawed to a point, and burnt into it was the words: *Salvation, 5 miles.* Squinting, she could just about see that small frontier town on the other side of the rippling heat. Hanging her stetson off the road sign, she mopped her brow. Then she knelt and collected up a handful of stones, letting them drop one by one until she was left with the one most round and smooth. This she wiped on the inside of her shirt before popping it in her mouth. It clinked off her teeth as she sucked. Then she returned the black stetson to her head and continued on.

*

When Martha woke, her whole body was throbbing, each body part putting forth competing claims as to which hurt the most. Her back had been dressed with white gauze through which a black-red spot had soaked and the precise pain the bullet had brought with it all those hours ago seemed to have mixed with her blood and that biting cordial dissipated throughout her body so that it now reached dully from her shoulders all the way to her posterior. Her head felt as though it had been scored straight down the centre and rendered in two. With her fingertips she gingerly touched where the backfire had gashed the fore and top of her head. Doctor Onabanjo had shaved away a strip of her hair and the skin had been sutured with yellow catgut so that the skin puckered up in a mangled kiss.

Doctor Onabanjo was sat across from where she lay, eyeing her. He smoked a pipe he had fashioned himself from a rusted, old-world kazoo. He crumbled a new lump of marijuana resin into the bowl and burnt it using a lit piece of kindling wood. He took a few draws, then shook out the kindling and placed it in a saucer wherein stood a white candle. He continued to regard Martha. After more than a minute had passed she realised he had not breathed. When he spoke, no trace of smoke came out.

'How are you living, Martha?' he said.

'Day at a time,' she said. Then, seeing his face, she said, 'It was just a ricochet, Banjo.'

'I'm not referring to the metal, Martha. Christ, you have the reaper himself sitting on your heart.'

He pointed to the tumorous mound bulging out from between her breasts.

'Oh that,' she smirked. 'I guess his black ass finds it nice and cool.'

Doctor Onabanjo was shaking his head. He rose and offered her the pipe. She smoked it prostrate and blew it out over the table. The smoke was so heavy it rolled off the edge of the table and tumbled to the floor, breaking in rolls like a spectral waterfall. The pain took a back seat, seemed to draw further away, until it was as if she was observing it in someone else. She began to chuckle.

'Why do you have all this voodoo on show, Banjo?' she said, nodding to the shelves of potions, the dried-up heads. 'You're no witch doctor.'

Doctor Onabanjo shrugged and smiled sadly. Looking at his pipe, he said:

'The people of this town just don't trust science anymore. They're scared of it. Half of them are drunk brutes. The other half all holier-than-thou. If I didn't masquerade as a magician, if they thought for one second I used the title *doctor* sincerely, they'd drag me through the streets today. As long as I have my ornaments and foibles, I'll always just be Banjo the crazy shaman. No harm to anyone. And if you die on my table, well what did you expect? You should have known better than to trust that hippie junkie. You've only got yourself to blame. But if you die on a doctor's table. No, no, no, that won't do.

Cause doctors aren't human. They're doctors. A whole other breed entire. Infallible. And yes, they may be gods while their patients live. But these days all it takes is a hundred-year-old leper croaking it on their watch and before you can say *penicillin* they'll be swinging from the rafters of their practice.'

'If that's the truth,' she said, 'then I'll have to ask you for another hit.'

Doctor Onabanjo smiled at her and, rising from his chair, brought the pipe to her lips and lit it for her. The heat from the kindling was fierce.

'I could have done with this before,' said Martha.

'You shouldn't have mocked me. You know how I hate that name.'

'You really are a petty sonofabitch, Banjo,' said Martha, dreamily, closing her eyes.

Doctor Onabanjo waited until she was asleep. Then he said:

'Don't you go and get yourself killed now, Martha. You're my last link to the old world. Oh Martha, how did we get from that to this? I miss it, Martha. I miss reason. I miss decency. It was a time of such promise. Why must that which burns brightest burn briefest? And it was so bright, Martha. So bright! When I shut my eyes, I can still see the afterglow.'

*

Martha's pursuer reached the town of Salvation and made straight for the saloon. The town was straight out of one of those Western movies she had watched as a child nearly half a century ago. Although it was less ornate. The buildings here were the stained wood you might expect; but they were patched up with corrugated metal, rotten cardboard, sheets of cloudy plastic nailed over windows in lieu of glass; Frankenstein's monsters of architectural endeavour. In the old Westerns, each speck of dust seemed placed in the name of beauty. For even dereliction in the movies was perfectly rendered. This town did not feel like that. This was a town of necessity. It was real. You could smell the cholera on the hot air.

The saloon was dimly lit. A hole in the roof patched up with some translucent tarpaulin let in a silvery oblong of light, bathing the splintered bar with a religious light, like it were an altar. Weak candle-flames burnt in the far reaches, profiling sorry wretches slumped over tables or lying on the dirt floor. The vinegar smell of impure opiate hung heavy on the air; as did the smell of human waste; as did death. Martha's pursuer approached the bar where a fat man turned a filthy rag round and round a cup of beaten tin. He paid great attention to his task, as though it were the highest of ceremonies. His eyes were all pupil, as though you could pass a finger clear into his skull without touching the sides. Sweat stood on his face in enormous, stationary beads that gave his features a knobbled look.

'Water,' she said.

The barman jumped and put a hand to his heart. The sweat leaped from his face in a scattering of jewels.

'Well ma'am if you didn't scare me half to death,' he said, and after he had taken a couple deep breaths, he beamed at her. 'Water, why yes, and a little whiskey on the side perhaps?'

'Just water.'

'Yes. Yes. Very good. I've got just the stuff. It's a little cloudy but it hits the spot.'

He held the tin cup he had been dirtying beneath a keg and turned the tap and a stream of bronze water trickled out. She was composed; but she gripped the bar real hard as she watched the cup fill up real slow like. She had gone twenty-something miles through the warm night and the hot morning and she was mad with thirst.

He tabled it in front of her. It whiffed of rum. She took it up and had a sip. Another. There was an audible plop as it hit her gut. She returned it to the bar and took a few deep breaths.

'You look like you come far,' said the barman.

She nodded, that big stetson accentuating the gesture. She took another couple of careful sips. Then she said:

'Where's the doctor at?'

'There ain't no doctor in Salvation,' he said flatly.

'Then where do you go if you ill?'

'Smart man'd go straight into the ground. But I suppose a desperate man might go see the old magic-man, Banjo, first. Y'know… and then into the ground.'

'Where's he at?'

'Other side of the road. Few doors down. It's the place with all the… funny stuff outside.'

She nodded and drained her cup.

'You don't look all that ill,' he said. 'I'd reconsider.'

She placed the empty cup upturned on the counter, as was the custom then in that part of the world.

'What do I owe you?' she said.

'What you got?'

She thumbed out a pistol shell from her fully stocked bandolier and stood it upright on the countertop. The barman stared at it. He cleared his throat.

'I know some who won't pay in slugs,' he said. 'They consider it a bad luck gesture.'

'Will it do?'

His wide eyes connected with hers, narrow, grey and cold beneath the brim of her hat. Like a scalded child, he looked down.

'It'll do,' he mumbled.

She nodded and stepped back out into the red street. The barman remained staring at the bullet, unsure quite what to do with it.

*

'Help me up, Banjo,' said Martha.

Though slight, there was a concealed power to Doctor Onabanjo and with great control and great care he raised her so that she was sitting. He allowed her a breather and then he helped her to her feet.

'I'm alright,' she said.

Doctor Onabanjo let go of her arm and she hobbled around the table and stopped at the dead man's side. Without hesitation, she fetched up those two gold coins that topped his eyes and presented them to Doctor Onabanjo, pinched between forefinger and thumb.

'I need a gun,' she said.

Doctor Onabanjo nodded solemnly and sauntered to an overhead cupboard from wherein he produced a Colt .45 revolver; around which, coiled like a brown snake, was a bandolier and holster of finest, old-world Spanish leather. Martha tabled the coins in a pool of her own congealing blood and Doctor Onabanjo did likewise with the gun. As she cinched the holster round her waist, he thumbed the black-red blood off those coins and made them sparkle again with his handkerchief. He inspected these hallowed objects by firelight and, satisfied, he placed them back atop the eyes of the deceased. Martha was loading the revolver. Doctor Onabanjo felt her eyes upon him.

'What?' he said.

'Nothing,' she said.

'I guess you best be going,' he said, walking to the door. He would not look her in the eye.

'I guess so.'

She walked towards him and holstered the revolver. He was crying. He hid his face behind his hand.

'Walters,' she said.

But as she approached, he turned his face away and opened the door…

And the long shadow of her reckoning fell in.

But both duellists were themselves unprepared. For Doctor Onabanjo had unwittingly pulled the trap away on this deadly game. Both drew with sleek, practiced movements. Both were swift. But Martha was the slower. The pursuer levelled her weapon at Martha's chest. Two gunshots exploded in quick succession, so close together they could have been one. That winy, tinnitus ring vibrated their eardrums. A revolver thudded against the pine floor.

The eyes of Martha's huntress bulged in their sockets, her face blanched and her mouth hung open in gaping horror. She was clutching her hollowed out leg and trying to hop backwards. Her good leg gave out from under her and she collapsed to the decking. The wind bore her stetson away.

The huntress looked up fiercely as Martha knelt beside her and disarmed her, tossing away a reserve pistol and a number of knives. Martha then drew her pursuer up into her arms as though she were but a child and sat herself on the porch steps, rocking her gently.

The denizens of the town were emerging and seeking the origin of the bangarang. A butcher came out of his shop wiping his bloody hands on his striped apron.

'That Banjo's up to no good again!' he said to everyone and no one, puffing out his chest.

In the next moment, a gang of raggedy street urchins filed out of an alley and the butcher started yelling at them to go home. They just laughed and threw sand at him. At this, the butcher disappeared back into his shop. When he returned moments later brandishing a huge meat cleaver, the larrikins scarpered, shrieking.

'Nettie, Nettie, Nettie,' said Martha. 'I always told you to opt for the lowdraw if the situation allowed it.'

The huntress, Nettie, spat.

'Guess I know for next time.'

Martha nodded.

'Damn this hurts.'

'You want me to end it?'

'Naw. It's okay.'

The noonday sun was punishing Nettie's eyes so Martha gestured to Doctor Onabanjo to retrieve the stetson. He beat the dust off it and gave it to Martha and she returned it to Nettie's head.

'Thanks.'

'How'd you know I was lying?'

Nettie snorted.

'That was a shambles of a cover up, Arty,' she said.

'Tell me.'

'Figured while I was there I'd pay my respects to Eddie and Bo.'

'So he knows they're alive, Cherry and Plum?'

'Yes.'

'He'll go after them?'

'Of course. What do you care?'

'She's a kid, Nettie.'

'So?'

'She's Bo's friend.'

In a flash of black and gold, Nettie patted Martha's cheek and left a bloody handprint there.

'You hokey old fool.'

Martha grabbed up Nettie's hand and held the fingers to get a good look at what had flashed before her eyes. On her marriage finger there glittered a ring of gold and obsidian. The devil's ring.

'You can talk. Oh Nettie. Which one?' she said.

'Lucien.'

'That pug bastard. Dear god, Nettie. Why?'

Nettie shrugged. Martha sighed.

'Mama would be proud,' she said.

Their eyes met sad and old and then Nettie convulsed and gripped her gored leg.

'Goddammit. Hold me, Arty,' she said.

Martha hugged Nettie as close to her as she could. They appeared the both of them two humongous children playing out some melodramatic game. In the next moment, Martha squealed and Nettie laughed.

'You bitch,' said Martha.

'Like a pig,' said Nettie, and died with her words.

Martha let go of her sister and she rolled off her and flopped down the porch steps like a ragdoll. She came to a rest face down in the red street to a rising of dust. Martha put her hands around the handle of the skinny flick knife sticking out of her side and drew it out and threw it skittering across the ground. In the next moment, she was howling with all her unadulterated rage. Cursing her sister; cursing the world. And the townspeople could not help but turn away from that shameful scene. In the electric silence that followed, a bold little street urchin ran to retrieve the flick knife to the cheers of her friends. Then the gang ran off together down the main drag, the sunlight glinting off the bloody little blade as the new owner waved it above her head, parrying away the sky. Martha watched as together the gang turned down the alley by the side of the butcher's and, by degrees, their gleeful screams died away.

FATHERS AND THEIR CHILDREN

That night, there was revelry. As darkness fell, the Brothers of The Messiah Caravan built bonfires and they slaughtered a great many of their pigs and erected their gutted carcasses over the fires on hand-turned spits. Before long, it seemed that barbequed pork was just what the world smelt of. Up rode a wagon and from under its awning was passed down barrels of ale and wine. One man offered to play barkeep but in less than an hour he was comatose on his back, drunk as hell. After that, it was a free for all and frequently came to blows.

Plum was all cut up from the explosion. She was sat by one of the barbeques, the flames dancing in her vacant eyes. She was not alone. A group of men more than twice her age were leering drunkenly at her.

'What's your name then?' said one.

'I bet you got a pretty name,' said another.

Plum did not seem to hear them.

'What's wrong? You a halfwit or something?'

'That's it. She's a retard.'

'Come on retard, loosen up.'

Still nothing.

'Women these days. No respect.'

'Her daddy must not have beat her hard enough.'

'Maybe he beat her too hard.'

They laughed at that. Then one rose to his feet, swelled up his chest and hitched his thumbs in the waistline of his codpiece.

'Look,' he said. Then two young women passed by arm in arm and stole his attention. 'Well would you look at these fine ladies,' he said, half to the women, half to his cronies.

With that, the five men leched after the pair, calling *What's your name then?* and *I bet you got a pretty name*, which got a giggle out of the women. Plum was left alone with nought but the woman turning the spit.

'You okay?' said the woman.

Plum looked at her but still said nothing. The woman looked around awkwardly and took a quaff from her tankard.

'My daddy used to beat me too,' she said.

'My papa don't beat me,' said Plum. 'My papa is Cherry Blossom.'

'Yes, yes, you're right. Cherry Blossom is our daddy now.'

Plum shook her head. That is when Hiroshi came ambling up out of the darkness with a couple of tankards.

'Beer or wine?' he said to Plum.

'Beer,' she said.

'Good,' he said. 'I'm more partial to the claret.'

The beer was warm and had bits floating in it but it was good. With that first mouthful, her brain was a clenched fist unfurling. Plum lit two cigarettes and handed one to Hiroshi.

'Thanks,' he said. 'Now, shall we finish cleaning those cuts?'

Hiroshi took her silence as a yes. Taking a rag from the bucket by her side, he wrung the pink water out and patted the dust out of the cuts on her arms. He had the cigarette in the corner of his mouth and the smoke was playing

THE MESSIAH CARAVAN

havoc with his eyes. The woman turning the spit watched them.

'Could I get one of those cigarettes,' she said.

'No,' said Plum.

'Jeez! I was only asking.'

'I was only answering.'

The three of them were silent but for the turning of the spit, the slop of the rag in the bucket. The party continued everywhere else.

'You're cut through your undershirt,' said Hiroshi.

Plum unhooked her dungarees, hitched up her undershirt, and leant forwards. Hiroshi dabbed the laceration, which ran across her back between her shoulder blades. It yawned like an envelope containing within a bloody valentine. Plum winced into her beer.

'You need stitches,' he said. 'I'll be right back.'

It was not long before he was trotting back with a catgut suture.

'Ready?' he said, a little out of breath.

She grit her teeth and nodded and Hiroshi went to work weaving her back together. She wished she had drunk more ale first. The skin around the cut was tender to the wet rag, let alone a needle. She kept her head between her knees and bit her knuckles and grizzled something fierce. She sounded like a wounded animal capable of massive and immediate violence.

Hiroshi tied off the suture and it was done. Plum took her fist from her mouth and replaced it with ale, the whole tankard. Her cigarette had gone out so she reached a shaking hand and drew a flaming branch from the fire in a shower of embers and relit it. She stood and clipped up her dungarees.

'Thank you, Hiroshi,' she said.

Then she walked off into the night.

*

She surveilled the tepee where they had carried her father. A lantern blazed within and the profiles of those inside played out across the awning like shadow puppets. One lay horizontally on a cot. Her father, presumably. Other shadows fussed over him like incubuses. The amber light fell out of the circular opening, illuminating those loitering outside. Some were drinking and cackling with laughter. Others were knelt in silent prayer. She watched, waited.

After a time, three Brothers exited the tepee and addressed the crowd, her father's lonesome profile the only one now projected.

'Our saviour has requested a little privacy whilst he convalesces. Come! Let us join in the festivities.'

The drinkers cheered and tottered off arm in arm, jumping on each other's backs, slapping each other's asses. Those on their knees finished their prayers in their own time. The three that had nursed her father idled and as those praying rose one by one they beckoned them towards the party. After a minute or so they said, 'Right, that's enough,' and hoisted the last of them up by their armpits and jostled them on their way.

In the ensuing fracas, Plum slipped into the tepee.

She knew her father had been crying in that silent way he had perfected where the face does not move and all the pain within falls in torrents out the eyes. Back home she had had a sixth sense about such things. Sometimes she would wake in the middle of the night, climb out her hammock, and get into bed with her father and spoon him. Only then would he break down into audible sobs and apologise for waking her. But this was different. He had stopped crying the instant she entered the tepee. In fact, he seemed happy. Exultant, even.

'My girl!' he said.

'How did you know it was me?'

'My dear, sweet girl, I know your sound by heart. Praise be. You're still here with me.'

'I'm still here.'

'And you're okay.'

'I'm okay.'

He flapped his hands, beckoning her to come close. She sauntered over to him and looked down into his face, so bald and scarred, like a cracked egg put back together. His blind eyes of perfect blue stared straight through her. She could not take it. She dropped to her knees beside him and buried her face into his chest, filling her mouth with his robe to muffle her moans.

'It's okay, little one,' he said, embracing her. 'Everything's alright.'

He held her until she calmed. Then he bid her sit beside him.

'Are we alone?' said her father.

'Yes.'

'Thank you. Thank you for saving me. Thank you for saving me *again*.'

'It's okay, papa.'

Plum reached and traced the bandages on his feet and wrists with her finger. Each had a red spot where the blood had seeped through and dried.

'Does it hurt?' she said.

'Yes.'

'Can you walk?'

'Not yet.'

'I'll steal us a wagon,' she said. 'And when they're all drunk and asleep I'll get us out of here.'

'No, darling.'

'Papa, we can't stay here.'

'And we won't. But don't you see? We have an army, Plum. Nobody'll be able to touch us ever again.'

'But, papa, they ain't loyal. They throwed out their old leaders just like that. They'll do the same to you.'

'I don't think so. Peter tells me that I am a most welcome change.'

'The same Peter who got you crucified?'

'My mind is made up.'

Plum folded her arms, huffed, and stuck her tongue in

her cheek.

'I know that sound,' he said, reaching for her face and poking the lump in her cheek so that it flattened. Plum gave the blind man a sad smile, her face smushed between his fingers. Then she sucked her teeth and shook her head free.

'I'm not going to be able to protect you forever,' she said.

'Who says?' he mocked.

'I say.'

'Little one, it's not your job to protect me.'

'No? Then why do I have to?'

Silence. Try as he might, Cherry could not think of an answer. Then...

'I found it! I found it! I found *The Messiah Caravan*!'

It was a giddy Peter, his face swollen from the beatings and garish in the lantern light. He came ducking through the opening of the tepee and then stopped dead upon seeing Plum there. The stocky book he hugged to his chest, he hugged all the tighter.

'It's okay,' said Cherry. 'Bring it here.'

Peter approached and handed the book to her father. He turned it over in his hands, smoothed his palm over its glossy dust jacket. Peter flared his nose at Plum. This was not how he wanted this moment to go.

'Tis a pity the devil took my eyes. I would have liked to have gazed upon this, to have read the words for myself. Read me some,' said Cherry, holding the book out to no one in particular.

'My holiness, I am sorry but I cannot read. None of the Brothers can. It was a privilege reserved solely for the Fathers. We were only sometimes allowed to gaze upon the pictures.'

'Yet another pity.'

'Can she read?'

'I tried to teach her. She didn't take to it.'

'How dreadful. To think she squandered such an

opportunity!'

'Reading is a terrible thing,' interrupted Plum. 'It steals the beauty out of things. Reading takes an apple, which is gold and red and green and brown, and turns it into black lines on a white page. Readers stop looking at the real apple; forget which the real apple is.'

Peter was horrified. He gaped at Plum and held his hand over his heart as though it might be vulnerable to her sentiments.

'How dare you,' he said.

Her father was chuckling.

'Behold my daughter, the illiterate philosopher,' he said. Then he said, 'Peter, go to your estranged Fathers. Tell them a single position has become available as my scribe and narrator. Select whomever seems most keen. I trust your judgement.'

'You flatter me,' he said, bowing his head and backing out of the tepee.

Once he had gone, Cherry felt for his daughter's hand and held it tight.

'Daughter mine,' he said. 'I am sorry but I need to ask something of you.'

'What is it, papa?'

'I need a doctor... A proper one. Do you remember Doctor Walters Onabanjo? He lives up at Salvation.'

'Of course. I remember Banjo.'

'Good. Good. I need his medicines. If possible, bring him to me also. It wouldn't hurt to have a doctor around. Tell him I'll make it worth his while.'

'What is it, papa? You reckon he can fix your eyes? Or did those fools bandage you up wrong?'

'No. No. It's not that,' he sighed. 'My pox is back. I can feel it. I can feel it *spreading*. I need those pills he has.'

'Okay, papa. Don't worry. I'll go first thing tomorrow.'

'That's my girl. And take this with you. He's a learned man. I'd be interested to hear what he makes of it.'

He peeled the dust jacket off the book and handed it to

Plum. She turned it over in her hands. There were those infuriating little lines that reduced the world to silent introspection. But also, on the inside cover, a black and white picture of a man's face. He was balding with scraggly whiskers on his lip and he held one of the temple tips of his spectacles in the corner of his mouth. Plum scoffed and stuffed it into her rucksack.

'I'll need a pony,' she said.

'I'll have Peter arrange one for you. Ah! Speak of the devil.'

'My lord?' said Peter, affronted. Cherry waved it off.

'I have tasked my Plum Blossom with a mission most secret and she requires a pony for her voyage.'

'That can be arranged, O divine one,' said Peter.

'Three,' said Plum.

'Excuse me,' said Peter.

'I need three ponies: one for me, one for the mission, and one for my companion.'

'Companion, aye? And who might that be,' quizzed her father.

'Yes indeed,' said Peter.

'Hiroshi,' said Plum.

'Oh no that won't do,' said Peter. 'Hiroshi is my underling. I'll not allow it.'

'The old religion is dead,' said Plum. 'You killed it remember? Hiroshi is free.'

'Lord, please...'

'She is right. Three ponies.'

'Yes, my lord.'

'Now, which of those mole-rats are to be my scribe?'

Peter was silent.

'Well?'

'None, my lord. They are so bold. They blaspheme. They spit. They desecrate your name to my face. None of them will ever work for you.'

Cherry sat up on his cot and passed his palms over his blind eyes. His mouth twisted into an abhorrent smile.

'Very well. Muster my disciples and wrangle forth the heretics. I wish to make an address.'

*

On Peter's orders, the Fathers were jostled out of the reeking pigpen that had served as a temporary jailhouse and were marched by spear-point across the hardpan. Their jailers called out to the rest of the Brothers who lay about inebriate, gorging on pig flesh, or else made up the mounds of naked, writhing bodies that were the fireside orgies. Gangs of children raced about through the night like desert poltergeists, throwing stones at the drunken adults, jumping over the fires and kicking the hot ashes so that fresh flames coiled upwards like blazing orange serpents.

'Come, my Brothers,' the jailers called. 'Come see what is to become of thy Fathers!'

The Brothers untangled themselves from their orgies and donned the vestments of their dead religion—the red skullcaps, the red vests and codpieces—before joining the procession. Others lumbered along behind clutching their swollen bellies. The children even came to heel and jumped and clapped and sang:

Ashes! Ashes! We all fall down!

'Torches,' called the jailers. 'We need torches!'

In answer to their cries, torches were lit and passed around and the night was cast in bronze. The procession came to a stop before the toppled basilica and the Brothers encircled the Fathers who hid their faces behind their black robes as though they might slip behind the curtain of night-time and escape. The Brothers hissed and spat and some brandished their torches at the Fathers who cowered back, falling over each other. One young man touched his torch to the tail of one of the Father's robes and the flames tore up his garments. The Father dropped and tried to roll but he was too cumbersome and he burnt up before them, his screams cutting through the blaze. The men looked on with devilish faces and whooped and patted the young arsonist on the back. The arsonist looked on with terrified eyes as his actions combusted before him. Then he turned and pushed his way through the crowd, his hands over his ears, screaming himself, so that he might drown out the screams of the man he was murdering.

*

In his tepee, Cherry sought council with Plum. He held out *The Messiah Caravan*. Plum took it from him.

'Search the pictures,' he said. 'Find he who I resemble. Find the one Peter called Jesus.'

Plum retrieved the book and leafed through its pages. There were many different glossy pictures of gods within. Not just men, women too. Naked women with long golden hair. Stone women with toned muscles sporting swords and shields. An ancient idol carved from browning ivory of a rotund woman with breasts that could feed an entire village. And animals. There were animals too. Cats and dogs and birds and snakes. Some with human bodies. Plum marvelled at a page of portly blue elephants who were either sitting cross-legged or lounging on couches. Then there was the moon, the stars. Then there was the sun.

She reached the back page without joy so she riffled the pages with her thumb and lo, did she imagine it, or had her father's face flashed out of the pages? She did it again, slower this time, and in doing so came upon the likeness of her father. He was long and thin and white and badly wounded. In the picture, he was nailed to a cross by his hands and feet, his head leant back against the wood, his sombre eyes taking in the heavens. There was an evil red smile below his ribs leaking a perfect line of blood and atop his head was a hat of thorns. On the opposite page, her father's likeness was repeated. Only this one had bronze skin more like that of her own and hair like sheep's wool. She tested the buoyancy of her own kinky hair with the flat of her hand.

'Have you found him?' said Cherry.

Plum nodded absentmindedly into the book. Then she looked up and said, 'Yes.'

'Do I look like him?'

In spite of the pain, Cherry was standing with his hands on his waist like a superhero.

'No,' said Plum.

'How about now?'

He took a deep breath, puffed out his chest and angled his chin upwards and slightly to the side in order to give a noble bent to his features.

'No,' said Plum, again. 'He's all hurt up like you. But he ain't proud about it. He looks sad. He looks meek.'

'I don't understand,' said Cherry, feeling blindly backwards for his cot and taking the weight off his tormented feet. His legs were shocked rigid from the shooting pain and his mouth was dragged across his face in a bitter grimace. The skin concertinaed on his forehead and around his eyes.

'That's it,' said Plum. 'That's what he looks like.'

Cherry scoffed.

'Sadists, the lot of them,' he said.

*

At her father's behest, Plum did not accompany him to the trial of the Fathers. When she asked why, he simply said, 'Appearances,' and would say no more. Plum climbed the ruins of the basilica and sat herself on a flat tablet of stone overlooking the crowded hundreds. The light from the torches did not reach up here and she sat invisible among the celestial canopy. She heard rubble shifting and rolling and turned to see Hiroshi clambering up the ruins behind her. He sat down near to her on top of a broken column. His eyes glittered with the stars and his teeth flashed briefly in the dark. She smiled back.

'We ride out tomorrow,' she said. 'Just me and you.'

'Yeah?'

'Yeah. I've got business in Salvation. After that, I thought maybe you might want to carry on. Take the pony and get your man Machiavelli. Live those dreams you spoke of.'

'Yeah?'

'Yeah.'

'Yeah. Okay.'

His teeth flashed once more, but briefly this time, and the glitter went out of his eyes. He turned away, looked down at those he had once called Brother, Father.

'What's wrong?'

'Nothing,' he said, wiping his eyes.

'It's what you wanted right?'

'Yeah.'

'Then don't put out the candles in your eyes. Not for those bastards.'

Hiroshi sniffed and ran his forearm across his nose.

'You don't understand,' he said.

'Dearest disciples!' cried Cherry below, stealing their attention.

The baying crowd fell silent. He stood atop a soapbox before the Fathers with both hands on Peter's shoulders for support. His face was mournful, his body broken, just like the man in the book. Atop his head was a garland of yellow and purple canal flowers.

'As I lay on my cot just now, God spoke to me. God said: *With your disciples' actions today, the tide has changed for humanity. The waves of evil that break over this land will begin to retreat. As they do, they will leave behind an earth capable of such bounty. For they were a tide of blood and filth. And blood and filth are fertilisers. Out of hate and badness will grow love and goodness.*'

The crowd cheered drunkenly. Though some within its ranks only frowned and clapped politely, confused as they were by the rambling metaphor. Cherry raised a hand for quiet, the torchlight illuminating the circle of blood on his bandaged wrist.

'But before love and goodness can grow, there is still

some filth in need of mucking,' he said, a wicked glint in his blind eye. 'I refer, of course, to the Fathers.'

The crowd roared. Cherry called for order.

'You have such rage in you,' he said. 'And who can blame you. For so long you have been lied to. Made fools of. My own stomach turns hot to think of the shame you must feel. You deserve satisfaction!'

The crowd grew hysterical. Their voices rose in ululations. Their hands clawed the sky. Cherry no longer begged for order. He let their rage grow, wielding it like a conjuror controlling a flame. He no longer looked like the man in the book.

'Never fear. I have a gift for you. A gift that will rid you of your rage. A gift that will exorcise the demon gnawing at your guts.'

Please, they moaned. *Please. Satisfaction.*

'First, throw off the clothes of the old religion. They are the relics of your slavery and while you wear them you are slaves to the past.'

The assembly hopped out of their codpieces and threw their skullcaps into the night sky. The vests were trickier. Their hands were shaking from the violence in their blood, making it impossible to navigate the ties of their corset-like vests. Individuals tore at themselves like they were trying to rip out their own hearts. In their frenzy, most only succeed in knotting their vests all the tighter and sought the teeth of their fellows and they worked on each other like animals feasting. Finally, knives were passed around and the remaining vests circumcised from their owners.

From above, the assembly was a pushing mass of naked bodies. Plum saw little children still clad in their red vestments crawling out on all fours between the legs of the naked and running off into the night waving to each other, calling to each other: *Stick together! Stick together! The grownups have gone mad!*

'Excellent. Excellent,' cried Cherry. 'And now for your gift. Your gift... Your gift is your Fathers. Do unto them what you will. Expend all your anger upon them. Let their bodies be the earth to your electric rage.'

The naked crowd moaned as a single unit and closed in upon the Fathers like zombies, biting, tearing, rending. The black robes of the Fathers were flung phantom-like into the air, revealing their tender white flesh ever so briefly before the naked mass fell back in upon them, their bodies dancing like maggots on meat.

Through it all, Cherry stood blindly on his podium, smiling, both hands on Peter's shoulders, as though he was giving him a massage. Peter was smiling too.

Plum watched and smoked. Hiroshi hid his eyes. After their time in the crucible, individuals would push their way through the crowd and emerge slick with blood, offal in their mouths, and those next in line would press in and have a turn mashing at the mound of gore at the centre of the assembly. Those on the periphery staggered naked and blood-drunk across the hardpan, collapsing into one another, clinging desperately to each other, crying, laughing.

As the frenzy dwindled, Cherry spoke into Peter's ear and Peter took him down from his soapbox and carried him back to his tepee; Cherry with his arms around Peter's neck as though they were a married couple stepping over the threshold together.

As the hundreds dispersed and migrated back towards the barbeques, the aftermath revealed itself by the light of the discarded torches. The red earth now stained a deeper red. The bodies of the mutilated Fathers sat in the blood like meat in a stew. The stragglers left one by one until there was but one man pounding his fists against a puddle of guts. Eventually, he too rocked back on his heels, took a deep, quavering breath, and began to cry.

The children had formed a group and were returning to the scene of the massacre. They made sure to keep well clear of the last man as he staggered past them towards the barbeques. Plum watched the children. They seemed to be looking for something. No, someone. Then, one of the children saw something in the darkness beyond the light of the discarded torches. He ran to whatever he saw and was swallowed by the night.

'No, no, no, no,' returned his desperate voice out of the darkness.

This was followed by a strangled squawking, like a crow or raven. The boy then came running back into the light of the torches.

'He's still alive,' he said. 'What should I do? I don't know what to do.'

He was pacing back and forth, pulling at his sandy yellow, bowl-cut hair. Plum got up and started to clamber down the rubble.

'Where are you going?' said Hiroshi.

When she did not answer, he followed.

Plum jumped down onto the hardpan and sprinted towards the children. They were very little. Half her size. They watched with wide, frightened eyes as she came charging up to them.

'Help! Help!' said the boy, his eyes aflood with tears. 'I don't know what to do.'

Plum took up a torch from the ground and explored the darkness. Rocks and dust and nothing else. Then she came to him. When Hiroshi caught up, he took one look and heaved up his wine. It was the same sandy haired boy, she thought. Only this one was lying on the ground, his arms and legs out at funny angles. He was lying on his front but somehow he was also looking up at her. His eyes were wide, scared. His mouth stuck like a tragic mask, out of which rattled that bird noise. He had been crushed. Crushed beneath the waves of those he had once called Brother. Plum stared at him, he at her. Then she dug her hand in her dungaree pocket, pulled out her .38, and shot him through the head. The back of his skull leaped out in a shower of grey and white and red and black and then darkness covered him for Plum had heaved the torch spiralling over the hardpan.

She emerged from the darkness and the other sandy haired little boy came charging at her, wailing, he ran his head into her chest and started hitting her with the bottoms of his balled up little fists.

'I'm sorry,' she said. 'I'm sorry. There was nothing I could do. I had to make the pain go away.'

And she was hugging him as he pummelled her in the sides. Hugged him all the tighter as he clutched her leg and bit it. When he slumped to the ground sobbing, she lifted him up and hugged him all the way back to the camp where the adults were starting once again to feast and to drink.

*

Plum stowed the desperate little boy in the hayloft of a barn where below the donkeys, ponies and horses lay dozing on their sides. The animals raised their heads at the passing of the children and watched them ascend the wooden ladder to the loft, their oval eyes black and starry. To look on those eyes is to look at the cosmos from the outside. Plum lay the boy in the hay and his friends nuzzled round him like a mischief of mice.

'Will you stay while we fall asleep?' said the sandy haired boy.

'Yes,' said Plum.

She and Hiroshi sat side by side and watched as the little children snuggled deeper into the hay and dropped to sleep one by one.

'I need to check on my father,' whispered Plum, once the last child had fallen asleep.

Hiroshi nodded.

'I'll stay here,' he said.

She shuffled across the loft on her hands and knees and eased herself down the ladder. As she touched down, a piebald shire horse rose up part way and snorted. Plum turned and looked it square in the black mirror of its eyes. There she was reflected. Doubled. Her image sealed behind their opalescent sheen. Wild and bloody. She could have been one of those half-animal-half-human gods in *The Messiah Caravan*. The horse lay back down in its bed of hay.

Outside, the festivities continued. There was a rumbling of bodhráns laced over with fiddle music and the Brothers danced naked around the fires. Plum found an abandoned barbeque and pulled fistfuls of pork, which she wrapped in the cornhusks that lined her rucksack before stowing them away for tomorrow's journey. She then took another handful of the blackened meat and ate it like one might eat an apple. There were several fistfights being waged by the beer barrels so she siphoned the part empty tankards dotted around into a single cup. She drank and she ate and she watched the revelry from the darkness.

The lantern in her father's tepee had burned low. She stood a little ways off and finished her meal. She drained her tankard and threw it at the revellers. It hit one of the fire pits and sent up a shower of sparks and the dancers whooped and clapped and sashayed around the fire. She spat and wiped her greasy hands on her dungarees.

She remained at the entrance of the tepee and ducked her head through the small opening. Her father lay on his cot in his white dress robe and in his arms was a naked Peter. He was running his hand over Peter's perfectly bald head and cooing to him and Peter could have been in heaven above going by the expression on his face. Plum sneered and shook her head. Peter's eyes opened and he saw her and he grinned a grin that made Plum want to go and put his teeth out. Plum spat and walked away.

*

Back in the hayloft, Hiroshi was sleeping. He lay on his side with his knees to his chest and his hands clasped before his face as though he was praying. The children were still sleeping peacefully. Some held hands. Some touched feet or heads. It was hot and musty up in the loft among the hay and they had little rosy cheeks the lot of them.

Plum grabbed herself a ball of hay and made her bed next to Hiroshi, setting her rucksack as a pillow. She lay down so they were back-to-back, a little apart. Then she shuffled backwards so that her shoulder was touching his, just barely.

THE DEVIL, A PROLOGUE

The lead 4x4 ploughed through the chain-link fence of the disused airfield, a section of the fence catching on the running board and dragging along the tarmac so that the rest of the convoy filed through in its sparkling wake. The airfield was still as a graveyard beneath the immaculate light of the full moon and the convoy roared across the runways, splitting the sacramental silence. Megalithic airplanes strewn in death's disarray remained standing in illusory operation, or were bowed low like monks with their noses smashed across the tarmac, or lay vandalised on their tubular sides next to their sheared wings, and the line of little vehicles passed beside each of them through that Ozymandian scene.

An aircraft hangar loomed ahead and the convoy accelerated in its direction. The cars stopped before it, the engines cut off, out went the headlights, and fifteen gunmen dressed all in black alighted swiftly from the four cars. They carried shotguns and assault rifles and after a quick check of their weapons they made their approach, the torchlights mounted on their weapons strobing off in all directions like some dreary disco ball.

A small red door to the right of the enormous white

shutters was the only entrance and they lined along the hanger as their captain tried the handle. Unlocked. He pushed the door and it opened silently and the group funnelled swiftly inwards into a blackness complete as starless firmament. The tail broke off searching for the lights as the rest of the group moved forwards. He found the mains; but when he pulled the handle, it clanged impotently, and he hastened to re-join the group. The captain stopped and switched off his torchlight. The rest copied him. When the tail caught up, he did the same. Out there in the darkness, a light was twinkling feebly. The captain hesitated, his eyes fixed on the little dancing light ahead. On account of the profundity of the darkness, the blinking light began to scintillate and he squinted against it and by degrees there materialised beside it the white oval of a head.

'It's him,' he said.

Without further ceremony, he moved forwards, his relit torchlight coring out the immediate darkness. The rest of the group followed suit and together they navigated that cosmic blackness like a single searching spaceship. All the while, like a moon, the white face hovered before them. As their torchlights touched and then reached over the scene, illuminating it, an agitation ran through the group as they attempted to comprehend the tableau to which they were witness.

There sat the devil, mouth open, as though lobotomised. He was leant forward regarding himself by candlelight in a freestanding cheval mirror of finest mahogany. His wrists and ankles were bound to the chair, a sturdy yet ornate creation, and his left shirtsleeve was rolled up, his arm hooked an intravenous drip that delivered a russet-coloured cocktail. The captain approached and knelt before the devil and was dwarfed by the devil despite being a big man himself. The captain looked up into the devil's emerald eyes but they did not comprehend him. The devil continued to stare at his own likeness in the mirror with a mindless obsession that suggested he perhaps saw something else there besides.

'Sir,' said the captain.

The devil did not move. The gunmen scanned their surroundings for signs of ambush as the captain examined the devil. There was no evidence of torture, no bullet holes, no blood. His clothes were ordered save for the drool that darkened his vermillion waistcoat and the urine that he sat in. His watch-chain still ran to his pocket and the pocket still bulged with its platinum timepiece. Rings of silver, rings of gold, still adorned his fingers. No injury. No theft. Even the devil's revolver with its handle of red jasper lay on a nearby table among the candles.

'What did they do to you?' mused the captain.

He peeled away the tape and drew the needle from the devil's forearm. A single bead of blood ran down from the puncture. The captain looked up from the needle and flinched for the devil was staring straight at him. He dropped the needle and it swung on its tubing like a queer pendulum, sending outwards a great many strange shadows in the variegated light. The devil surveyed his rescuers, his walrus moustache bristling. Then, turning back to the captain, he spoke.

'Where is my brother,' he said. 'Where is Lucien?'

'He's searching a factory building on the outskirts of the city. We've been getting a lot of false leads.'

'Did he tell you to say that?'

'Sir?'

'He should be here.'

'We'll take you to him directly.'

'He should be here. To see. To see.'

'To see what? Sir, what does he need to see?'

'That there is no phoenix. Only ash.'

'Sir, who did this to you?'

'Why, old sport, the godkillers, of course.'

'Who?'

'The godkillers.'

'Who are—'

'Who? Who? What are you a fucking owl? I'm gonna fucking—'

The devil cut his tantrum short and took a deep breath through his nose, exhaling slowly. The wood of the chair creaked beneath his almighty grip. The devil noticed this and relaxed his hands.

'I'm sorry, old sport, still a bit of the old me coming through.'

The devil turned back to the mirror and said no more. The captain looked back at his squad and then pulled out his knife and cut the devil's binds. It took a moment for the devil to comprehend his release. He stared absently down at the severed ropes and then he rose rubbing his wrists. The captain took a few steps backwards. The devil towered above them all. His neck clicked as he rolled his head about his shoulders. Then he bowed and conspired with the mirror, whispering goodbyes, secrets. The gunmen looked on.

'Sir,' said the captain. 'Shall we go?'

The devil paused, eyed the captain suspiciously, then nodded. Drawing himself back up to his full height, he walked towards the gunmen and their torchlights danced around him as they cleared his path. The devil's revolver glinted in the candlelight and the captain grabbed it and caught up with him.

'Sir,' he said, offering the revolver by its barrel.

The devil turned and screamed. 'No!' he said. 'No! No!' He swiped the revolver from the captain's hand and it went clattering along the floor and was swallowed by the darkness. 'No! No!' And he was beating down on the captain with the bottoms of his fists like a gorilla. The captain raised his arms in defence but it was futile. When the devil finally stopped, the captain lay crumpled on the floor of the hangar. The devil squinted in the light of the torches for they were all of them fixed on him and all of them quivered in the shaking hands of the gunmen. The devil was snorting like a hog; the captain's breath could be heard rattling in the wreck of his rib cage. Then, all of a sudden, a change occurred in the devil and he became timid, childlike. He looked upon what he had done and he began to whine. He shuffled anxiously from foot to foot and he pinched and pulled at his crotch through his trousers.

'That was bad,' he said. 'I oughtn't have done that. Bad. Very bad. Sorry. I'm so sorry.'

The devil beat his head with his fists. The gunmen edged away.

'So stupid,' he said. 'Don't be mad. Please don't be mad.'

He started to blub, his arms straight and tense by his sides. The gunmen held a silent conference behind their torchlights and then one came forwards and addressed him.

'We'll talk about this… when we get home,' she said.

The devil sniffed and nodded.

'Let's go,' she said.

She set the pace and the devil followed close behind her, his head bowed. Every now and then, he would look back over his shoulder at the rest of the gunmen. Outside, she held the car door open for the devil and as he boarded there proceeded a race amongst the other gunmen to get a seat in a different car. A tussle for the last seat ultimately broke out between the two gunmen lugging the captain's broken body. As soon as the captain was stowed hastily in the trunk, they grappled and one quickly fell to the floor with the wind knocked out of him. The defeated party rose and shut the boot on the captain who would therein die. He then took his seat in the rear of the 4x4 alongside the devil.

*

The tenements and skyscrapers of New Sodom towered above them and the devil gawked at them as though seeing them for the first time, his forehead on the glass, his breath steaming up the window of the 4x4. Fires burned high up in these dark buildings in old drums lugged up stairwells or hoisted by rope up the disused elevator shafts. Around them would crowd the cold and the weary, the hungry, and if they were lucky there would perhaps be a little mulligan stew brewing in blackened pots. Down below, the harlots and the gigolos lined the streets beneath lanterns that filtered the light scarlet. Inebriates swaggered across the road with jars of moonshine, the labels of which read: *MARTHA'S SILVER CORN WHISKEY*. The convoy blared their horns and the drunks cleared the way or else were knocked down. The devil started pounding his head against the window and the pane reverberated in its frame. The driver and her fellow gunman exchanged glances in the rear-view mirror.

'We need to get off this street.'

'The road ends when it ends.'

The devil was pulling at his trousers and the swelling that bulged beneath them was causing him noticeable discomfort. The rhythm his head was keeping on the glass quickened in time with the beating of his heart, the throbbing of his blood. Then, all of a sudden, he was gone. The driver looked back in time to see him disappear out the door. She saw him out the rear window rolling in the road. The jeep skidded to a stop and so did the rest of the convoy but by the time the gunmen had alighted the devil was already up and a ways down the road, snatching clumsily at the courtesans who fled screaming before him. The pimps and the dueñas emerged and herded their boys and girls inside and some of them warded off the devil with their canes or with baseball bats crowned with barbed wire and the devil would recoil covering his face and move on to torment those further down the street. Ultimately, a madame dressed in a dirndl and of great stature stepped out into the street whirling a morning star flail like some nefarious milkmaid and ran the devil off for good shouting, 'Verlassen, verlassen, du bist hier nicht willkommen!' The devil fled wailing and passed from that scarlet scene into the outer dark. The gunmen pursued and so too were swallowed by the darkness. The madame shouldered her flail and watched them go. Then she turned and went back inside.

*

The gunmen lost the devil in the dark. They scanned the alleys and the side streets but to no avail. All the while, the constellations rotated above them through the vertical vistas of the serried buildings. Human time was abandoned and all were whisked away by its cosmic cousin who makes a comedy of the parcelling out of lightness and of darkness. All went blind to their individual spotlights; and as their torches died one by one, the gunmen sought out the light of their comrades. They rallied in an old plaza, the moonlight shimmering on a dead fountain: the cherubs holding their peckers, the women thrusting out their breasts, their nipples barren fountainheads. Beneath them, the water was black and still.

'What do we do?'

'We're so fucked!'

'Why didn't you lock the door?'

'Don't you dare blame this on me. You just stood by and did nothing, coward.'

'This isn't helping. We report in. We get help.'

'If we go back empty-handed Lucien will execute us and hang our bodies from the highest building.'

'She's right. We carry on looking.'

'And what happens if we don't find him?'

'If we don't find him I don't plan to stay around to find out. I suggest you all do the same.'

'We could lie. Tell him it was a hoax. Tell him his brother weren't there.'

'We've been gone for hours. How'd you explain that?'

'Look, we're wasting time. You four get the cars. Meet us back here. We'll keep looking.'

The four set off as bidden and the rest of the group

conferred and assigned themselves directions before dispersing outwards once more. The search continued fruitless. The streets were deserted. The night grew darker. Dawn was approaching. They passed from street to silent street. A baby started barking like a seal somewhere out there in the velveteen morning and the mother hummed a song of soothing on which the gunmen converged like sailors to siren song. The mother was sat on a crate behind a reeking metal bin and the gunmen passed her unawares on their first tour of the alley for she ceased her singing with the approaching footfall. The baby gave a rasping cough and the gunmen spun around, the mother squinting fiercely through the light and clutching her baby to her ragged dress. The infant was not yet three months old and its airwaves were swollen from an infection, each breath dragged down into its little lungs. The mother tried to shield it from the light but it craned its head, mesmerised, its black eyes glittering.

'Has anyone passed by here tonight?'

The mother said nothing. They would have dismissed her as dumb if it was not for the keen and knowing glint in her eye.

'Has anyone passed by here tonight,' the gunman repeated.

'Anyone? Aye. Aye. Anyone he says and he might be right in that it could have been anyone in that death comes to anyone and everyone and in coming to them becomes them so that I guess that in the reverse anyone could be death when I saw death running by back when the moon was yonder.'

'This hag's crazy.'

'Which way did he go? Did he say anything?'

'He went the way you're all headed, which I think you already know, and I guess it's my duty to tell you to leave such assassinations to the almighty, but I can see you'll not listen. Eh, my darlings? Anyhow, my duties done. See, lord? I thought he'd maybe come for my Mary but of course he wouldn't come for something so little when a fairy woman could take one in each hand. *Gomorrah! Gomorrah!* he was wailing. *Gomorrah! Gomorrah!* And I realised he was not my Mary's ruin but the ruin of our sister city entire. But ruination so massive is by no means stable, which is how come this curse comes to be lodged in my Mary's throat.'

The gunmen conferred behind their torchlights.

'Do we go on?'

'No. We regroup as planned. There's but one road to New Gomorrah.'

And like that, the gunmen were gone, their torchlights flitting back the way they came, regressing once more into the night, as though the mother had been visited by a band of yellow orbs and nothing more.

*

As the convoy roared out of New Sodom the sun was rose before them and behind them was illuminated the city in all its derelict and gunmetal grandeur. In the new light could be seen the tallest building and the bloody cornrows wig it wore, which upon scrutiny revealed itself to be the hanged dissidents of the devil. The road to New Gomorrah stretched out before them, a single grey tablet part reclaimed by the desert. The red dust moved in swathes across the blacktop, snaking in the sultry morning air, cycloning in the wake of the convoy. The roadside was strewn with agave, desert spoon and prickly pear, and all rotated slowly by as the defunct telephone pylons did their best to maintain a little perspective through that seemingly endless waste. The road ran squarely to the horizon and disappeared over its rim directly into the calamitous heart of the sun and as the convoy passed over that barren landscape at great speed there began to materialise by degrees a dark speck silhouetted against the sun, like an impurity floating in a crucible of molten gold. There was no doubt in any of their minds. They drove on and the sun ascended and hung an infernal halo above that fleck of darkness, which grew before them and as expected grew into the devil. He was jogging, a weary shuffle, his head bowed, as though at the tail end of a marathon. His waistcoat was unfastened and his collar yawned, exposing his chest; sweat glistened in the curling black hair. The convoy slowed to a crawl and the devil kept on. His trousers were unzipped and he had them hiked up by the belt hole with one hand whilst the other hand massaged beneath his breeches. He wore the same countenance of pained frustration he had adopted in the back seat of the 4x4 as they rolled through the red-light district all those hours earlier. He was oblivious to the convoy. He kept pace, kept rubbing himself in the same furious manner. The lead 4x4 pulled alongside and the driver wound down the window.

'Sir, sir, you really need to come with us,' called the driver.

With that, the devil removed his hand from his undergarments and beat himself over the head.

'Shut up! Shut up!' he cried, as though the driver's words came from within his own head.

The gunman riding shotgun, grim faced and growing impatient, reached across and sounded the horn. It echoed out across that sparse landscape. Prairie dogs communing in a pocket of baked grass ducked back down their burrows. The devil stopped and faced them, his head cocked as though unconvinced of their materiality. The convoy pulled ahead and blocked the road and the gunmen alighted. At all times their guns remained pointed impotently at the ground.

'Sir, please get in the car.'

The devil seemed confused, intrigued.

'Sir, please…'

'I will not be going back,' said the devil.

'Sir, you're not in your right mind.'

'But I am. You see, in my bondage, god came to visit me… She blessed me… Can you fathom the import of this? *She* blessed *me*! Her blessing… it was a thought… a single righteous thought… and she said that if I nourish this thought it would certainly take and more would follow… like a single seedling proliferating outwards into a meadow. But I cannot protect it there, the thought; it dies, it dies in my own kingdom. I need to protect it from the forces inside myself… My compulsions… My creations.'

He was rubbing himself again and he started to moan as though in pain and then he was screaming, screaming at his swollen genitals, commanding them to 'Stop it! Stop it!'

'Sir, what is this thought you must protect?'

The devil calmed. He looked up and his lips spread wide as a wave of serenity washed over him. His eyes lit up and he beamed down at them.

'Yes. Yes. The original righteous thought. Why, that I am her son and that through this relation I am forever kin to the stars that burn against the terrible cavity that darkens both our days and dreams. This is what I must protect… what I must never forget… what I must always praise within the tabernacle of my skull.'

Then he raged into his crotch once more before composing himself with these words:

'I am no phoenix… only ash… and the wind blows me yonder.'

The gunmen looked on confounded as the devil measured his breathing and recaptured his capricious zen.

'Sir,' piped up one of the gunmen, 'what should we do? We cannot return without you.'

'That decision is not mine to trouble over. We are no longer each other's concern. You are hereby released from my influence.'

The gunmen looked at each other.

'Now,' he said, 'I must be going. The leaf is turned. A new life waits for me at the end of this road.'

He approached them and sluiced through the blockade unhampered and the gunmen watched him slowly diminish down the highway to New Gomorrah.

A DEAL WITH THE DEVIL

The devil is dead. Long live the devil. All hail Lucien, devil of New Sodom!

That night, as the Brothers celebrated their emancipation, the new devil paid a visit to the town of Salvation. Three of his black 4x4s rolled down the main drag, their headlights bleaching the night. The denizens of the town cowered by their windows, watching, waiting.

The cars stopped outside the house of Doctor Walters Onabanjo and the devil and his cronies alighted. They were a motley crew of roughhousers with faces full of tribal tattoos or sugar skulls sat over their features. Nose-bones, gouged earlobes, and mohawks of electric green abounded. Some wore biker leather of an age gone by. Others were dressed in chequered harlequin outfits like circus freaks. One man wore lipstick and a white wedding gown; when he hitched up his dress to draw his desert eagle, he flashed his lace panties.

The devil stood front and centre whilst his cronies loped about baring their teeth at the darkness like hyenas. His face was pocked with bloody indentations where the broken glass had been pulled. He took a step forward and hailed Doctor Onabanjo's house.

'Doctor, come now, don't be shy.'

The door to the house creaked open and Doctor Onabanjo stepped out onto his porch. He was wearing a pair of brown chinos and nought else but still his body glistened with sweat. They shone their torches on him and he held up his hand against the glare. His eyes were red as hellfire and in his hand he clutched his kazoo pipe from which rose a thin strand of grey smoke.

'Doctor, I am looking for Martha Biobaku. Is she on your table?'

'She was.'

'And where is she now?'

He shrugged.

'Only she knows that. She rode out before the sun died.'

'Rode out?'

'Yes sir. She done bought herself a horse with her sister's clobber.'

'And what of her sister? What of Nettie Biobaku. What of my wife?'

Doctor Onabanjo coughed into his fist and looked over his shoulder through the open door of his home and practice. Therein was the silhouette of Nettie Biobaku, deceased.

'Well?' said the devil.

Doctor Onabanjo turned back and stared into the pristine torchlight.

'I suppose you best come in,' he said.

Doctor Onabanjo stepped aside and gestured through his open door into the dark house. The devil stepped up onto the porch followed by three of his cronies. As he drew level with Doctor Onabanjo, the doctor could not meet his eye.

The devil went in and his rage came out, as though the house itself were possessed, the door a screaming mouth. His cronies hung around on the porch. None dared follow him in. The screams continued. Then a shot was fired through the roof of the house and Doctor Onabanjo cowered behind the stone gargoyles that decorated his porch. The devil's cronies pointed at him and laughed, flapped their arms like chickens, pecked at the night air. *Bok, bok, bok!* Then a bullet whizzed out the open door and a bald-headed woman in harlequin chequers crumpled to the floor. At that, the cronies shut up and ran for cover behind the 4x4s. The devil fired until all chambers were spent, the bullets splintering the wood walls of Doctor Onabanjo's home, dinting off the row of cars.

The devil came storming out of the house, his pudgy face purple as a fig. He found Doctor Onabanjo cowering among the gargoyles and stood over him, levelled his revolver and pulled the trigger. It clicked impotently, the bullets spent. Doctor Onabanjo opened his eyes in time to see the butt of the gun arcing towards his face. He jumped backwards and the devil succeeded in clubbing the horns off a nearby gargoyle. The devil then dropped his gun and leapt on top of Doctor Onabanjo, straddled him, and started shaking him by the shoulders.

'Which way did she go?' he screamed in his face. 'Which way did she go?'

'That way. That way.'

'Gomorrah? Gomorrah. Yes, of course.'

The devil stood and snapped his fingers thrice at his cronies and two of the 4x4s loaded up and went roaring off across the hardpan. Doctor Onabanjo remained on the floor, shaking as the devil paced the boards of his porch, kicking over his ornamental gargoyles. The devil's revolver lay at the doctor's feet—but what use was it? The devil saw the doctor looking at it and approached him, a malevolent grin on his lips.

'Pass it to me,' he said.

'What?'

'Pass it to me.'

'Please. No. No.'

'Pass. It. To. Me.'

Doctor Onabanjo sat up and collected the revolver and, holding it by the barrel, offered it up, the empty cylinder rattling with the shaking of his hand. There was still a void between them, which the devil refused to reach through, and the doctor yielded and shuffled forwards on his knees. The devil snatched the gun out of the doctor's hand and started feeding fresh rounds into the cylinder. With each click, the doctor winced. He had his eyes tight shut now and tears beaded down his cheeks. His hands were clasped together like a man of faith.

'Please don't kill me.'

'Come now, doctor, you must do better than that.'

'I will help you.'

'How could you possibly help me?'

'If she comes back. *When* she comes back. I'll take care of her for you. She always comes back here, beaten up, stabbed up, shot up. I'm always putting her back together. She's a revenant you see. Bullets and knives, it's like she's immune to them. Strychnine on the other hand, no one immune to that. I'll do that… for you.'

'Ha! For me?'

'Yes. For you.'

'I suppose you'd expect to live for such a gesture?'

Doctor Onabanjo gargled on his words.

'Okay. Okay. How about this then? Are you a gambling man, doctor?'

'The way I see it, everything's a gamble. Things might happen, things might not, and people stake accordingly.'

'Good. A man after my own heart. So, here's the game. You have a week for Martha Biobaku to return. During which my beautiful assistants will keep you company. If she does, you drug her. You then give her to me. I want her alive. If this happens, you keep your life. However, if she does not materialise, I will have to assume that she has made it to New Gomorrah and you, doctor, will inherit her fate.'

'But. But. But,' stammered Doctor Onabanjo.

'Or you can forfeit your life now. A swift one through the skull. Why not? Grief has made me soft. Although I think neither of us wants this.'

'Please. Don't.'

'Well?'

Doctor Onabanjo nodded.

'Come, come, that is not enough. Where is your gambler's honour? Stand and shake, man!'

Doctor Onabanjo pushed himself up. He was unsteady on his feet, as though he stood in a dream. The devil hawked a good gobful of phlegm onto his palm and held it out. The doctor spat what little spittle he could muster onto his hand and clasped the devil's. They shook and the deal was done.

'Very good. Seven days, doctor. Seven days. Fear not, the world was made in less.'

DELIRIUM TREMENS

After leaving Salvation, Martha had stormed across the hardpan on the horse she had traded her sister's guns and bandolier for. It is true she had paid a high price. The bullets alone could have bought the horse. The gun perhaps another two. At least one and a pack-donkey. But she had not the time to barter and was anyway satisfied with the horse and the supplies she had secured. What's more, she needed no more enemies in this life. The devil was foe enough.

The horse was an Appaloosa mare with a coat like a Dalmatian. She had good legs on her and she made many miles with the last light of the sun. Martha rode her hard into the dusk and into the beginnings of the night but as the country grew dark and unfamiliar she slowed it down to a canter and then a trot. The rocking of the horse grew rhythmic. She pulled her sister's stetson down over her eyes and by and by she fell into the semblance of sleep. Though her eyes were closed, her legs were locked to the horse's side, her hands tight on the reins. She rocked with the horse like they were one beast.

The cosmos rotated overhead. The moon rose waning gibbous.

Martha came to with a snort. The horse had stopped and stood patient as a steward. Martha rubbed her eyes and sought the North Star and their relation to it. She took a double take. The horse had not veered at all. Its nose still pointed in the direction of New Gomorrah. 'Good girl,' she said, patting the mare on the neck. Then she nudged it in the sides with her boot heels and they trotted onwards.

The night sky was perfectly clear and the moon and stars endowed the red earth with a strange blue luminosity. It looked another plain entire and she rode that spiritual realm until the moon passed overhead and began its descent. Then she stopped.

She swung herself off the horse and pushed the bones in her back straight with the palms of her hands. Her shoulders popped as she rolled them. She cracked her knuckles. She was like a golem reanimating.

From the saddlebags, she produced a waterskin. The horse's black eyes were on her as she drank. Martha saw this.

'Girl,' she said, 'we've only just got going. You'll get yours soon enough.'

At this, the horse whinnied and dropped its head.

'Ah, come on now, don't sulk. We'z just beginning to get along,' said Martha, patting the horse's neck.

She rummaged through the saddlebags and pulled out an apple. Cutting it in half with her knife, she held a section beneath the horse's nose. The mare flared its nostrils and clopped it out of her palm; then came back for the rest. Martha got herself a smoked sausage from the bag and stood alongside the horse, both of them grazing and looking off towards the purple-black horizon.

'I'll tell you this,' she said. 'I could do with a proper drink.'

Finished, she sucked the grease off her fingers and once again returned to the horse's side. This time she pulled the saddle off the horse's back and lay it on the hardpan. Taking a rope out the saddlebag she made herself a cow hitch round its front leg and pulling on the hitch got the horse to back up and lie down, talking the mare through every movement. The mare rolled onto its side without much fuss at all and Martha told her she was good and ran her palm along her side as it rose and fell with each titanic breath.

'Now I'm afraid we ain't that close yet so I'm going to leave the rope on tonight. You stay put and it'll be the first and the last time you have my word.'

The horse lay serene and tucked its head in between its feet. Martha watched it a while, matched her breathing to its own. After a time, though its eyes were still open, Martha knew it was sleeping. Martha took the other end of the rope and hitched it to the saddle. Then she lay her head in the curve of the seat and, pulling her sister's hat down over her eyes, fell asleep.

*

Martha woke just before the dawn. A terrible coldness had seized her body in the night and shook her as she lay on her side hugging her shoulders. Great beads of sweat stood on her forehead and her shirt was sodden under the armpits and down the length of her spine. She garbled something nonsensical at the night and the night spoke back.

'Hello, Arty, did you miss me?'

'No! No! No!' said Martha

A perfectly black shadow with empty white eyes grew out of the ground before her. It was distinctly human, its body hulking, familiar, but with two demonic horns rising out of the temples of its skull. Martha moaned and clamped her eyes shut but the image remained upon her eyelids.

'No! No! You're gone. I got rid of you,' said Martha.

'Got rid of me? Oh no, Arty, I never left. When you started drinking you just stopped seeing is all.'

'I want you to go.'

'Arty, Arty, I will not leave my wife alone in this cruel

world. I know the vow said with death us'll part. But I guess on this matter god and I will have to disagree. Heh, heh.'

Martha was shivering and sobbing like an ill child. She blew her lips out and kicked dust up with her boot heels.

'Damn you! Leave me alone!' she screamed at the phantom. But at this it only bared its brilliant white teeth in a nefarious grin.

'Oh god, what's happening?' mumbled Martha, her lips wet and trembling.

'My love, you've got the whiskey horrors, the drunkard's dread. But don't worry; your loving husband is here to see you through.'

The phantom started cackling and its mouth expanded so that it filled all of Martha's vision and the turncoat earth shrugged her off its Atlas-like shoulder and Martha was falling, falling through the phantom's mouth, past its blade-like teeth and into blackness terrible. The sounds of the living world passed away—the myriad notes of the wind, the dawn chorus as sung by those scrawny hardpan birds—all put out in an instant. All that remained was the phantom's laughing. That and her own screams.

The Appaloosa mare watched her new master writhe about making garbled pleas to the morning. It then rocked up onto its feet and stood over her, leant down and dragged its pink tongue over her face. Martha snapped to and drew her revolver, finding herself outnumbered by her reflections in the horse's black eyes. She dropped the gun and clutched her heart, which was crashing like a cymbal.

The horse bowed its head and Martha stroked its face and hugged its neck and it raised her to her feet. Martha cinched the saddle back onto the horse, untied the cow hitch, holstered her revolver, and scrambled up onto the mare's back. She made to take a deep breath but the air was stolen from her mouth. She gawped like a fish. The phantom had followed her out of her reverie and now stood beside her horse, its smile perfectly white, evil.

'Get,' she stammered.

Nothing happened. She dug her heels into the horse's side and cracked the reins.

'Get!' she shouted.

The mare bolted forwards and in mere moments it was galloping full speed across the hardpan. Martha looked back over her shoulder and still the phantom stood there, grinning. Then, as the sun came shooting horizontally over the dust bowl, the phantom dissolved from the feet up until it was but a set of shadowy horns hovering in the air and then nothing at all.

*

The sun beat down something vicious but still Martha's body could not lose its terminal chill. The horse kept on towards New Gomorrah straight and true and Martha murmured in its ear words of thanks, words of love. As the day grew on, two riders leading a third animal appeared to her forward-left and scurried along the horizon no bigger than mites. Probably just Brothers of The Messiah Caravan with business in Salvation, she thought. With the distance between them, it took a while for them to pass, but pass they did and she was once again alone in that recurrent plain.

*

The horse had slowed once again and Martha rocked unconscious atop it. She was leaning to the left and with each lurch the angle grew ever more obtuse until she slumped sideways off the mare. She hit the ground and was dragged, her foot caught in the stirrup. She kicked herself free and lay face down, sipping the air, the wind knocked out of her. The horse, ever dutiful, came to a stop, waited.

Still the whiskey horrors shook her bones. She dug her fingernails into the hard earth and waited for her breath to refill her lungs like the arroyos after rain.

No one living ever been this cold, she thought. *Your body dead and just don't know it yet.*

She sighed and heaved herself up onto her hands and knees.

'If you going to quit on me then hurry up about it,' she said aloud, her mind to her body. 'Or else get the fuck out my way.'

She clambered to her feet and hobbled after the horse, beating the dust off her sister's stetson as she did. After she had got herself a drink from the waterskin, she filled the hat and held it under the horse's mouth. The horse buried its nose inside the hat and Martha could hear the liquid trickling down into the horse's gut.

'My, my, your insides sound just about sundried. Don't worry, there'll be more soon, I promise. There's a town not half a day's ride. Sooner you get us there, sooner we both drink.'

Once the horse had drained the stetson, she returned it to her head and the damp material made her shiver all the more. Swinging herself up on top of the horse, she pushed back her hat, raised a hand against the sun, and eyed the journey to come. That is when she saw it.

The phantom. Dead ahead. A hundred metres out. Two dimensional, like an upstanding shadow. The same white Cheshire cat grin occupying most of its black, featureless face.

'It's just the bottleache, Martha. It ain't real,' she told herself as she slapped her face. 'You go ahead and ride that sonofabitch down and you just watch as nothing happens. Get!'

She dug her heels in and the horse jolted forwards. The phantom just smiled. She rode that mare hard, her arms working the reins like pistons. The phantom smiling, always smiling. She should have bore down on that shadow, it being the size of a man and no more, but its blackness began to dilate like a pupil, and as she drew close it bore down on her, its mouth impossibly wide, dwarfing even the horizon. It was inevitable. Martha rode into that howling blackness.

'Yar! Yar!' she cried.

And she rode clear through the mouth of the phantom, its blackness breaking easy as a soap bubble.

But the world was changed.

A boundary crossed.

She saw the world as its negative. The earth, once rich and variegated as saffron, now was electric blue, electric black. The turquoise sky now a burnished bronze. Her own black hands now cast in platinum. Over her shoulder, the only thing unchanged in that spectral plain was the phantom itself. As she fled from it, it diminished to its former size and then glided after her, matching the speed of her exile.

In this new realm, the coldness was unbearable. Previously, the chill had only been in her blood. In this place though it seemed the sun's negative refrigerated the air around. Her teeth chattered in her skull. An invisible membrane of frost layered her skin. Her bones locked together like frozen machinery. Still she rode that mare as hard as she could.

'You watch as nothing happens... You ever get tired of being right, Martha?' she said, the words turning to vapour on leaving her mouth.

It was then she heard the rumble of engines reverberating over the hardpan.

'Fuck me, what now?'

She turned to see two of the devil's 4x4s shimmering ethereally and raising a trail of blue powder. They were still a ways off, but closing, fast. The blaring of horns and crackling of gunfire signalled they had spotted her, the muzzle flash from their pistols a pearlescent black like the whipping of crows' wings.

The roughhousers sat out the windows of the cars and cried their ululations, slapping their mouths with their palms to quaver the note like injuns in those old-world westerns. In their harlequin outfits and biker leather they looked like the maleficent ghosts of dead carnies. Martha was not sure to which world they belonged.

'Just when it was all going so well too,' she said to the horse. 'Come on, get. Get! Quit your dawdling.'

The mare seemed already to be going flat out but Martha managed to squeeze a bit extra juice out of it. The horse was mad eyed and snorting something fierce. It was trying to shake its head, trying to stop, but Martha drilled its nose straight. It looked like she was wringing its mighty neck.

'That hoss's heart is going to explode if you're not careful, Arty.'

The phantom was gliding at her side.

'Not now,' she ordered.

'Looks like you're in a bit of a situation. Heh, heh.'

'Not. Now.'

'Okay, okay… Want some advice?'

Martha was silent.

'Well?'

'Yes. Fine. What?'

'Say *please*—'

'Fuck you.'

'Heh, heh. You didn't let me finish. Say *please, won't you stay?*'

Martha glared at the phantom. It smiled back. A crackle of gunfire and bullets whined past, spiking the hardpan. Potshots at best.

'You don't have long, Arty.'

'Fine. Please, won't you stay?'

'Love to. But first, why don't you head for those ravines yonder?'

As he said it, a holy golden light spiked out from a snaking fissure in the earth a quarter mile away. Martha looked at the phantom and its grin was less pronounced, less malevolent. Did she imagine it or was the blank shadow of the phantom's face beginning to wax over into the familiar features of her dead husband: his beer-brown eyes and angular cleft chin; his chestnut skin; his cropped black afro with its distinguished greys. Martha loosed a hand from the reins so that she might run her hand through his hair.

'Don't get fresh, Arty. Heh, heh. There's a job needs doing.'

She snatched back her hand and changed course for the ravine. The 4x4s adjusted also.

'Slow down. Let the hoss get a look-see at the jump,' said the phantom as they approached.

Martha obliged. About five metres of golden light was the break in the electric blue earth. The horse flicked its ears.

'There you go, she's twigged it.'

Martha felt the horse resist but she tightened up on the reins and set it straight.

'Don't fret now. If you drop, I'll catch you.'

'Does it hurt?' said Martha.

'Death? Naw. Dying's a sonofabitch though. But from this height you won't be doing much of that.'

Martha creased up over the pommel in deranged laughter.

'Yah! Yah!' she cried, whupping the horse on its rear. Then right before the earth fell away the horse broke hard and sprung its hind legs and together as one beast Martha and mare leapt over that ravine of golden light.

The landing threw her from her saddle but she rolled and was up in a moment, drawing Banjo's Colt .45 revolver. The horse trotted on shaking its head and stomping its foot. She faced down the 4x4s. They seemed not to notice the ravine. They must have thought she had been thrown by mistake. In actual fact, seeing her down, they sped up, the roughhousers hanging from the windows yelping and firing their pistols. Bullets were whizzing all about but they were poor shots the lot of them.

Martha picked the furthest car and took aim at the tinted windshield. She fired off her rounds in steady succession. Holes appeared in a tight group on the driverside section of the windscreen. The car slalomed, throwing one of the harlequins from the window she sat, then careened, rolled, crushing the others who had managed to hold on. The other 4x4 ploughed onwards. Seeing the ravine open up beneath its wheels, the driver hit the brakes, but there was no earth for to stop it and it smashed into the far side of the ravine and nosedived down into it, grinding down the stone in a swell of screaming metal until finally it wedged itself.

Martha walked up to the ravine edge, thumbing new rounds into the revolver. She took a nosey over the side and saw one of the leather clad roughhousers climbing out of the shattered boot window of the 4x4. Once he had pulled himself free, he just sat there on the rear of the car, suspended in the belly of the earth. In this world of negative colours, she had to squint to make out this scene below, for the ravine was bright as a crucible of liquid gold and the car and man mere flakes of silver floating in it.

Looking up, the harlequin that had been thrown from the car was scrabbling about on her knees for her pistol. She picked it up and pointed it at Martha but before she could pull the trigger a little hole appeared in her breast out of which ran an alien's blue blood. She doubled over into the electric blue dust.

Martha turned away from the massacre and went after her horse, which stood obediently a little ways off. The phantom was by its side.

'That sure was impressive, Arty,' he said.

Martha feigned a curtsy and flashed her teeth.

'How's the horse?' she said.

'Good as new. Least she will be after a sup of water. She a fine animal indeed… like her owner. Heh, heh.'

Martha raised an eyebrow at him.

'Now who's getting fresh?' she said.

Her hat had come off in the fall. She went and picked it up, beat off the dust, and set it back on her head. Returning, she pulled it down low over her eyes to hide the tears on her cheeks.

'Look, Martha, it's time for me to go. You got something to say, now's the time to say it,' said the phantom.

She coughed and shook her head.

'No? Okay.'

The phantom began to drift away.

'Why you?' Martha called after it. 'Why not Bo?'

'What do you mean?'

'What I mean is… where's Bo at?'

'He playing.'

'Playing?'

'Yes ma'am.'

'Playing where?'

The phantom surveyed the empty hardpan all about.

'It's hard to say,' he said.

'How'd you mean?'

'Cause he's sort of everywhere.'

And in that moment the dry breeze blew over the hardpan and in the shifting of dust and stones Martha heard the padding of bare feet. Feet she knew by heart. Feet she had made. Feet she had learned to walk. Feet she had listened to every day while the Earth daydreamed its way round the sun twelve and a half times.

She dropped to her knees and clawed at the earth where she had heard the incorporeal feet go pattering by as though she might catch them up by the ankle and hold the world steady just a moment. But the breeze broke through her fingers and rocking back on her knees she returned to the old pleas so long unuttered, cried her bargains to the indifferent heavens.

Her moans turned to whimpers turned to sobs. She shook, not from the cold but the warmth returning. She stood and embraced the phantom.

'What now?' she said.

'I don't rightly know. Expected dying was the only closure you'd get in this world. Guess I was wrong.'

She shut her eyes and buried her face into the phantom. She did not pass through him as before but was received by his slab-like chest. He stood on his tiptoes, as he had always had to in life, so that he could comfort all of her bulk. She took a deep breath and sighed.

She could smell the corn on him.

*

When she finally opened her eyes, she held air and air only. The earth had returned to red, the sky to blue. She collapsed upon the hardpan in her penitence and cursed the enduring heart inside her chest.

THE MUDLARKS OF SALVATION

Hiroshi nudged Plum awake at dawn and together they slipped out of the hayloft. As Plum felt with her foot for the first rung of the ladder, the little sandy haired boy opened a single, crimson eye. She paused and held his gaze, as though he were a ferocious animal best not awakened. Only once he had shut his eyes and nuzzled further into the hay did she disappear through the hatch.

In the revelry, no ponies had been readied for them, so they took the liberty of choosing their own. Plum was instantly taken with a skewbald Chincoteague pony with a cotton coloured mane that fell across its eyes like a fringe. It was powerful and sort of mean looking but seemed compliant enough. Hiroshi was fussing over a Shetland pony a third of the size of the Chincoteague, rubbing its nose and hand feeding it the hay at its feet.

'Aren't you just the cutest thing,' he said.

He straddled it bareback and his feet all but touched the floor. Plum had her tongue in her cheek.

'Onwards noble steed!'

'*Shhh*! You'll wake the kiddies.'

Hiroshi clapped his hand over his mouth, a puckish

glint in his eye. Plum was surprised to find herself
snickering at his antics. Above, the heads of the children
appeared around the loft hatch. Each still wore the red
skullcaps of the old religion. Spotting them, Hiroshi
removed the hand from his mouth.

'Adventure, here I come!' he cried, pointing to the barn
door.

The Shetland took a few steps forward, stopped, and
then would not budge no matter how Hiroshi rocked upon
it. He looked a proper fool. At his performance, the
children overhead broke into fits of cherubic laughter. All
except the sandy haired boy that is, who could only shake
his head at the audacity of mirth.

*

They each rode out on Chincoteague ponies with Plum
leading a third. For the children's entertainment, they
stormed out the barn something dramatic, the children
running after them through their dusty wake, jumping and
cheering. The sandy haired boy was the last out into the
steely light of the new morning. He alone was silent, stoic.
As the riders disappeared over the horizon so too did they
vanish into the dark tunnels of his eyes and the image of
such freedom would live forever in his mind thereafter,
both as a dream and a nightmare, an innocence and a guilt.

*

Hiroshi led their little caravan for he was the more
familiar with the Salvation road, which was not a proper
road by any stretch but the faintest desire line beat out by
horse hoof and pony. What's more, he had committed to
his memory where the land kissed its hazardous bridges
over the dry-gulches, which scored this landscape like the
cracks of hell.

They dallied on the road, enjoying the quietude of the
desert plain and each other's easy company. The children
had scouted them the necessary provisions before they had
left and they rode side-by-side and passed back and forth a
waterskin and the pork Plum had pilfered the night before.

Plum had stowed her tattered undershirt in her saddlebag and rode bare chested to let the air at her wounds, which ran across her body like runes writ in blood. Hiroshi was making a point of ignoring her nakedness, his eyes fixed firmly on the horizon or on the trail, so when she offered him a cigarette she had to thump him to get his attention. Hiroshi turned, rubbing his bicep, scowling, but quickly perked up when he saw what was offered. They stopped the ponies and Plum lit their smokes without dismounting and then they trotted on trailing puffs of smoke behind them that danced down to the ground and then up again before coming apart all together.

Hiroshi smoked his halfway and then, hiding it behind the body of the pony, covertly dropped it upon the hardpan. He took a furtive glance at Plum and found her looking at him with raised eyebrows.

'What,' he said.

'Where's your smoke at?'

'I finished it.'

Plums eyebrows were now so high on her forehead that they had disappeared into her hairline. Hiroshi's eyes darted to the cigarette still in her mouth.

'I meant I dropped it,' said Hiroshi. And then he coughed and said, 'You know, by accident.'

She took a draw on her cigarette, then another. She smoked it right down to nothing at all, pinching it between mid-finger and thumb, so that when she clicked her fingers there was but a sprinkling of grey ash and nothing more.

'Don't waste my toby,' she said.

Hiroshi pulled a face at her.

'Don't sass me, boy.'

When Hiroshi pulled the face a second time, she went to backhand him across the chest, but he shifted in his saddle and she swiped the air and lost her balance. Clutching the pommel of her saddle at the last moment, she managed to save herself from hitting the ground, but she hung undignified off the side of her pony. Hiroshi snickered. Plum heaved herself back into her saddle and glared at Hiroshi something fierce. Grinning, Hiroshi kicked forward his pony and went galloping across the hardpan.

'You best pray I don't catch you,' she hollered after him and then, laughing, she heeled her pony and went racing after him.

She never did catch him. The pony she led thrashed its head and fought her the whole time, no matter how hard she pulled on the lead rope.

'Fine. Be like that,' she said, and brought it back down to a trot. Hiroshi stopped lengthwise ahead and goaded her.

'Yeah, yeah,' said Plum. 'You're lucky. You'd have no chance in a fair race.'

'Oh yeah.'

'Yeah.'

'First one to that big rock over there.'

'What big rock.'

'The only… Hey!'

Whilst Hiroshi was busy pointing out the finishing line, Plum had dropped the lead rope and snapped the reins of her pony. By the time Hiroshi had his pony turned, she had a lead of several lengths and she maintained it all the way up to the big rock.

'Told you,' said Plum.

'Hey now, what happened to a fair race?'

'You not satisfied?'

'You bet your thumb I'm not.'

'Well I guess everyone's got their own opinion on what's fair.'

'Let's go again.'

'Naw, I think I'll retire champion.'

Perhaps seeing a chance of escape, the third pony went galloping passed them and across the hardpan, trailing the lead rope.

'First one to wrangle it wins,' said Hiroshi, winking, his

pony taking a few eager steps forwards.

'Naw, like I say, I'm retired,' said Plum, but walking her pony after him all the same.

'Well this should be easy then,' he said, and his pony went springing forwards.

'Oh no you don't,' said Plum, and she kicked and whupped her pony until it was running flat out after him.

Hiroshi drew alongside the runaway pony first and tried to catch it by its hackamore but the pony fixed him with a single crazy eye and went shying away. By the time Hiroshi had brought his pony round in a great arc, Plum was now hot on its tail. She kicked her right foot free of her stirrup and eased herself towards the earth. The hard, red earth rushed by below. She reached for the lead rope, which dragged between the pony's legs and out across the hardpan. Her fingers touched it but the runaway altered its course and the lead rope went snaking away from her. She tried a last-ditch and foolhardy snatch but only succeeded in unbalancing her own pony and if she were any heavier would have pulled it down on top of her. The reins slipped from her hand and by luck she managed to grasp the seat of her saddle and she rode horizontally, hugging the pony's barrel chest with her face buried in its hot fur and its mighty heart drumming against her eyes.

'Need a hand?' called Hiroshi, pulling alongside her.

Plum shouted her unintelligible dissent into the pony's side and tried to scramble unaided up onto the pony's back. Trying for a better grip, her hand slipped from the saddle and she was falling backwards. The azure sky stretched perfectly across her vision like a blue blindfold. The thundering of the hooves under which she would be crushed was all she heard. She did not hear Hiroshi cry war-like. But she did feel his spidery fingers lace around her upper arm and clamp like a vice, suspending her above that ultimate and lingering trauma. She hung between the two ponies as though she swung within an invisible hammock, her arm held by Hiroshi and her left foot caught in the stirrup.

'What are you waiting for,' cried Hiroshi, his slight frame quivering from the strain.

Hiroshi heaved and Plum reached and she regained her grip and together they hoisted her back up onto the saddle. She caught up the reins and wound them about her fist. Turning to Hiroshi with bright eyes, she looked like she might say something, but instead she broke out laughing and howled like a wolf.

'Hey. Hey! That pony's heading straight for that ravine yonder,' Hiroshi hollered at her. 'Stick close and get ready to pull my pony up.'

They thundered on together over the hardpan, chasing the dust of the runaway pony. They were swiftly upon it and Hiroshi kicked his feet out of the stirrups and drew them up under him so that he was riding crouched on the saddle like a circus rider. The three of them rode abreast: the runaway, Hiroshi, then Plum. Together they raised a storm of red dust.

'Ready?' said Hiroshi.

'Are you?' said Plum.

Hiroshi looked back at her and winked and then sprung through the air like a bullfrog. He managed to straddle the pony but his momentum kept him going and he rotated anticlockwise about the pony and dropped under its feet. On his way down he caught up the lead rope and it burnt through his hands as he went skidding along through the pony's legs and out behind. The pony dragged him along on his belly for a good hundred feet but Hiroshi hooked the rope around his arm and held tight and the pony quickly grew fed up of the weight on its nose and came to a stamping stop not ten feet from the lip of the ravine.

Plum pulled up her and Hiroshi's ponies so they stopped a little ways off. She watched as Hiroshi dredged himself up off the hardpan, bloody and bruised but grinning all the same. Plum jumped down from her pony and approached him and before she knew what she was doing she was pressing her face against his, their faces hot and sweaty and slick with blood. She withdrew, his blood on her face, and then she made to kiss him again. He pulled back.

'Plum. Wait. I'm sorry. It's just... Machiavelli.'

Plum was dumbstruck; as though she had been accused of a crime committed in a dream. Then she coughed and said, 'Yeah. That. What? I don't care,' and she leapt back atop her pony and cantered off, leaving Hiroshi standing there red-faced from the blood without, the blood within. The ponies beside him had their heads bowed, as though they were all of them embarrassed.

*

They rode the rest of the day in silence, Plum smoking one long line of cigarettes, lighting each on the dying embers of the last. On several occasions, Hiroshi licked his lips and opened his mouth as though he might speak, might put in a smoker's plea, but each time he just shut his mouth and rode on.

Darkness fell and still they rode. Without saying a word, they transitioned as though they were both passengers on the same train of thought and Hiroshi took the lead once more and navigated them over that dicey terrain by memory and by starlight, every now and then making sure to look back and check the filament of Plum's cigarette still smouldered out there in the darkness like it was its own orange star. And though each time it was there ready to confirm her closeness, to Hiroshi she was as distant as Antares or Betelgeuse.

*

Salvation manifested silver-blue beneath the reeling constellations like it was a ghost town and they two beggarly spooks who had finally found their way through to the land of the dead. They entered Salvation via the main drag and they clopped down the dirt road with their ponies snorting, weary and petulant, stumbling over that corrugated thoroughfare wrinkled by the perpetual comings and goings of prairie schooners. The cloudy plastic sheeting that passed for the saloon windows glowed a dim amber and inside could be heard an inebriate soloist serenading his fellow lollygaggers. They passed by with his maudlin oration keen in their ears for they had heard no human voice so far this night; only that internal voice which chatters its misgivings; but even that is strangely quiet out on the hardpan; muted by muscle ache, drowned beneath the thunderous hooves manifolding through the reverberant nothingness. This is the song the old drunk sang:

> *You can wait and wait for something,*
> *and wait and wait for something,*
> *and not know why but be waiting for something,*
> *and something may never happen.*
> *I used to think there was a little meaning*
> *to this little drinking song we call life.*

They passed side by side down the thoroughfare and the lush's song died with distance. Lanterns burned in the paneless windows of that wooden town and they could hear shuffling and mutterings in those bleak bedrooms. Eyes glittered in the dark alleyways, which contained shadows blacker even than the night, and as the riders passed these eyes would flit out of existence, giggling like poltergeists, only to reappear in alleyways further down the road.

The house of Doctor Walters Onabanjo with its gargoyles and other supernatural accoutrements loomed up on the left-hand side. A cigarette was flaring on the porch partway illuminating what looked at first glance to be a bearded harlot dressed in a white bodice with flat chest and wide shoulders.

'Eyes front,' Plum hissed.

They trotted passed the house as though it were any other. The figure rose and walked out into the street and stood there smoking and watching them, his feet planted wide apart. It was the devil's man dressed as before in his ransacked bridal gown. He squinted their shapes out of the darkness, the rumps of their ponies sashaying down the thoroughfare.

They took a right down a side street that ran between two houses, one reduced by fire long ago to nought but charred stakes sticking out of blackened ground, the other still standing, still occupied, but with scorched and honeycombed walls. They dismounted and led their ponies behind the houses back in the direction they had come, passed reeking hills of compost and oblong plots wherein grew potatoes, courgettes and bell peppers. The fugitive eyes of the townsfolk glanced from the outsiders to their vulnerable plots and back again, but the alien riders led their ponies without incident back up to the saloon, there to water them from the galvanised trough and tie them to the hitching post out front.

'Who was that?' said Hiroshi.

'I don't know.'

'Why are we here exactly?'

Plum pulled needlessly hard on the hitching rope and acted like she had not heard.

'Plum, please.'

'I'm here for the doctor.'

'The magic-man?'

She nodded.

'Why? Are you okay?'

'It's for my papa.'

'Oh.'

He cast a furtive look back down the thoroughfare where still could be seen the man in the white dress standing in the middle of the road, watching them.

'Looks like someone else already got to him,' he said.

'What do you care?' said Plum, without meeting his eye. 'You're free. Go get your man. Go get Machiavelli.'

She walked off up the side of the saloon. She did not

know where she was going. Hiroshi caught up with her and grabbed her arm. She turned and shook him off.

'What do you mean?' said Hiroshi.

'You have no obligation to me.'

'Yes I do. You said it yourself. We have business to settle here first.'

'No. I have business. You are just… a liability… and a scrounge.'

In her passion, she had her finger pressed into his chest, as though she pointed to some malady rooted deep in his heart. With the ensuing silence both of them grew awkward and Plum dropped her finger, turned, and continued walking up the side of the saloon.

'Plum,' he called after her.

'Don't bother,' she said, flapping her hand as though swatting away an irksome fly. 'Just leave me alone.'

She disappeared from view behind the saloon. Hiroshi stood there a while, watching the dark vista down which she had passed. He shuffled forwards, like he might go after her. Then he sighed and entered the saloon instead.

*

Plum sat on a barrel behind the saloon and retrieved her makings from her pocket. A teardrop struck the paper she held between her fingers and absorbed itself into it. 'Shit,' she muttered, scrunching it and casting it to the night before pummelling the tears from her eyes and bringing forth another paper. Her hands shook as though the Jekyll of her rage was trying to fit its hands into hers, striving for agency over her body. But she knew rage and knew it well and knew it would pass like everything passes. What disturbed her more was the interloping of an old emotion, which had stolen its way inside dressed in the cloak of her rage. An enigmatic emotion, both tender and tremendous, which had once been reserved solely for Bo, stirring in the seat of her stomach before surging up through her guts and blowing through her heart like gales through a windsock. She breathed deep through her nose, filling out like she were in fact an inflatable rendering of a girl. Then, poking the stringy tobacco into the u of the paper, she licked it shut and brought it to life with a match.

Behind the sulphurous flare of the match three little shadows carved profiles out of the dark like ghouls surfacing out of that deeper region where exists the combined and nebulous dread of humankind. Their eyes reciprocated the celestial glimmer above and in the hand of the leader glinted the skinny blade of a flick knife. They kept their distance for they were children only.

'Handy over ye goodies,' said the girl with the knife. 'Or I'll cut the smoke out ye lungs.'

Plum carried on smoking. The little vagabonds shook in the hide strappings they called shoes, the leader aiming the quivering knife point between Plum's eyes as though it were a magic wand. Plum took the cigarette from her mouth and spat on the floor between them.

'Fly away little mudlarks,' she said. 'Else.'

'Else what?' said the leader, stepping forward into the amber light dribbling out of the saloon window. She was a child of eight summers, no more, with a blotchy flea-bitten scalp; the town barber, out of pity, having razored off her yellow hair at no charge.

'Ye deaf? I said *else what?*'

The leader of the mudlarks feinted with the knife and Plum flicked her cigarette at her and it hit the little girl's face in a puff of hot yellow cinder. The girl swiped at the embers and brandished the knife blindly before her. When her vision restored itself, she discovered her comrades had deserted her. She was alone with this stranger to her town and the stranger held a snub-nosed .38 in each hand, both of which were trained on her heart.

'Oh,' said the girl.

There was a black spot on her right cheek where the cigarette had hit, like a beauty spot too liberally applied. She lowered the switchblade.

'Should I drop it?' she said.

'Sup to you.'

She closed the knife and put it in her ragged pocket. She then coughed into her fist and scratched her bald head. Plum crossed the pistols over her lap.

'You're not from here are ye,' said the girl, more statement than question.

'No.'

'Then I'm guessing ye come for the magic-man. Whenever there's a sneak in town they're here for him.'

Plum blinked and nodded slow. The mudlark nodded also. She then looked over her shoulder and stuck her tongue in her cheek as though she were considering something. When she turned back, there was a sly glint to her eye.

'I got counsel if ye willing to parley?'

'Okay. What do you want for it?'

'What ye got?'

'You smoke?'

'If it burns.'

'How about some bacco roles?'

'Real bacco?'

'Yes.'

'How many?'

'Name your price.'

'Five?'

'Okay. Now halve that.'

'Not fair.'

'Take it or leave it.'

The child was counting out the math on her fingers, swapping between two and three fingers upheld. Plum smiled.

'It don't work anyway,' said the little girl, furrowing her brow.

'You're right,' said Plum. 'Tell you what, I'll give you two now and a third depending on the wisdom of your counsel. Deal?'

'Okay.'

'Deal?'

'Deal.'

Plum set about rolling four cigarettes whilst the child danced on the spot and looked over her shoulder. As Plum rolled the last cigarette, the girl's comrades came sallying forth out of the darkness with reinforcements, clutching sticks and stones, but the girl straddled the ground before them and held up her hands and called for them to cease. They stopped dutifully before her and commenced giggling and rubbing their noses. Snickering a little herself, Plum passed the girl her prepayment of cigarettes and the girl collected them. She put one straight in her mouth and, sharing a match, they both lit their smokables.

'So, what have you got?'

The girl took a draw and squinted against the rising smoke.

'I suppose ye heard of the devil?' she said.

'I've heard of him. Also hear he's dead.'

'No. No. Ye can't kill the devil, only the form he takes. The new devil visited here this very night. That man-bride on the step of the magic-man's home is his. So's the two jesters inside. And they all strapped up with pieces bigger than yers. Ye best leave him alone. Word is he made a deal with the devil, one which he'll never make good on, and one which he'll pay a sorry price fer sooner than he'd care to. Mm-hmm. Ye should leave before ye share his fate.'

Plum tapped the ash from her cigarette and watched the wind carry it off into the darkness.

'Banjo never seemed the type to make dealings with the devil,' she said.

'Mm-hmm. Ye might be right. He was forced into it. The devil was mad after his woman got deaded by another.'

'Huh?'

'Yuh. They was gun fighting outside the magic-man's place. This big woman shot down the devil's woman and rode off for New Gomorrah.'

'Big woman,' said Plum, smiling and nodding.

'It's the truth. This be the devil-woman's knife,' she said, wagging the switchblade at her before stowing it back in her pocket.

'I don't deny it,' said Plum.

'Then why ye mocking me?'

'I'm not. She is a big woman.'

'What? Ye know her?'

'I think so. Yeah.'

The mudlark grinned, a mouthful of smoke escaping through the gaps in her yellow teeth.

'You all hungry?' said Plum.

'Always,' said the girl, and this was backed up by the nodding of her comrades.

'Well then,' said Plum, as she conceded unto the scallywag the supplementary payment of one cigarette. 'How's about we parley some more?'

*

It was the dark hours of early morning and the lead mudlark with the shaved head stepped out of the darkness and up the boards of Doctor Onabanjo's home. The man-bride was reclining on the doctor's porch-side bench with a demijohn of mescal propped on his belly. When he heard footsteps, he startled and raised the desert eagle lying on the bench next to him. Upon seeing it was just a child, he lay it back down and scoffed.

'Whaddayerwant, mudlark?' he slurred.

He made to spit but the mucus didn't have the legs and it dribbled down his chin and onto his shoulder, which were both bare above the sweetheart bust of the dress. He wiped it away with the flat of his palm and then his palm on the hem of the dress.

'I got counsel if ye prepared to pay for it,' said the mudlark.

The man-bride flared his nostrils and blew out his lips.

'Fuck off, kid.'

'It's true. I'm sure yer bossman would want to hear it.'

The man-bride eyed her drunkenly.

'You don't know nothing,' he said.

'Yeah? Ye know the devil-woman's assassin? Well I got a buddy of hers holed up with my crew. Ye grease my palm and I'll handy her over to ye.'

The man-bride sat the sloshing demijohn next to him and levelled the outrageously big handgun at the child.

'Take me to her or I'll blow your heart out,' he said, as the handgun swayed from side to side, up and down.

'Nah. Ye don't wanna do that. Think what yer bossman'll say when ye deliver him the assassin's buddy. He'll be liable to kiss ye.'

'You dare slander him?' he said, shaking the gun at her.

'Okay. Okay,' she said, holding her hands up and taking a step backwards.

'Where's her buddy at?' said the man-bride, laying the gun between his legs and leering at her with dead eyes.

'Payment first.'

'Where's. Her. Buddy. At?'

'Pay. Ment. First.'

The man-bride ran his tongue along his teeth.

'You little punk. Fine. What do you want?'

'Well, way I see it, there are two things in this world that equal power. Knowledge and money. I got the knowledge. And seein' as yer kin to the devil I'm guessing ye might have on you some of those coins that would buy just about anyone anything or out of any situation they might find themselves in.'

'You think you're smart, I can tell,' said the man-bride, snarling.

He reached his hand into the cleavage of the dress and pulled out a little leather poke that hung by a string around his neck. He fingered a coin out and flicked it with his thumb so it landed before the child and rolled between her legs as she snatched at it to save it from falling between the cracks in the boards. She slapped it to a stop with her palm and gathered it up and turned it over in her hand. It was

130

crudely minted but solid gold nevertheless. On one side was inscribed an x and on the other a y and the similarity of these inscriptions had caused a great many altercations in the past—would cause a great many more to come—whenever something consequential is wagered on the tossing of these talismans in the often dark, inebriate arenas of debate.

'If you're lying to me, you're dead,' said the man-bride.

'I ain't lying,' she said. 'She's roasting corn with my fellows. Rode in this very night she did. Ye must have sawed her. Follow me, I'll bring ye to her.'

She stepped off the porch and waved for him to follow and he rose drunkenly and lumbered after her, rocking his shoulders like a hard-man. At the sound of his heavy boots dragging on the boards, one of his harlequin compatriots came out and quizzed him where he was going. He just waved her off without regard and when she spat and called him a fool for wandering off drunk alone in a hostile town he wheeled around and shouted, 'It's just a kid. Grow a fucking pussy.'

'O idiota merece morrer,' muttered the harlequin, crossing her eyes and jutting out her chin and putting her closed fist to her forehead. Then she spat once more and went back inside.

The child led the man-bride up the main drag and then, like a flower girl who had long scattered all her petals, she led him down the aisle that was the saloon alleyway. Halfway down, they stopped. At the other end of that dark vista, out past the vegetable plots, burnt a fire on the hardpan, around which crouched an assembly of urchins roasting corncobs as foretold by the child. The corn cooked on a sheet of metal gauze suspended over the little fire and the biggest of the urchin's was turning them over with a stick. She had dungarees on and her back to them.

'That's her, the big one tending the grub.'

The man-bride made to go after her but the child grabbed him by the wrist.

'What?'

'Don't bloody up our food.'

At this, the man-bride pushed her down and the child fell on her face in the dust of the alleyway. She looked up, her lip cut, and spat blood after him as he walked away. As soon as he was out of the alley there were two flashes, *pop, pop*, and the man-bride went down on one knee and clutched his gut. He swung up his desert eagle and fired and its detonation was one of terrible reckoning. In the reverberant clangour of its aftermath there was another two lesser explosions, each preceded by a flashbulb-like flare, and as the man-bride keeled over sideways into the dust, Plum walked from behind the saloon wall in nought but her ragged undershirt and shorts and shot him one last time through the head.

Plum walked towards the child where she lay on the floor and stood over her. Then she hitched one of her .38's under her armpit and offered the girl a hand.

'You okay?' she said, as she pulled her to her feet.

The girl nodded and wiped the blood from her lip, smearing it across her cheek.

'Good. Here,' said Plum, and she palmed her a handful of crumpled cigarettes she had had stowed in the pockets of her shorts and pushed her back down the alleyway towards her friends. The girl looked back once and then ran to her fellows. Plum ducked back into the shadows and circumvented the building next to the saloon. Before going down the parallel alley, she looked for the urchins; they were retreating into the darkness of the hardpan, their hot food wrapped in one of their filthy shirts, just as she had told them to do.

In the alleyway, she crouched behind a beer barrel and unloaded the spent shells of each pistol into the dust and thumbed home fresh rounds. She gently clasped the chamber of the second gun shut with her palm and steadied her breath. Voices. There were voices on the wind, echoing down the alleyways so that they seemed to come from all about.

'The shots came from this way. Lucille! Lucille! Are you there?'

'Pisso. Keep your voice down.'

Plum peeped over the barrel and saw the two harlequins on the main drag pass by the mouth of the alleyway. They held their pistols sideways in one hand, their arms fully extended, as though it was the pistol that led them, courted them, like debutantes escorted to a dance floor. They disappeared. Then one doubled back and started up the alley. Plum dropped her head back below the rim of the barrel. She closed her eyes, charted in her mind the slow padding of the harlequin's steps. The night was silent as a church. The harlequin's approaching footsteps was all she heard. That and the harlequin's nervous breath rifling in and out of his dry lips. When he was not twenty foot from the barrel, Plum leapt out onto her side and lit up the alleyway with her pistol fire. The harlequin, his pistol trained on the space above the barrel, fired off a single shot, which went splintering through the wood wall beside the barrel and set the occupants of the building screaming. Then he dropped to his knees, bent over into the dust, and died.

Plum was quick to her feet and backtracking down the alley at a sprint. She flung herself against the corner of the building for cover and as she did so too did the last harlequin on the other side. A moment of reckoning followed wherein both sets of eyes widened. Then came a flourish from both duellists. Plum turned to fire but the harlequin bore down upon her and gathered her up in her stout arms and locked her hands behind her back and squeezed her and brought her forehead crashing down upon the bridge of her nose, knocking her swivel-eyed and sending two hot jets of blood squirting from her nostrils. The harlequin dropped her into the dust between two vegetable plots and Plum looked out of muddled eyes at a grayscale night, choking on her own blood. The figure of that nightmare clown stepped over her and raised its pistol so that she was looking straight down the bore. Plum clutched her shaking hands to her chest. Though her .38s lay at the feet of her enemy, her fingers were curled as though still she held her pieces. In her bewilderment, she aimed these pistols immaterial up at the harlequin and her twitching fingers told that she spent every last hallucinatory bullet. The harlequin sighed and lowered her gun. Then she said, 'Isso é muito triste. I am sorry,' and she raised it once more so as to shoot.

Plum shut her eyes.

A scream, short and shrill. Then another.

Plum squinted out of one eye. She watched through a fog as the harlequin danced in pain, in terror, ravaged by some wily djinn making serpentine twists about her body, delivering its havoc with both a rock and a shard of mirror-glass. The harlequin fired her pistol and the muzzle flash burnt a resplendent fried egg into her corneas, which jittered away, returning to its centre each time she blinked. The djinn ducked beneath the harlequin's gun-arm and made a pass about the backs of her legs with the mirror-glass. The harlequin dropped to her knees and clutched her ribboned ankles. Looming darkly over her, the djinn then stove her head in with the rock and she went taut as though strung up by the stars, her head capped with a dark and surging spume. She toppled over sidewards, convulsing in the dust and her own weltering blood.

The djinn then descended upon Plum and her face was one of gaping terror. The lanes of blood on her face made roads into her eyes and she saw the world as though through a lens of wine. She thrashed and kicked and tried to swipe the hot, thick fluid from her eyes, smearing it across her features like some tribal rite, but to no avail. She tried to scream, but could only gargle on the blood in her throat. The djinn grabbed her, raised her, held her like a friend. It then spoke to her in Hiroshi's voice.

'It's okay,' he said. 'You're okay.'

Plum was shivering, her hands frantic over his body, as though trying to find there a hold to cling to, to keep her from falling into that metaphysical void known only to her in her blood-blindness.

'Come on. Come with me,' he said, and with his arm around her, he was her tender guide to the house of Doctor Walters Onabanjo. The urchins came running in off the hardpan and caught up with them, Plum's dungarees flapping among their ranks like it was their stonewashed standard. They fussed over her and asked her if she was okay. Then they asked Hiroshi if she was okay and he said she was. They returned to him her articles for safekeeping, pushing them into his palm like donations from the faithful. They remained with her right up to the door of Doctor Onabanjo's house. They then scampered off into the darkness, there to spend tenebrous hours trying to chronicle her story, endeavouring to synthesise a singular truth from the parallax of their realities, disputing the order of events, the events themselves, as though they were not witnesses at all but the descendants of witnesses; she of another age, another Earth, a citizen of that perfect planet which shines as bright as turquoise when set against the darker cosmos of the human mind.

It was in this way she was delivered.

THE DUST JACKET

D octor Walters Onabanjo sat gagged and bound to a chair when Hiroshi burst through his door, Plum propped up beneath his arm. At the site of these bloody intruders, Doctor Onabanjo fought his binds and shouted muffled denouncements. On registering the girl though, he stilled, as though she were some wonder to behold. He jutted his chin at Hiroshi, beckoning him to come untie him.

Hiroshi sat Plum on the doctor's table; the same table on which Martha had been remedied; the same table that had bore the cadaver of Martha's sister, Nettie; both a surgeon's and a mortician's table, therein that wood the sisters' blood reconstituted, a death-mother, one sibling conceived thereby, the other aborted back to life. The other table in that room still bore the father of Lily-Jane, he who had received his end assisting Martha on the hardpan, his body beginning to sour. Hiroshi went to Doctor Onabanjo's side, dropped the gag and pulled the balled-up handkerchief out of his mouth. He then knelt behind the chair and set about undoing his binds.

'That you, little Plum Blossom?' said Doctor Onabanjo.
'Hello, Banjo,' she said.

'Up to your old tricks I see.'

'What, this? This is nothing.'

She was pointing to her face, which in the lantern light was recast in some horrorshow mould. The blood upon it thick as paint. Her eyes badly bruised so that she could discern only the outlines of things through the swollen, purple folds of skin.

'Why are you here?' he said.

'I'm here for you.'

'You're not here on account of the malcontent Martha Biobaku?'

'Let me put you right. I am only here on her account. I'd be dead if not for her. So, I dare you, *dare you* to speak ill of her again. But to take your meaning, no, I am not in your house a-cause of her.

'She didn't send you here to save me?'

Plum scoffed.

'Save yourself, shaman,' she said.

The rope binds dropped to the floor and he rose rubbing his wrists.

'I meant no offence, little Blossom. She is my friend also.'

'I know she is. And I have never understood how people talk so behind their friends' backs. It's as though they do not think themselves heard. But our friends always hear. Always they are tuned into our frequency. You watch, when you next meet her, something will be changed.'

Doctor Onabanjo approached and bent to look at her battered face. He tutted and tightened his lips in a twisted grimace.

'You always have been loyal to a fault. Now I know I must just be an old crazy to you, little Blossom, and you'll do with my advice what you will, but let me tell you this so that I might at least sleep tonight: a noble life does not guarantee a noble death. In fact, I might go as far to say that death is never noble. Yes, yes, I would go that far.'

'My death has naught to do with me, Banjo. Nor yours you.'

'A bold claim indeed. But confidence is no warranty for truth, little Blossom.'

'Nor is experience, old man.'

'Ah! Touché.'

He walked from the room without another word and a moment later the creak of a hand pump and the splashing of water came drifting in from out back. He waddled back into the room clutching the handle of a sloshing bucket in both hands. Hiroshi leaned on the wall and watched as Doctor Onabanjo plonked it down on the table next to Plum and commenced cleaning her face with a rag.

'The wisdom of children, it is such a thing to make you reappraise how little you've come in your long life,' said Doctor Onabanjo as he worked. 'Even now, close to death as I am, the starting line of this race to understand is still in sight. And you know what the damnedest this is? I'm not even sure I'm looking backwards on it.'

He walked to the shelving that contained thereon a great many vials and jars, each containing therein some anonymous and vibrant creation. He drummed his fingers on his chin as he traced with his finger from the upper-left corner, snaking down until he came to the flask he sought, it a honey-coloured number, suspended in it a galaxy of air bubbles.

'Ah. Wolf's bane,' he said. 'Arnica. It will help with the swelling.'

At his approach, Plum held up her hand.

'I'm not putting no wolf killer on my face.'

'Suit yourself,' he said, and returned it to the shelf. Then, with his back to her, he said, 'Why are you here, little Blossom?'

'I'll get to that,' she said. 'Sit down. Let us idle a moment.'

'No offence, but I'd prefer to stand, I've been tied to that thing all night.'

'Okay. Hiroshi, my bag if you will,' she said, reaching out a hand towards his blotchy form. He obliged and Plum, half-blind, took it and rooted about inside.

'Maybe if you tell me what you're after I can get it,' said Hiroshi.

'It's alright,' she said, and she pulled out the glossy dust jacket of that text arcane, *The Messiah Caravan*. 'Will you read this for me?'

'Is that…' said Hiroshi.

'What is it?' said Doctor Onabanjo.

'Read it and you'll find out,' said Plum.

'Alright.'

Doctor Onabanjo took it from her and then retreated to the wall, there to lean, his eyes flicking over the page.

'Out loud, Banjo,' she said.

He cleared his throat.

'With over twenty million copies sold and translated into thirty-five languages, *The Messiah Caravan* is the best-selling, international phenomena by Professor Arnie Arnoldson. With his trademark dry humour, Arnoldson provides a frank and even-handed history of religion. Its origins, its successes and failures, right through to its place in an increasingly post-religious planet. This book is a comprehensive topography of what Arnoldson dubs "The Messiah Caravan"—the long line of groups employing the god-myth as a basis for reality—and its travels across the desert sands of human time.'

Banjo turned over the dust jacket.

'Arnoldson's is a considerate and much needed voice of calm in an increasingly divided and raucous world, says Neil deGrasse Tyson.' Then he read ahead, scoffed, and continued. 'A rigorous, riotous and righteous romp through the world of religion. Every atheist needs this book in their armoury. Five crucifixes! Says Stephen Fry.'

Chuckling to himself, Banjo turned the dust jacket over and back again but said no more.

'What does it mean?' said Hiroshi.

'It means that you're even greater fools than I gave you credit for.'

'I don't understand.'

'All this time.' He slapped his knee. 'All this time, you and your brethren have been worshipping an irreligious text.'

'I don't…'

'It's ironic.'

'What is?'

'You believed this the word of god. This book says god is not real.

'But this man Arnoldson writes of god, he writes of The Messiah Caravan.'

'Yes. To discredit it.'

'That's not my point. What I mean is… How to say it… How can it not be real, The Messiah Caravan, when it is written? How are we talking about it if it is not real?'

'The Messiah Caravan is real. It is history. God is not. God is only real as a lie. A ghost story.'

'Aha! But stories are real. That's my point.'

'What? No…'

'And if I understand right, it is the gods which drive the wagons that make up the caravan in this man's story?'

'In a sense. But…'

'Then how are they moving if the drivers aren't real?'

'It is the believers who drive the caravan.'

'Ah! But the believers are driven by god.'

'The believers drive themselves. They just don't know it.'

'So, the wagon is god and the believers drive it?

'Confound you both! I am too old and whipped and not nearly high enough to unpick these knots of yours.' He threw his hands up in the air in his passion and then caught them up under his armpits as though to stay them, like they had a mind of their own. 'I'll just say this. It's all just a crazy hustle. The whole lot. Not just god. Life. Everything. Now, some people deep down want to be hustled.' Here he looked at Hiroshi. 'Some'll hustle without a quarrel on the half of others.' He looked at Plum. 'The rest, like Martha, like your pappy, like the devil and the devil before him, well they just go ahead and hustle for their own damn selves.'

His breath whistled in and out of his nose, his flared nostrils big as gun bores.

'And you? What about you, shaman?' said Plum.

'Me? I just try to stay out of it as much as I can.'

'Yeah. How's that working out for you?'

He sucked his teeth and turned away. He stared at the black square of window.

'Why are you here, little Blossom?' he said, without looking at her.

'My papa needs his meds.'

'I see. A little premature is it not? His last prescription should have run through to summer's end.'

'Which leads me on to my next request. Through no fault of our own, my papa and I find ourselves on the lam from the devil. Much like your present situation, now I think about it. But unlike you, my pa has been busy hustling. He's managed to recruit himself an army of zealots who sure as the setting sun believe him to be the next in line on The Messiah Caravan. Course, they're not privy to what you just read being illiterate every last one of them. My papa wants to invite you to be his confidant, part of his inner sanctum.'

She had his attention.

'You mean to tell me the Brothers of The Messiah Caravan are now in the employ of your father?'

'Yes.'

Doctor Onabanjo glanced at Hiroshi who with open mouth was digging his tongue into the grooves of his molars. He nodded.

'And what of the Fathers?' asked the doctor.

'Dead. Every one,' said Plum.'

'My word. I never thought I'd see the day. This is

uncharted territory.'

'Will you chart it with us?'

'What choice do I have?'

'You have a choice.'

'What. Stay here and be brutally murdered, run and be tracked down and brutally murdered, or join you and, more than likely, be brutally murdered?'

'It's still a choice.'

'Well thank you very much.' He sighed. 'When do we ride out?'

'When you're done jabbering.'

*

They camped on the hardpan in the predawn darkness. They set no fire and the scale of things was such that they were infinitesimal and lost in that cosmic crucible. Doctor Onabanjo was abroad in the darkness, drunk on his kazoo pipe, and he circled the children like a shadow puppet against a backdrop of spangled firmament. Two-dimensional and of a blackness perfect, he erased whole constellations as he danced before them, a performance akin to those titanic mouths that hurtle through space, silently screaming and cannibalising the universe.

He was communing with the ghosts of his practice, reciting the names of dead doctors and chemists, which to the children were as fanciful as fairy names:

Hippocrates! Faraday! Curie! Nobel!

When they shushed him and begged him to re-join them, fool that he was, he merely blew a raspberry and sang those old names all the louder. At this the children dismissed him and lay back down and muttered curses under their breath, willed his feet to find their way over one of those winding dry gulches which dogged their path.

Plum and Hiroshi lay side by side, a little apart, audience to the celestial theatre overhead, the silver incisions of shooting stars, the electric green snaking of the aurora. The swelling in her face had already begun to subside, as though after all the beatings and injuries she had sustained in her short life her body was now expert at fixing itself.

'I'm sorry about earlier,' said Hiroshi.

Neither looked at the other. Plum sighed.

'Do we have to talk about it?' she said.

'Not if you don't want to.'

'I don't want to.'

'Okay.'

Plum sat up and got out her makings and set about rolling. She sprinkled the tobacco into the paper and then stopped a moment, pinching the paper closed to save its contents being carried off in the night wind.

'Look,' she said. 'I shouldn't have done what I done. You told me your situation soon as we met near enough. It's just, in that moment, it was like you was somebody else, somebody I used to know, but also someone new as well. But hell, that don't excuse it. What I'm trying to say is it's not your fault… and I'm sorry.'

She licked and stuck the cigarette and offered it out to Hiroshi who was stunned both still and silent.

'Do you forgive me?' she said.

'Way I see it, there's nothing to forgive. You was only following your red heart.'

Plum smiled.

'That some corny line from your old religion.'

'Not quite. We were always told beware the red heart. Ignore its passionate rhythms lest ye forsake your Fathers. I guess you can only ignore it so long.'

She nodded and wagged the cigarette at Hiroshi who took it from her and received a lit match cupped in Plum's hands. Plum then rolled one for herself and lit it from Hiroshi's while it was still in his mouth in the manner of kissing ducks. Soon they were leant back on their elbows, gazing up at the stars and talking about other things.

'What do you make of the doctor?' said Hiroshi.

'He is the most brilliant mind I have ever met. Pity he's also an idiot.'

They watched his silhouette conclude its contortions out there in the gloom. Then, all of a sudden, he stopped and hung his head and beat his brains with his balled-up fists.

'Stupid,' he said. 'Stupid. Stupid.'

Returning to their higgledy-piggledy camp, he slumped to the ground in a single fluid movement, like his bones had been tricked out of him, and in an instant he was fast asleep and snoring like a pig. Hiroshi flared his nostrils in disgust.

'Do you think he was right earlier... about my Brothers and I?'

'Probably.'

Hiroshi looked at her and then turned away and did not say anything.

'What does it matter?' she said.

'No one likes being wrong.'

'Yeah, well. Everyone and everything is proven wrong in time. Only kindness and cruelty endure. They are the only constants. Everything else has always been liable to change. Banjo himself has even said the multiverse is infinite and every occurrence accounted for somewhere in its iterations. Which means your gods must exist. Just maybe not in our universe. He'll be proved wrong before long just wait and see; and once he is buried beneath the collapse of his adamance he'll regret ever being cruel to you.'

'Well I look forward to that day. You hear me you arrogant shit?'

Doctor Onabanjo did not even break the stride of his snores. Hiroshi scoffed and pitched his cigarette at him but it sailed comfortably over him and it was clear he had never meant for it to strike him. He grinned weakly at Plum who raised her eyebrows at him.

'Good night, Hiroshi,' she said, douting out her

cigarette in the dusty earth and rolling onto her side.

'Yeah. Good night, Plum.'

*

The next day, when they rode into camp, all was changed.

A GOODBYE, A GREETING

They rode into camp a ragged band of exiles in the last light of the demising day. They had set off in the cold hours before dawn and the going had been slow and without event. Doctor Onabanjo, who inebriate had earlier toppled from his pony, was now tied to the body of the Chincoteague like the rest of his cargo, as though he and his effects had been pillaged by these rapscallion children. Hiroshi uncoupled his binds and slapped his chops and the doctor erected himself on his saddle and yawned like a cat.

Plum, having left Salvation half-blind on the back of Hiroshi's pony, was now astride her own and led their little caravan between the campfires and bemused onlookers towards her father's tent. The Brothers now wore a new uniform, plain robes of unbleached linen, and they tutted and narrowed their eyes as Hiroshi rode past them still clad in the red vestments of their dead religion. As he drew alongside, an old man took a step forward from the crowd and spat a rancid cord of brown chew so that it zagged across Hiroshi's bare leg. Bewildered, Hiroshi looked back at him but said nothing.

Peter came ducking out of Cherry's tepee at their

approach. He too was now dressed in robes, but his were bleached and gilded with a golden thread. A single dove stood on the hem, multiplying up the robe until it became a flock of doves in full flight across his breast. It was a true masterpiece of stitching.

'You're back,' he said.

His hands were clasped behind his back and he sneered wickedly up at those wretched revenants atop their ponies, filthy and bone-tired. His eyes locked onto Hiroshi.

'Boy, how dare you desecrate this ground by wearing those foul remnants!' he said.

'I didn't know!' said Hiroshi, but his words were drowned beneath the hisses of the crowd. His cheeks turned purple and he ducked his head. A stone came whizzing out of nowhere and glanced him in the side and he flinched and took a sharp intake of breath but he held his cool. Plum surveyed the crowd and turned back to Peter.

'I guess you got what you wanted,' she said.

He regarded the milling crowd, his chin held high, proud. A smile stretched snake-like across his face.

'I always do,' he said. 'Eventually.'

'Peter, what the hell are you waiting for? Invite them in,' cried her father from inside the tepee. Peter's smile broke and he blinked hard as though woke from a daydream.

'How brief, the eventual,' said Plum, her lips arranged in a small, pitying smile.

He glared at her, hesitated.

'Peter!' shouted Cherry.

Peter resigned. He coughed into his fist and stood aside. Then, bowing his bald head toward them just a fraction, he beckoned the riders through the opening of the tent. Dismounting, they filed in, Doctor Onabanjo last of all somehow managing to tread hard on Peter's foot after making a pratfall out of the short walk. He backed up and regarded Peter with dark, sympathetic eyes as he hopped clutching his sandaled foot.

'Terribly sorry,' he said. 'I'm a bit wobbly. It's been a long ride and I got horse legs. Tell you what, bring my bags in and I'll fix you up something for the pain. Honestly, what a first impression!'

Peter ignored the doctor's request and followed them in. As he entered, Plum was saying, 'Pa, we need one of those swanky socks for Hiroshi before they stone him to death.' To which Cherry responded, 'Of course! Hiroshi, are you alright my darling? I bet they gave you hell on the ride in. Peter. Peter. Is he here? Peter, get Hiroshi a robe. One of the nicer ones. Pronto!'

'Yes, my lord,' said Peter, and bowed out, snarling at the lot of them. Smiling, they watched him go.

'Doctor Onabanjo, are you there?' said Cherry, his blind eyes skyward, like it were a séance.

'Yes.'

'Ah, my friend. Welcome. I suppose Plum has caught you up?'

'Some.'

Doctor Onabanjo rattled a small plastic pillbox and Cherry felt out the noise with his hands and clasped the doctor's hand and held it a moment before retrieving the pillbox enclosed therein.

'Thank you, doctor,' he said. 'Come. Come. Let us sit a moment.'

A small fire burned in the centre of the tepee and the four of them sat around it.

'Did you read it?' said Cherry.

'Yes.'

'And?'

'It's some old atheist's manuscript. A denouncement of religion. The Messiah Caravan is not a single pilgrimage at all, but rather a metaphor for the history of all dead religions.'

'You don't say. Not much help to my present situation then, being the second coming and all?'

'Depends on what you are trying to achieve.'

'I'm just trying to stay alive.'

'Then no.'

Cherry pulled out the text from beneath his robes of golden yellow and smoothed his palm over the cover.

'Shame,' he said, and tossed it on the fire. 'Plum, the dust jacket.'

'Already got rid of it, pa.'

'Good girl. Now I suggest you all get some rest. The true messiah caravan rolls out tomorrow.'

*

'Why'd you tell your daddy you got rid of the dust jacket?' said Hiroshi, from the towpath. His new robes flapped gently in the soft breeze. They were fine indeed, embroidered with suns and moons and stars, but they were too small for him, ending above the knee like a tunic; a product of Peter's pettiness, no doubt about it.

'Nice digs,' said Plum.

'Why'd you keep it?'

Plum was sat on a slender bough that shot diagonally out of the bank and over the still, black waters of the canal. A blood moon was at her back, filtered red by the desert dust. She tapped the ash from her cigarette and watched it dance down to settle with the tiniest ripple upon the lonely profile of her reflection.

'I have my reasons,' she said.

Hiroshi lingered on the towpath a moment, kicking the stones.

'Come sit with me awhile,' she said.

Hiroshi grinned and, deft as you like, traversed the bough, which was young and flexible and yielded beneath his weight without even a threat of breaking. He lowered himself down beside her and their forms were married upon the surface of the water before a valentine of weltering moonlight.

'You'll be leaving in the morning,' said Plum.

'At dawn.'

'You packed?'

'I am.'

Plum nodded.

'That's good,' she said.

She lit and passed him a cigarette she had pre-rolled, as though she had been expecting him. They smoked a while. Then Plum took a small fold of paper from her dungaree pocket and nudged Hiroshi in the sides.

'What's that?' he said.

'It's for you. I thought you might like it.'

'A going away present?'

She nodded and spat some baccy off the tip of her tongue. He took it from her and unfurled it like it were a map.

'The dust jacket?'

'Yeah.'

'You kept it for me?'

'I guess so.'

'I don't know what to say.'

She nodded and turned away. The tear in her eye, she turned it out with the palm of her hand before it the chance to fall. All about the stars were strung like fairy lights and the canal-side ferns were lush and radiated a dull orange in the light of the red moon. His arm fell across her back and she sighed and leant her head on his shoulder. And then they just sat there, the universe revolving around them.

*

That night they slept back-to-back in the hayloft of the barn. When Hiroshi rose before dawn, Plum did not stir. He tiptoed across the boards and lowered himself through the hatch and paused.

'Plum,' he whispered.

She did not move. He made as though he might speak again but he just took a deep breath and disappeared through the hatch. As soon as he was clear, Plum opened her eyes. Though still she did not move. She just lay on her side listening through the boards to him saddling up the Chincoteague below. As he rode out, she buried her face into her pillow of hay and finally allowed herself to weep.

'No. I'm not okay, Bo,' she said, rising from the hay and wiping her eyes. ''Cause I don't want him to go. Why do my friends always have to go? But you're not here, are you? Okay, so you're here and you're not. That's not the point. Look, don't be jealous. Okay, I'm sorry I kissed him. I really am. Shut up. Don't be mean. Just shut up, alright? Shut up. Shut up, shut up, shut up!'

*

When Plum stepped out of the barn into the light of the new dawn, final preparations were already underway. Eggs and bacon were frying over cook fires, loads were being tied to the packhorses, and a solitary woman was studying the wheels of the prairie schooners. She paced back and forth, stroking her chin with one hand and with the other she would lay her fingers against each spoke in turn as though able to detect some pulse in the wood and thereby tell if it was healthy or defective. If she was unsatisfied, she would motion to her crew who were idling about nearby smoking and drinking coffee and they would set to work removing the great wheels and replacing them with new ones certified by she, the master carpenter.

Plum went over to the nearest cook fire and drew a plate and shovelled down eggs and bacon and wiped up the yolk and the fat with a triangle of tortilla. Afterwards, she decided to dawdle on over to her father's tent and it was then she noticed the dust cloud on the horizon in the direction of Salvation. She walked a ways out onto the hardpan so as to get a better view and when she squinted she could make out little figures mobilised within that red strata of dust, their forms drawn and wavering through the rising heat. She set off at a run.

'Papa!' she cried, as she bowled through the opening of his tepee. 'Somebody's coming.'

Her father had been asleep in the embrace of Peter and

he rose with a start flapping his arms like a crazed flightless bird, stumbling over the extinguished fire in the centre of the tent. Plum caught him up in her arms and they fell together, he knocking the wind out of her.

'Who is it?' he whispered, still atop her.

'Dunno,' she said, in between sharp breaths.

'Is it him? Is it the devil?'

'I. Don't. Know.'

'Peter!' he cried, rolling off her.

'My lord?' he said, pulling on his robes.

'Somebody approaches. Quick! Send out a scouting party. And ready our horse should we need to make a quick getaway.'

'Yes, my lord.'

As Peter ducked out, Plum made to follow. As though he sensed it, Cherry said, 'Stay with me, my girl.'

'Papa, I need to know what's going on. I can't help otherwise.'

'Please.'

And so she sat, her chin in her hands, and waited with him as outside the commotion grew louder, closer. Cherry sat down on the floor also, his knees pulled up to his chest, patting them, playing out an anxious rhythm.

'Who do you think it is?'

'I don't know.'

'But who do you *think* it is?'

'What's the point guessing? We'll find out soon enough.'

'Are you okay?'

'Fine.'

'I thought you'd be with your new friend.'

'I was.'

'He seems nice… I said he seems nice.'

'He is. He was. He's gone.'

'Oh.'

Cherry cleared his throat. Outside, people were hollering and there was the sound of hooves and wheels.

'Who could it be?' said Cherry.

'I'm going to find out,' said Plum.

'Wait.'

But she was already clambering out of the tepee. The second she was out and up, she spat. There was a violence to the action, as though the spittle contained her vehemence, like a gypsy curse. Her knuckles shone white through her clenched fists.

The scouting party were riding in and shouting, 'Friendly! Friendly! Calm yourselves, my Brothers. It's the Salvationites.' They pulled up before her father's tent and dismounted.

'What happened?' said Plum.

The lead scout walked straight past her and into her father's tent. She listened at the entrance.

'A horror befell them last night, my lord. The devil. The devil has driven them from their homes.'

'Ah! I see. Then welcome them. Welcome them with open arms.' Then he qualified this by whispering, 'But make sure they know who's in charge.'

'Yes, my lord.'

The lead scout came ducking out of the tepee and the scouting party mounted up and rode out once more in a flurry of hooves and driven dust. Plum followed in their wake, spitting out the fine grit settling on her teeth. The Salvationites were close now and she watched as the scouting party rode out and headed off their procession and rode them into camp. At the back of the column, behind the schooners and the horsemen, stumbled the exhausted pedestrians of their outfit. And at the very rear were the mudlarks. It was to they that she went. They were each of them wretched and sunburnt but they welcomed her with great enthusiasm. A hero's welcome. They crowded all about her and those near to her embraced her and those behind reached in any way they could so that they might just grace her dungarees with their fingertips. She responded by patting some of them on the head and this gesture was welcomed such that she was required to reciprocate it for all.

Among their number, their little leader was not. When Plum queried this, they grew solemn. Then they told her what happened.

THE SALVATION EXODUS

On the morning of Plum's narrow escape from Salvation, a detachment of roughhousers was seen entering the little frontier town at dawn. Upon finding Doctor Onabanjo gone and their compatriots dead in the alleys, they loaded the fallen into the boot of the 4x4 and departed. All that morning, Salvation was a ghost town. No one came. No one went. Everyone just hid and waited for the devil's return. The wind and the dust scoured away the blood of the slain until there was no record of the night's drama. Then, at high noon, the devil's convoy rolled in. Five cars containing nineteen roughhousers and the devil made twenty. They alighted and the devil commenced monologuing about this and that; judgement, pain, death, and the like; but also of reward for the acquiescent. Still none emerged from their homes or hidey-holes. The people cowered in the shadows or twitched at their windowsills. Then the devil said, 'Fine. Be that way,' and his roughhousers took his meaning. They spread over that town like a plague, rooting out whomever so was first to be found and dragging them by arm, by hair, out into the thoroughfare for all to see. There the devil interrogated them. He would start out kind. All nicey-nice. Telling them he did not want to do this. Then, in the next moment, he would be yelling in their faces. Slapping them. Over and over. Mindless drunks who never saw nothing ever. Mothers clutching their children, humming to their babies throughout the beatings. He worked his way along the line and had quickly had enough. That is when he drew his revolver and levelled it at some poor mother and you know what she did? She cupped the babby's ears and hummed all the louder. That is when the leader of the mudlarks stepped forth.

'Stop it!' she had cried. 'Just stop it!'

She was walking up the thoroughfare all by herself, courage coming out of her ears.

'Let her go. I'm who ye want.'

The devil was intrigued. He approached the mudlark and they each stopped a good ten paces off like duellists, the devil with his revolver, the girl empty handed. It was a strange sight, seeing him remain a ways off like that. All tentative. He looked a big man reduced.

'Tell me what you know,' he called out to her.

And she did. She told him about Plum. How some brown skinned girl with a purple splodge on her ear had turned up in the middle of the night and deaded his men easy as that. Told him they had rode out thattaway, towards the Red Basilica. And then she even told him the girl knew the big bad woman that shot down his woman on the steps of the doctor's home.

'Is that so?' said the devil.

But he was nodding, like he knew it was so.

'Mm-hmm,' said the leader of the mudlarks. 'And I know one more thing too. But I don't think ye'd like me shouting it to ye in front of all these folks.'

The devil looked back at his men and then approached the girl cautiously, like she was something of unreckonable power. He did look a coward. Then again, considering what happened next, perhaps he should have taken better care.

'Go on then,' hissed the devil, when but a step separated them. 'What is it?'

The mudlark looked over her shoulder as though concerned for the devil's privacy and then stepped forwards and magicked forth her switchblade out of her ragged sleeve and stuck it through the waistline of his trousers. It took the devil a while to realise what was happening. There was the same sincere girl about to tell him a big old juicy secret, only now she was trying with all her might to pull free the switchblade lodged in his pelvic bone. He commenced a screaming torrent at her; and his roughhousers, who were not privy from their angle to the intimate scene before them, looked from the devil to each other without a clue as to how to proceed. The devil then shoved the girl in the chest and she fell onto her backside. She just sat there, right in the middle of the thoroughfare. She did not even try to run. The devil limped off to the side, wincing and sucking his teeth, trying to pull free the knife. A moment passed where all watched only him. What was to happen next? He then looked up at his roughhousers with bewildered eyes.

'What are you waiting for?' he shouted, indicating the girl with his finger.

At this, every roughhouser present turned and unloaded their pieces on the leader of the mudlarks and that little child burst open like a party popper.

In the wake of that most disgraceful scene, the town held its breath. Even the roughhousers hesitated to reload their pieces as though in reverence to their most abominable crime. The only sound was the bawling of the baby whose mother the mudlark had saved. The mother, like everyone else, was frozen, fixated on that scarlet smear in the dust, which just a moment ago was composed and living and beautiful. Even the devil stopped his dancing, his stupid wounded dancing, and gave his regards.

Then the knives started flying.

'Motherfucker!' cried the butcher, as he heaved his

meat cleavers at every roughhouser near at hand. Most of them missed. But one lopped the ear off a harlequin and he went down clutching the spurting chasm on the side of his head. Next, some great big monstrosity sluiced down through the shoulder blade of one of the devil's men nearly splitting him in half. The butcher then ran riot with a lengthy butcher's scimitar, wielding it like a samurai.

The roughhousers were in a tizzy. They had spent their bullets on the child and it was all they could do to keep themselves alive as the butcher, then the barber, joined the fracas. The barber with her cutthroat razors, ambushing roughhousers as they crouched trying to reload and slitting their throats and pushing them forward into the dust.

A breakaway of roughhousers went and grabbed the devil and dragged him back to the line of 4x4s. It was then that the barkeeper emerged. His pistola loaded with the only bullet he owned, the bullet the devil's own woman had traded him a glass of silt-water for. He took aim at the devil and fired. Though his aim was true, the sight on the old pistola was not, and one of the roughhousers taking the weight of the wounded devil crumpled. A roughhouser near at hand had then finished reloading and spied the barkeep with his empty pistola raised and murdered him outright. The cycle complete. A bad luck gesture indeed.

The remaining roughhousers succeeded in stowing the devil into the 4x4 and they were away. Of the twenty women and men that entered Salvation that day, only the devil and two more escaped. The rest lay slain in the thoroughfare of Salvation. It was then that the townsfolk knew they must flee. That their best hope was to follow the enemy of their enemy and make for the Red Basilica.

GARGANTUA

S he heard their tale to its end and remained among them until their sorrow burnt itself out. As they wiped their eyes, a little girl among their number felt the need to explain that their leader had not meant to forsake Plum and that she had only offered the information as a means to get close enough to stick the devil. Plum said she knew this and that their little leader was very brave and that they should all, herself included, honour her bravery by remembering it and trying to be as brave as her when situations allowed it. Then the little girl brought forth that coin from the devil's own mint, the one their leader had traded for, and said they would like Plum to take it, for it was evil and no replacement of a friend. Then she said:

'If anyone can put evil to good use, it's you.'

Plum accepted it in silence for there was no thanks right or worthy for such a gift. She then bid them follow her and they all linked hands in a line and filed after her. She led them to a prairie schooner wherein dozed children of The Messiah Caravan, their arms tucked inside their robes, each using the other for a pillow.

'Not fair,' complained the children on seeing the

159

mudlarks. 'There's no room.'

'Make room,' said Plum, and she leant each mudlark in turn a hand up into the schooner and then left them to work it out. As she walked away, the two tribes of children faced each other across the schooner; the mudlarks, exhausted and raw-eyed; the children of The Messiah Caravan, wriggling, huffing and puffing. Then one of the mudlarks broke wind quite out of nowhere. You could tell it was an accident too for she sat up straight and her eyes went wide. Then, one by one, each child gave way to snickering until the schooner was full of laughter and the pinching of noses and the wafting of hands.

*

The caravan finally rolled out before morning's end after a series of setbacks, which included the rousing of hungover parishioners, final arguments from a vocal few who thought they should stay and rebuild, and a tantrum from the master carpenter upon inspecting the shoddy work of her crew. Reeking canal water was chucked over the inebriate; the remainers were told, *Stay if you want, but we're all leaving*; and Cherry took the master carpenter aside and delicately advised that there was only room in the caravan for one prima-donna, and that was he.

Azure skies stretched uninterrupted to the chilli powder mesas on the horizon and the sun was a searing white branding iron overhead such that after only an hour on the hardpan the caravan was forced to stop and siesta away the noonday sun. Those unfortunates consigned to their feet found shade beneath the schooners or else erected their robes on sticks and sat naked beneath their slipshod parasols. Those inside the schooners dared not step out even to make toilet lest their place be stolen and the passengers took to relieving themselves over the rear-edge of the wagons. A small gazebo had been raised for Cherry and his closest disciples at the head of the caravan and he lay in the shade with his head on the lap of Peter who was tenderly tracing the scars on his head with his

160

index finger. Doctor Onabanjo sat a little aside, smoking his kazoo pipe, his legs laced up like a pretzel beneath him. Plum, having been to check on the mudlarks, came walking up and took a seat and lit her cigarette off the burning draw in the bowl of Doctor Onabanjo's pipe.

'Where exactly are we going?' said Plum.

'Wherever our brave father leads us,' mused Peter, looking down on his lord and saviour with puppy dog eyes.

'Last I checked you were my pappy's eyes, not his mouth.'

Peter scrunched his face up at her rebuke but said no more.

'We make for the town of Hope, then on to the Rivers of Paradise. From there, who knows?'

'What's at the Rivers of Paradise?'

'An old friend I am hoping might be able to help us.'

'With what?'

'Weapons, little one. Weapons for our army.'

Plum considered the caravan, which snaked out behind them.

'What army?' she said.

'Why, Peter tells me we have as many as a thousand fighting fit women and men in our number.'

'Does he now?' she scoffed. 'I make it nearer five hundred, including the young, the old and the sick.'

'Either way, a force to be reckoned with, surely it is.'

'You expect them kiddies to fight for you, eh, papa? Die for you?'

'We're all fighting the same battle, my girl.'

'Is that so?' She shook her head. 'I swear, when you lost your eyes, you lost your mind.'

Peter sat bolt upright and glared at Plum, his eyes venomous.

'How dare you, you—'

'Calm. Can't we please have some calm? It's too hot,' said Cherry.

'She can't talk to you like that, my lord.'

'It's okay. She's just upset because your boy Hiroshi took off on her.'

'Oh, I see!'

Peter was delighted. He giggled into his hand and gave Plum a coy look.

'Is it *love*?' he crooned.

Plum's face flushed with hot blood and she could feel her heart pounding in her head. She balled up her fists, crushing the cigarette out in her hand as she did, but she did not even notice. She was so mad. She imagined grabbing Peter by his throat and jamming her .38 down his throat. She could have demanded him to repeat what he had said and as he garbled his apologies around the borehole of that pistol she would blow the top of his spinal column off anyway. She could have done it too. Why didn't she?

'Don't be cruel, Peter,' chuckled Cherry. 'O, my girl, we're only playing.'

Throughout all this, Doctor Onabanjo never said a word. He just sat there looking concerned. Plum took a deep breath, relaxed her hands and brushed her palms together. Down danced the tobacco and the ash. She studied the little black burn stamped over the lifeline on her palm. Then she stood up and looked down at them.

'I do love him. Ain't no shame in it,' said Plum. 'I love him like I used to love you, papa.'

Then she turned and sought the shade further down the caravan.

*

When they rode out, Plum remained a ways back. Although she rode wide of the advancing column so that she still had eyes on her father's schooner at the head of the caravan. The remains of the afternoon passed in a blistering haze and the scintillating heat conjured forth a silver-blue lagoon on the horizon. The poor and the bedraggled consigned to their feet began one by one to falter under the relentless sun. Only then were allowances made and disgruntled passengers ejected from the schooners to be replaced with the sun-stricken pedestrians. Plum eyed a boy in his teens holding up his grandmamma and she rode up and alighted in a single fluid motion and held the pony steady whilst they mounted up in silence. The boy sat himself behind his grandmamma and let her recline on him like he was the back of a chair. Plum passed up the waterskin out of her saddlebag and they each took grateful, tender sips of the warm liquid. The grandmamma then passed it back down to her. As Plum received it, the grandmamma caught up her wrist and gripped it with her soft, cool hand. Plum looked the grandmamma in her face. Her skin was tan and rugged and seemed as enduring as the desert about. The grandmamma stared at her with blue and vital eyes but never said a word.

'It's okay,' said Plum.

The grandmamma leant forwards and cupped Plum's face with her hand. A single silver tear broke and rolled down the old woman's face. Plum tried to hold her gaze but it proved too difficult, the nudity of it and all, so she half-smiled and dropped her eyes and the old woman let go, nodding, as though in this brief interaction she had acquired a truth about the girl, a truth that perhaps she did not know about herself yet.

Plum walked before them the rest of that day leading the pony. Evening fell slowly, the sun sinking into the earth like a buzz saw, bleeding the horizon. The caravan continued long into the night, the travellers relishing the cool dark, the moon and stars pulled over the heavens like a magician's robe. All plodded dutifully on until their messiah stopped. When the call came to set up camp, many lay straight down on the hardpan and were asleep in but a moment. Others set about building cook fires and pitching tents. The boy and his grandmamma got down off Plum's pony. The boy smiled at her with wet eyes whilst the old woman wrung her hands and then they took their leave.

Plum ate among the mudlarks. As they passed round tortillas and bowls of bean stew, the mudlarks asked her where they were headed.

'For the Rivers of Paradise, or so I hear.'

'I never see'd the rivers,' said one boy, grinning. 'All I ever see'd is desert.'

Plum looked him square in his fair little face. His skin was more freckle than not and his hair the colour of sweet potato.

'I only ever seen them once,' she said. 'And I was little. Too little not to be sure I'm making it all up in my head. But if the picture in my noggin is right, they're bluer than you can imagine. Bluer even than the sky. But also green. Yellow. Brown too. Black and white. You name it. It's like all life is mixed up in them.'

'How about red?'

'You best believe it. But it's not like desert red, dead and dusty. It's a living red, like blood. Where the rivers get shallow, thousands of fishies snake over the pebbles and they red as flame. It's like the water's on fire.'

The children *oohed* and *aahed*. Then the boy said, 'Will you take us? Please. To see the fishies,' and Plum said she would. In the ensuing chatter she slipped away to find herself somewhere to sleep, somewhere altogether more lonesome.

She led her pony a ways out onto the hardpan and hobbled it where it stood. Unhitching the saddle and the bags, she slipped them from the pony and piled them on the ground. Against this she sat and, lighting a cigarette, she watched the shepherds driving the caravan's livestock pass back and forth distributing hay and grain to the cows and bucketing out slops for the pigs. On this scene, her mind winked out. Her chin dropped to her chest and the desert wind carried away the cigarette from between her lips.

*

When she awoke, it felt as though no time had passed but there was the sun crowning the horizon. Beside her, the hobbled Chincoteague lay on its side, the breath gusting in and out of its huge nostrils. She got up and stretched and rolled her stiff neck about her shoulders. Leftover bean stew was already being put to warm and there was a little pig meat roasting too for the lucky ones. Her belly rumbled as the smell reached her on the sultry morning air so she ambled over and got herself a bowl before the masses stirred.

They rolled out within the hour, the cook fires left burning on the hardpan. Plum rode her pony with a full belly, a cigarette between her lips, and watched a pair of cook-hands washing bowls and spoons in the back of a prairie schooner. It was a gleeful affair, the vehicle rocking side-to-side, pitching one cook-hand into the other, and the buckets sloshing about. They were the both of them drenched with dishwater and they fell into one another's arms like actors in a melodrama, and they were laughing, laughing all the while, and Plum thought perhaps they were in love.

A small skyline grew out of the ground ahead so they pressed on without a siesta and rode into the town of Hope at the meridian of that day. It was a frontier town, much like Salvation, but wealthier and better kept, and on the outskirts was a corny sign that read: *WE LIVE IN HOPE*. The townsfolk came out to gawk at their arrival and they were a smartly dressed bunch and some of them were wafting ornate folding fans in an attempt to beat the heat. Even the children were wearing collared short-sleeved shirts or else wore bright sundresses. They were a far cry indeed from Cherry's proselytes in their plain robes.

A portly fellow in a felt top hat stepped forwards, his hands wide in greeting, and blocked the way down the town's thoroughfare. He wore a waistcoat in spite of the heat and his white shirt showed up damp under his arms. Sweat stood in beads on his hairless face and this he dabbed with a handkerchief before returning the top hat to his head with a pat of the crown for good measure.

'Well halloo there. Welcome. Welcome!' he cried out. 'My name is Noddy and I have the privilege of representing these fine peoples in the office of mayor. Now, may I ask, what brings such a… *profound* assembly to our humble town?'

'Redemption,' called Cherry. He was riding shotgun on the lead schooner. The mayor sought his voice amidst the crowd and when he found him sat there all cut up it was all he could do to stifle a little gasp behind his damp handkerchief.

'My word,' said the mayor. 'Well, I don't suppose we'll be wanting any of that. You're welcome to spend your coin in our stores and taphouses. If you have no coin, then you can trade. But y'all make camp yonder. And when you roll out *tomorrow* you take your redemption with you.'

A silent standoff ensued. Peter whispered in Cherry's ear.

'Well?' said the mayor, his eyes flicking between the two conspirators. Cherry, who had his ear bent to his advisor, nodded and held up his hand and Peter sat back in his seat.

'A fair proposition, for we are strangers on this road and who would not be wary.'

At this, the mayor breathed a sigh of relief and dabbed his face with his handkerchief. He looked back to his people for support but they were edging away and it was apparent he stood alone. Cherry spoke on.

'I see that you are a wise and courageous man, Noddy. Your people are fortunate to have such a mayor.'

'Well. I mean…'

The mayor's reply trailed off into a series of throaty coughs and his cheeks flushed up scarlet. As the caravan rode around the town to the designated campsite, the mayor turned back to his people with his belly puffed out and his thumbs tucked in his belt as though he were a regular badass.

*

The caravan idled away the early afternoon heat under the fretful watch of the townsfolk. None came to welcome them. They were left very much alone. Hope, however, was a rumour mill.

'Bunch of wackos like that. Devil-sent. Gotta be,' said the tailor.

'Refugees. Exiles. Proof of the war beyond the desert!' said the blacksmith.

'A traveller once told of a mountain cult that wore a similar get-up and who feasted on their young. Perhaps this is they,' said the barkeep.

Though incredible, there was a modicum of truth to be had in all their stories.

In the lull, Plum walked abroad and entered the town's thoroughfare via the back alleys. She passed down the street unmolested. But followed she was by the whispers and darting eyes of society-ladies out on the verandas and cafe-fronts. No doubt remarking at the child's ragged, blood-stained dungarees and outlandish aviator goggles which hung around her neck like some uncouth necklace.

She turned into a store, the sign of which read: *Urkel's General Store and Apothecary*. Though of course read it she could not. The owner was behind the counter crushing out a fine white powder in a pestle and mortar and as she entered a bell tinkled against the door and he looked at her over the rims of his half-moon specs.

'What can I do you for?' he said.

'Bacco.'

'Come again?'

'To-bac-co.'

Nodding, he moved his work aside and wiped his dusty fingers on his apron. His movements measured, pompous. He knelt and retrieved a box from beneath the counter and, opening it, took out a little drawstring pouch of green felt.

'This is the way they come,' he said. 'I ain't measuring you out nothing smaller.'

'Did I ask you to?'

He closed the lid of the box and placed the pouch on the counter.

'Suppose you'll be wanting matches.'

'You suppose right.'

'Is that all?'

Plum started gazing around the store.

'Look, I haven't—'

'How about a big bag of those sweeties over there? No, not those ones, the yellow ones.'

The shopkeep huffed as he came back with the sweeties. As soon as they hit the counter, Plum said, 'Jerky. You got jerky?' In this way things proceeded until Plum had a regular bounty piled atop the counter: breads and cheeses, fruits she had seen before and fruits she had not, medical supplies, toy horses and bears and wolves whittled from wood and between them painted every colour, things of the old world, things of the new, and a waterskin freshly filled from the shopkeep's own well. When he returned from the well, he was out and out pissed. It was then that Plum said, 'And what about that?' She was pointing to a display of toilet paper stacked up like a pyramid.

'What about it?' said the shopkeep.

'What is it?'

'Toilet roll. You mean you ain't never seen toilet roll?'

'What's it for?'

'It's for…' the shopkeep blushed but still went ahead and made a charade of wiping his arse.

'Well ain't that the shits,' said Plum, and called for half a dozen.

'And pray tell, what will you be trading for all this?' said the shopkeep, as he loaded the lot of it into a pair of gunnysacks.

'Trading. Who said anything about trading? I aim to buy it outright,' she said, slapping down the devil's coin.

The shopkeep just stared at it.

'That ain't no regular coin,' he said to himself. 'Why that's the devil's own.'

'It is.'

'And how come you by it?'

'Never you mind.'

'I ought not to serve you. It could be stolen.'

'Could be? It is.'

The shopkeep's mouth opened and closed but he did not say anything. A bead of sweat broke and trickled down his forehead. His spectacles fogged over.

'Look,' said Plum. The devil will be rolling through here in a few days' time. When he does, you can return it to him yourself. Won't he be pleased?'

'He's coming here?'

Plum nodded.

'Oh my.'

'So, what do you say?'

∗

Plum returned to camp hugging the gunnysacks and made for the schooner wherein the mudlarks dozed.

'What you got there, Plum?' called a little girl as she approached.

Plum dropped the gunnysacks and took out the tobacco and matches. These she stowed in her own dungaree pocket.

'A gift,' she said, hoisting the gunnysacks into the back of the schooner. The mudlarks jumped to their feet and swarmed around the gunnysacks. Amidst the bustle there were calls of 'Pass'm round! Pass'm round!' and it was a festive scene indeed as the little ones doled out the presents amongst themselves.

∗

That evening, as the sideways sunlight drowned the world beneath a sea of blood, a beer barrel was hauled forth near the outskirts of Hope and Cherry Blossom, lord and saviour, was hoisted atop it. Stood there like the god of drunks, the caravan gathered round and those closest did indeed put their mouths to the tap and siphon away a little of the podium's ballast beneath the blind eyes of their messiah.

Plum ducked and elbowed her way through the crowd until she was at the front, her father before her with his back to her. She eyed the crowd, her hand on the pistol in her dungaree pocket.

Cherry took a huge breath and seemed to swell up twice his size. There he stood scraping the red sky, all china skin, gold robes and scars. The crowd might be forgiven their deception, for he was indeed messianic, no doubt about it.

'My disciples!' he cried and the crowd threw up their hands and cheered. 'Look at us here at the start of our journey. I may be blind, but still I see your passion, your belief, it flares on my eyelids like the sun once did. O the brilliance of it!'

The crowd roared and amidst the din could be heard cries of *We believe in you!* and *Praise him!*

'But I also spy a shadow. A creeping shadow looming over the very brightness of your faith. Doubt. Doubt, my children.'

No lord! they cried. *We trust you! Death to the doubters!*

'Doubt is the devil,' continued Cherry. 'And when you speak of the devil, do you exorcise him? No! You *exercise* him. You make the devil stronger.'

Forgive us lord!

'Speak not of it. Seal that doubting devil within you and watch him soon die.'

We will! Thank you, lord!

'You. Do you believe with all your heart?' said Cherry, pointing blindly at someone in the crowd.

I do!

'And you?'

With all my heart!

'And what about you, my child?' said Cherry,

pirouetting atop the barrel and pointing square at Plum, his blind eyes strangely seeing. 'Do you believe?'

All eyes were on her. She sucked her teeth and gripped the pistol in her pocket tight. Her father's lips stretched into a snakelike smile.

'Well?'

Plum opened her mouth as if to speak.

'I believe!' boomed a voice directly behind her. Plum span around to find herself in the wake of a gigantic woman, an easy six-foot-wide and double that in height. Her skin was a-swirl with greasy, darkling rainbows, like oil on tarmac, and she was altogether naked.

'Forgive me, lord. I have doubted all my life. Doubted myself. Doubted the world. I have lived in Hope all my life and yet hope has never lived in me. But now, seeing you, for the very first time, I truly do believe.'

Tears ran down the giant's cheeks and rained upon Plum.

'Step forth, child, and tell me your name?' said Cherry.

The giant stepped clean over Plum and approached Cherry. Even atop the barrel, she loomed over him. Noticing this, she took a knee.

'They call me Gargantua, my lord.'

'They?'

'The people of Hope.'

'And do you hold this name as your own?'

'I ain't never held another.'

'I understand. I too was once given a name I did not want by those who sought to control me. You know what I did? I gave myself a new name. What name would you give yourself?'

'I don't know. I just don't know,' she said. 'I used to dream of names. Names fit for great warriors and lovers. But they were make-believe and are now all but faded away. Now I am nothing.' At this, she broke down whimpering.

'Come. Come. Let me see you,' said Cherry, searching

the air with his hands. She rose and allowed him to trace her shoulder-span with his palms, to hug her arms, which were the size of tree trunks

'But my word, child. You *are* gargantuan.'

'I am?' she said, blinking away the tears. There was something in the way he said it. She was not a thing to be insulted but a thing to be revered.

'Indeed, you are. My child, you are the opposite of nothing. You are… *abundance*. In fact, if you permit it, I think I will give you a new name. A gift. And when I give it, it will be yours. It will not belong to I, nor the citizens of Hope. And rest assured, it will be both a warrior and a lover's name.'

'Please, lord,' she said. 'Give it to me.'

'From this day, you will be…'

'Yes,' she moaned.

'Gargantua!'

'Yes. Yes,' she cried. 'Now I understand. I am Gargantua!'

Gar-gan-tu-a! Gar-gan-tu-a!

And as the crowd began to chant her name and close in around her, Plum slipped away.

*

That night, Plum found herself on her back outside the Hope-town saloon with a belly full of sweet cider, a bust lip and a bloody nose. She had been cussing someone. Cussing them good. For what? Who knows? But whoever it was had boxed her twice in the face quick smart before she knew what was happening. She had gone down and someone had stepped in and broke it up before it could go any further.

'For the love of man, Sid, what are you doing?' they had shouted. 'It's just a dumb kid!'

Maybe it was the barkeep. Who cares? Then she was dragged from the place and as she was she told them all to go to hell and spat blood and tooth at their feet to seal the curse.

As she lay there, tonguing the new gap in her teeth, she heard the boards strain under a pair of approaching feet. Then the twinkling stars went out overhead and were replaced by the great milky whites of Gargantua's eyes.

'Plum, is that you? My name's Gargantua.'

'Oh. Now I see how it is. Go on then, G. Get it over with, motherfucker.'

'Excuse me.'

'Just make it quick.'

'Make what quick?'

'He's sent you here to kill me.'

'What? Who?'

'My papa. Cherry Blossom.'

'Cherry Blossom's your daddy? Your real daddy?'

'He was.'

'Well then, things are starting to make a little sense round here. But never mind that. I'm not here to kill you, kid. He asked me to get you. He says he's sorry and he needs you back. Told me to say he was just mad at you for breaking his heart.'

'*I* broke *his* heart. Ha!'

Plum turned her head away and spat but the bloody spittle clung to her lip and dribbled down her chin.

'Look,' said Gargantua, lifting Plum up and propping her against the saloon wall. Gargantua then knelt and looked at her directly. 'Look,' she said again, but Plum belched in her face. Gargantua scrunched up her nose and wafted away the reek.

'Gawd almighty! What you been drinking?'

'Same as your mama.'

'You're drunk.'

'So was your mama.'

'Right.'

With that, Gargantua hoisted her up and trod the boards down to the watering trough, Plum wriggling in the crook of her arm.

'Let me go!' shouted Plum.

Gargantua shooed away the two horses taking water there as though they were no bigger than dogs. Then she upended the girl and, holding her by the ankles, dunked her head first up to the shoulders. Plum came up raging like some reluctant baptismal candidate.

'You cooled off?' said Gargantua.

Plum blew the water out her mouth.

'I swear. I swear I'm gonna shoot your a—.'

Before she could finish, Gargantua dunked her another turn, then pulled her out coughing and spluttering. In the next moment, Plum was laughing, caught upside down like some hysterical fish.

'You cool?'

'Yeah. Yeah, I'm cool.'

Gargantua set her down right ways up.

'Let's take a walk.'

They left the saloon behind and made their way down the thoroughfare. Being that Plum had to take three strides to Gargantua's one, for her it was more a drunken jog.

Glancing up, Plum noticed that Gargantua was no longer naked but had about her waist two adult robes spliced together to form a skirt that rode up around her knee and in it she looked altogether Amazonian.

'He needs you, you know. Cherry. Your daddy. He says you are the only one who speaks the truth to him.'

'What good is the truth to people who don't want to hear it?'

Gargantua paused a moment. Then she said:

'Tell me. I want to hear it.'

Plum looked up at her.

'No, G,' she said. 'I don't think you do.'

'You don't believe he is the messiah.'

'I know he isn't.'

'But you were there when he killed the devil, were you not? You were there when he raised the Red Basilica to the ground.'

'I was there when I killed the devil. I was there when I

raised the Red Basilica to the ground to save his skinny ass.'

'It was you?'

Plum nodded. Gargantua walked on in silence.

'I'm sorry,' said Plum, catching up. 'I know you want it to be true. But the truth is he's worse than all those people in Hope who've put you down all these years. Cause he'll raise you up. He'll raise you up and then he'll let you go. And the way down will be much further than you've ever known. And when you hit the ground it will hurt so, *so* much more.'

Gargantua stopped and studied the stars.

'You know what,' she said, at long last. 'It doesn't matter. I want to see what's up there.'

'Okay,' said Plum, shrugging, and they walked on together.

As they exited the thoroughfare, Plum set about rolling a cigarette by the light of the moon and stars. She clocked Gargantua looking her way and she offered the cigarette out to her.

'You don't have to,' said Gargantua.

'It's alright,' said Plum. 'Come on. Let's smoke them up over here.'

They made their way over to where a big old chunk of rock lay out on the hardpan. Atop this, they sat and Plum lit their smokes from the same match. Plum then watched, mesmerised, as Gargantua raised that teeny cigarette up to her lips and sucked it down to nothing in one colossal breath, the glow burning along the cigarette like the lit fuse of a boomstick. The giant brushed her fingers together and the remains of the cigarette disintegrated, falling like black snow. She then proceeded to blow three massive smoke rings in quick succession, big enough Plum could have jumped through them had she had the inclination.

'Well that's something I ain't never seen before.'

Gargantua smiled at her, smiled like a dragon, the remains of the smoke escaping through the gaps in her teeth. Then they leant back and watched the stars.

'You weren't lying to me just now was you? About Cherry... That he's your daddy.'

'Naw. Why?'

'Don't matter.'

'Okay.'

'Let just say I put two and two together and I didn't get four.'

'You reckoned me his lover?'

'Hey, I've seen worse... heard worser still.'

Plum scoffed and shook her head.

'Gross,' she said.

'Can you blame me? Your daddy is the whitest man I have ever seen. So white it's like he's not even there. And you... Well... Let's just say your mama must have been blacker than black to mix you up the way you is.'

'Nope. My mama was white also.'

'Go figure!'

'That's the honest truth.'

'Well how do you account for that?'

'Mama told me before she died that once upon a time all people were brown people. Then at some point out popped a white baby. She said god must have outright regretted that decision, the world being how it is a-cause of them. That's how white people come to be having brown babies.'

'I've said it once, I'll say it again. Go figure.'

'Yup.'

Plum screwed her cigarette out on the rock with her thumb.

'I'm sorry about your mama,' said Gargantua.

'What?'

'That she dead and all.'

'Oh. Yeah. Well. Thanks.'

'My mama's dead too.'

'Yeah?'

'Yeah. I killed her, so my daddy says. The day I came

out was the day they lowered her in. She was a normal size woman, you see. She wasn't like me. It's my fault she's dead. That's why my daddy called me what he called me. It was he who started it all off. He hated me then. He hates me still.'

Plum shook her head.

'There ain't one thing in this world that's a baby's fault.'

'You think?'

'I know.'

Gargantua sniffed and nodded her head.

'What was your mama like?' she said.

'My mama… She was smart. Well, sort of. She was a history professor at the University of New Sodom. Was, anyway, until the devil burnt it all down and she along with it. Her eyes were always on the past is what I mean. She wasn't looking where she was going.'

'Naw, you don't mean that. Nobody knows when the devil's gonna come knocking.'

'Maybe. Shit,' said Plum, turning out the tears with the heel of her hand.

'You okay?'

'Yeah. No. I don't know. It's just… I haven't thought about her in a long time.'

'I'm sorry. I didn't mean to upset you.'

'I'm not upset. I'm just angry.'

Some time went by, Gargantua watching the stars, Plum picking at the rock with her thumbnail.

'I bet it must have felt good… killing the devil… avenging your mama. I bet you couldn't believe your luck when he turned up on your doorstep.'

'It wasn't him.'

'It wasn't him?'

'Who killed my mama. It was the devil before him who gave the order. Maybe even the devil before that. I don't know. That man was nothing to me when I shot him down. I guess, just like the messiah, so too does the devil have his own caravan and in it there are many carts splintered and broken.'

'What are you talking about?'

'Doesn't matter. Come on, let's go.'

They ambled back together, Gargantua timing her lengthy strides against Plum's easy gait. As her father's tent loomed ahead, Plum stopped.

'You okay?' said Gargantua.

'I suppose you're going to rat me out to him, aren't you? Tell him I've been spouting off... about him not being the messiah and all.'

Gargantua looked up at the night sky as if for a sign. In that moment a shooting star cut across the firmament and Plum saw its tracer reflected in the sweat on Gargantua's breast.

'Naw,' said Gargantua. 'You heard him earlier. He don't want to hear doubt from anyone. Why would I risk telling him yours?'

'Okay,' said Plum. Her lips twitched a half-smile. 'Thanks.'

Plum set forth for the tent and Gargantua lingered behind. Before entering, Plum looked back over her shoulder. She could still make out Gargantua's prodigious profile, rimmed with the afterglow of the diminishing cook fires, and those eyes–big as eggs–watching her.

She ducked under the awning and into her father's tepee. As she did, Peter sprang to his feet and pointed at her.

'Get out!' he cried. 'Guards! Guards!'

There was shuffling and clanking outside and then a band of four robe-clad machos came crawling into the tent dragging farming equipment, shovels, scythes and the like.

'Settle down, settle down,' said her father, as they rose looking for the fight.

'But sir, she *embarrassed* you,' hissed Peter. Cherry ignored him. The guards looked awkwardly one to the other.

'Leave us,' said Cherry, waving his hand, and the guards

bowed and shimmied back out on their hands and knees. Peter watched them go.

'You too, Peter,' said Cherry.

'My lord,' implored Peter. But when Cherry said no more he acquiesced. 'My lord,' he said again, this time with a curt nod of the head, and left.

'So,' said Cherry.

'How long you been able to see?' said Plum.

'Ah. That. It was the morning we woke up on the canal.'

'All this time. Why didn't you tell me?'

'I never got the chance.'

'Bull shit. Why didn't you tell me?'

'I don't know. I just didn't.'

'Are we not on the same side any more or something?'

'Of course we are.'

'Then why you treating me like we not? Why you treating me like one of those sorry fools?' she said, pointing her finger in the direction of the caravan. 'My word that was some lousy trick you pulled on me earlier.'

'You're right. You're right. I'm sorry.'

'Who else knows?'

'Doctor Onabanjo. He called it hysterical blindness.'

'Hysterical blindness. What's so funny about it?'

'Your guess is as good as mine.'

'Who else knows?'

'No one.'

'Does Peter know?'

'No. Course not.'

'You sure?'

'Yes. God. I already told you he doesn't.'

'Good. I don't trust him.'

'He's okay.'

'He's a no good thimblerigger.'

'You don't know him.'

'Neither do you!'

Silence ensued. They both took a few breaths.

'Look,' said Plum. 'No more lies. Not to me. Or I'm gone. You hear. *You hear me?*'

'Okay. I hear you. Quiet down.'

Plum paced back and forth, her fists clenched. She turned to face him.

'What you playing at anyhow?'

'What do you mean?'

'You know exactly what I mean. Why are you lying to these people?'

'What makes you think I'm lying?'

'Papa, if you don't know your lying, then I swear you've played yourself good and proper.'

'You don't understand.'

'What's there to understand? This was supposed to be about you and me... looking out for each other... like the old days. Time was all we ever needed was each other. When did that change?'

'But Plum, darling, don't you see? I... *We* have an opportunity here. To make the world a better place.'

'What the hell are you talking about? So far, all we done is uproot a whole bunch of people. Their lives weren't perfect by any stretch but they was comfortable enough. Safe, at least. And for what? So that they can die out on the hardpan with hearts and bellies empty of all but the devil's metal. And why? So you might live.'

'That's not true. You just don't understand.'

'What? What don't I understand?'

'You'll only mock me.'

'Papa, tell me.'

He sighed.

'I can see it, Plum. I see in myself the same thing they see in me. And it's glorious.'

Plum shook her head.

'Papa,' she said. 'Mark my words. When the devil took your eyes, he gave you his.'

MARTHA PICKS UP THE TRAIL

'Do you see that, Brother Lesley, yonder?'
'I see it, Brother Quinn.'
'What do you make of it?'
'I make of it what it is. A hoss.'

They approached the Appaloosa mare, two Brothers of The Messiah Caravan still dressed in the red vestments of their dead religion. The mare's piebald coat bristled at their approach and its eyes were wide and knowing. As Brother Lesley extended her hand to stroke it, the mare snorted and shied away.

'Curious,' she said.

She eyed the perimeter, the barren hardpan to their right, the lush foliage to their left like a green wall between them and the canal.

'Where's the rider? Quinn, Brother, I said where's the rider?'

'I heard you the first time. How the hell am I meant to know?'

'Alright, alright, don't shit your codpiece. Hey, check those saddlebags, there might be food.'

'You check'm. That hoss has killer written all over it.'

'Seriously, what's wrong with you?' said Brother Lesley,

181

driving her spear into the ground.

This time she approached the mare side on, careful not to brush it, for it was tense as a coiled spring. Dipping a hand into the saddlebag, she came out with a package of dried meat. On her next pass, the horse whinnied and shook its head. She backed up.

'There's more where that came from,' she said, returning to her Brother and offering out the jerky. Brother Quinn took a handful and stuffed the lot in his mouth. He shut his eyes and sighed his satisfaction.

'That's good,' he said, mid-chew.

They stood grazing and watching the mare, the mare watching they.

'It's a sign,' said Brother Lesley. 'A sign from god we made the right decision.'

'You think?'

'Mm-hmm. Oh man, you're right, it is damn tasty.'

She swallowed and took a bite of another piece. Then she continued, the jerky balled up in her cheek.

'It's got to be. The Fathers forewarned of charlatan messiahs, remember? God rest their souls. I bet this hoss is our reward for heeding their warning and getting out of there when we did.'

'I hope your right.'

'Oh, Quinn, don't be so dramatic. Hold this.'

Brother Quinn received the package of jerky and held it to his heart like a valentine.

'What are you doing?'

'*Shhh!*'

'Be careful.'

'Dammit, be quiet.'

Brother Lesley approached the mare once more but it backed off crabwise before she could get within a couple metres.

'Right,' she said, and she snatched up a handful of grass from the canal bank and held it before her as she closed in once more. The horse flared its nostrils but its eyes could not see past the grass. The second it clopped down on it, Brother Lesley had her foot in the stirrup and was hoisting herself atop. When it felt that familiar human weight, the Appaloosa bucked and twisted full circle but Brother Lesley kept hold of the reins and dug her knees in tight and it was not long before she had the mare subdued.

'There. There. Atta girl,' she said, patting its neck.

The mare blew out its lips in contempt.

'You okay?' said Brother Quinn.

'Do I look hurt? Get up here.'

Brother Quinn did not reply. He was looking straight past her.

'Don't be a baby,' she said.

'Les,' he said, real sober-like, nodding at something behind her.

She turned in the saddle to find Martha, gaunt and hunched, crawling out from beneath a huge rhododendron bush like some lesser troll. Martha was much reduced; her once blue-black face now had a deathly pallor as though powdered with lime. She struggled to her feet. In her jittery hand she clutched her revolver and this she trained on Brother Lesley's heart.

'Who the hell are you?'

'Get down off my horse.'

'Your horse?'

'That's right.'

'Why should I?'

Martha rattled the revolver.

'If you don't know that, sweetheart, you've no hope in this life.'

'Come on now, that ain't no real gun. And even if it is, the bullets won't be.'

'Look. I'll give you to the count of three. That's how these things usually go, isn't it?'

'Quinn, Brother, pass me my spear.'

'Don't move,' said Martha, recalibrating her aim.

Brother Quinn froze, his hand on his comrade's spear,

which was still dug blade-down in the hardpan.

'Quinny, look at her, she's a rascal and a vagabond. Ain't no way that gun is real.'

'I don't want to kill you but I will. Now get down off my horse. One.'

'Brother, my spear,' said Brother Lesley, gesturing for her weapon.

'Two.'

'Quinny!'

'Three.'

Brother Quinn pulled the spear from the hard earth, a shot rang out, and the spear clattered shaft-wise against the ground. He looked down, confused.

'What?' he said.

His belly started belching blood out onto the dry earth. He laced his fingers over the tender puncture and the claret sluiced through the impromptu and ineffective gauze.

'What?' he said, again. 'I don't understand. You said it was fake.'

'I thought it was! I thought… Oh man, Quinny. I'm sorry. I'm sorry,' she said, and then she was calling 'Yar! Yar!' and kicking the horse. But the mare would not budge. Not an inch.

Brother Quinn sat down on the hardpan. The blood had drained from his face and he was starting to shiver. Martha struggled on over to him.

'I'm sorry,' she said.

'Help me,' he said.

'I meant to shoot you in the heart. My aim's off. I'm not well. I didn't mean for you to suffer.'

'Please,' he said, placing his blood-soaked hands on Martha's jeans.

'I'm sorry.'

'Ple—'

Martha discharged her revolver and his brains burst out the back of his skull. He toppled backwards, leaving two bloody handprints on her trousers.

'No!' said Brother Lesley.

'This is your last warning,' said Martha, turning and aiming. 'Get down off my horse.'

Brother Lesley looked from Martha, to the gun, to her fallen comrade, as though relearning the working of things. Then she unhooked her foot from the stirrup and slipped down off the horse.

'Back up. Further,' said Martha, and she did.

Martha dragged herself up into the saddle. As she did, the would-be-thief edged towards her but Martha was quick with the revolver.

'Get back. I swear. Oh my god, don't you learn? Why won't you listen?'

The girl stopped and stared daggers. Martha winced and clutched her stomach. She had been laid up three nights and days beneath the rhododendron bush racked by the whisky horrors. She was starving.

'I'm looking for a girl,' said Martha. 'Brown girl wearing dungarees. Purple birthmark on her ear. You seen her? She should have passed by this way.'

Brother Lesley shook her head.

'She's travelling with her father. White man. White as milk. Skinny as a reed. Last I saw he was wearing a white nightgown. Blind.'

Brother Lesley's eyes went wide and her lips parted.

'You've seen him, haven't you?'

She nodded.

'Where is he?'

She hesitated. Then she said:

'Who is he?'

'What?'

'That man, who is he to you?'

'Just a friend.'

'He ain't nothing special?'

'He ain't my husband if that's what you're asking. You trying to tell me he dead in some roundabout way?'

'This is gonna sound stupid. Is he your god?'

'What the hell are you talking about?'

'Then it's true. He's a no-good liar.'

'Cherry? Cherry is the best liar going.'

'I knew it.'

'I think I'm beginning to understand. What has he done?'

Brother Lesley shook her head.

'They rode out for Hope three days ago. No saying they'll still be there.'

'They? You mean Cherry and the girl?'

'No. I mean Cherry and the Brothers of The Messiah Caravan.'

'I see. He really done a number on you, didn't he?'

Brother Lesley sniffed hard, cleared her throat. She could not stop shaking her head.

'I'm sorry. Not for what he's done. That's on him. I'm sorry for your friend. Things should have been different.'

Brother Lesley scrunched up her nose in disgust and spat at the horse's feet. Martha looked to where the spittle landed, sighed and nodded, as though this summed everything up nicely. Then she took up the reins and turned the horse in the direction of Hope.

'You do realise, as soon as you kick that horse forward, I'm running for that spear and mark my words I'll skewer you where you sit.'

'I hope for your sake that that's not true,' said Martha and, clicking her tongue, the horse set off at a gentle trot. Brother Lesley watched her go, watched her chance for revenge draw further away. Then she went and knelt beside Brother Quinn and cried into his chest.

Martha did not look back once.

MACHIAVELLI

The soldier of fortune was leant back on the bar, thumb in his belt, surveying the barroom. He wore no shirt and his black, matted chest hair glistened with sweat. Across his back he wore an ill-fitting military jacket of black and gold that clung to his thick arms and would not button up for he was a barrel-chested sonofabitch. Beside him, on the countertop, lay his tricorn hat and a cut-glass tumbler of silver mescal.

The barroom was empty but for a game of five card stud operating in the corner and a vicious looking woman with a face full of tribal scars who was idling on a couch waiting her turn on the gigolos upstairs. The soldier of fortune turned and sank his mescal in one smooth motion. He made no face. It could have been water for all anyone knew.

'Boy,' he said, setting his empty glass down.

The boy cutting limes behind the bar put down the knife and walked over, wiping his hands on his apron. His skin was rich as lacquered walnut and a green paisley neckerchief set off his emerald eyes. He brought the bottle of mescal from the display and poured the soldier of fortune a generous serving, pushing the wiry spectacles back up onto the bridge of his nose as he did so. The soldier of fortune leaned in close and breathed in deeply through his nose. The boy could feel his eager eyes boring into his skull. He set the bottle down and looked the mercenary full in the face. The soldier of fortune snarled, lecherously.

'How long's that game been going?' said the soldier of fortune, jutting his chin toward the poker game.

'I'm afraid I couldn't tell you.'

'You sassing me, boy?' said the soldier of fortune, tonguing a gap in his teeth.

'No sir. Just it's been going since before I found myself gainfully employed.'

'That so?'

'Yup. Players come and go but that game has never broken.'

'What about the players then?'

The boy leaned in close. The soldier of fortune wet his lips with his tongue.

'The white-haired feller. That's Jonny Fishguts. He arrived shortly before you. He's what that smell is. He's a fishmonger y'see. Comes straight from work. He'll be broke and home within the hour. Only reason they put up with him. See that lady all in black. That's Saint Helga. Watch out for her. She's in here eight days a week. They say she's blessed. Only ever seen her lose once and that just so happens to have been to that girl on her right. The one in the denim with the cut throat. That's Laika Rawlins-Stone. Her daddy was Jimmy Rawlins. You must of heard of him if you a card player. She's somewhat irregular. Plays all over. Story goes she was cheated recently in the big game up at the Rivers of Paradise. Afterwards, they opened her neck and shoved her into the Vida. Yet there she sits. Though of course this is all conjecture. Lord knows she can't validate it. The knife cut the words right out of her throat. My advice, don't tangle with her. She beat Helga so bad I'm surprised they let her back in.'

'What about that guy?' said the soldier of fortune.

He nodded at a roughneck leant back on his chair, his foot on the poker table. He was dressed not unlike the soldier of fortune but with two bandoliers crossed over his chest. His rifle was propped up in the corner behind him. He was drunk as all hell and was singing some lairy drinking song around the cigar he was chewing. A crass tune about all the different coloured titties he had known, having once been a sailor and all.

'That guy? I don't know that guy. He's like you, if you pardon my candour. He came in here looking for a game and he found one.'

'How long for a seat to open up?'

'You want to sit down?'

'I want to sit down.'

'Helga,' called the boy. 'This man wants to play.'

Helga gave a single solemn nod in their direction and turned back to the game.

'You'll be next. Fishguts won't be long.'

'You're a good kid,' said the soldier of fortune, and lay his ham-like hand over the top of the boy's. The mercenary's hand was cool, cracked, covered in purple spider-veins. 'What's your name?' he said.

'Machiavelli, at your service,' said the boy.

'Mac, how about you and me get a room until that seat opens up?'

'I can see about a companion for you, if you'd like?'

'No,' said the soldier of fortune, who began to trace his sausage-like finger over the back of Machiavelli's slender hand. 'I want you.'

'I see. My mother warned me about men like you,' he said, flashing a coquettish smile before slipping his hand from beneath the soldier of fortune's touch. He grabbed up the mescal bottle and sashayed back down the bar.

'Men like me?' said the soldier of fortune after him, leering over the bar, smiling like a shark. Machiavelli looked at him over his shoulder.

'Relentless men,' he said.

The soldier of fortune laughed, cold and hard. There was no humour in it, only the semblance of mirth.

'She was right to do so,' he said, striding down the bar until they were face to face once more. He drained his glass and placed it in front of him. Nodded at it. Machiavelli uncorked the mescal and filled it.

'Come on, Mac,' he breathed, lustfully. 'I'm a soldier off to war. I may never come back. You could be the last man I ever love.'

Machiavelli raised one of his dramatic eyebrows at the soldier of fortune.

'What war?' he said.

The soldier of fortune raised the glass to his lips, took a whiff, lingered, and then sipped, enjoying the attention.

'Don't you know? Somewhere out there is the saviour of our time. Salvation. The Brothers of The Messiah Caravan. They've all joined him.' The soldier of fortune then leaned in real close. He looked left, right, checking for eavesdroppers he knew weren't there. 'Word is, he's the messiah,' he whispered, before straightening back up, nodding, his hands on the lapels of his military jacket. 'As you can imagine, the devil does not like this one bit. He has mustered himself an army never before seen in this brave new world. A thousand bona fide killers bought and paid for. Among them, yours truly.'

The soldier of fortune winked and drained his glass. Machiavelli stared off into the distance.

'So what do you say?' said the soldier of fortune, slamming his glass back down and oozing himself over the bar. A rush of lavender cologne preceded him, which failed to mask the rot. Machiavelli took a step back, looked at him as though he was only half there.

'Don't make me mad, boy,' said the soldier of fortune, the mask of humour falling from his face. 'You won't like me when I'm mad.'

Just then, a commotion started up over at the poker

table that drew both of their attentions. The roughneck was mouthing off at the player known as Laika Rawlins-Stone.

'What did you have? Bitch, I said what did you have?'

Laika paid him no mind, just raked in the pot and started stacking her chips. Her up-cards were showing the six, seven, eight, nine of diamonds.

'Not talking, eh?' said the roughneck. 'Well fuck you.'

He reached over and grabbed up her hole card. Looking at it, it was like he could not believe it. Then his face flushed up cherry-red and he threw it down face up. Deuce of spades. A stone-cold bluff.

'You dare fucking bluff me, woman? Three kings. You made me fold three fucking kings. You think you're a hard man or something. Look at me, cunt!'

Laika carried on stacking her chips as though nothing at all was going on.

'Right,' said the roughneck.

He turned for his rifle. Before he even had a hand on it, Saint Helga was on her feet, all seven foot of her, and subsumed the table in her dark shadow. On her hip glittered a silver magnum. Without hesitating, she drew and shot the roughneck in the back. He hit the wall and skidded down the brickwork, leaving a smear of dark blood.

The soldier of fortune turned back to Machiavelli.

'You're lucky, boy,' he said. 'Seems a seat just opened up.'

*

The sun was rising by the time Machiavelli was relieved of his duties. With his glasses atop his head, he pinched his nose and rubbed his eyes and slogged the steep and narrow staircase up to his attic room. Reaching his door, he laid his forehead to the cool wood. At his touch, the door creaked open. He hesitated. Then with wide, terrified eyes, he shoved the door so it flung back and clattered against the wall. There, in the centre of his modest room, by the leaden light of dawn, sat a dark silhouette upon his bunk. The figure rose and strode silently towards him, embraced him, kissed him, like some incubus loosed out of his own imagination. Machiavelli moaned softly. Then he took his love by the shoulders so that he might look him full in his soft, grey face.

'Oh, Hiroshi,' he said. 'You're okay.'

He kissed him again and pressed his body against his.

'I have heard such terrible rumours,' he whispered into his ear. 'I thought I wouldn't see you again.'

'It's okay. I'm here.'

They held each other there in the doorway for some time. Then, upon taking a step back, Machiavelli noticed Hiroshi's ill-fitting robes. He scoffed and shook his head.

'What *are* you wearing?' he said.

They retreated inside and closed the door. Sitting side by side on the bunk, they held hands and watched each other in silence, in awe, and it was as though there was a secret dialogue between them that only they could hear. Machiavelli raised a hand to Hiroshi's face and with his thumb traced the slight downward slant of his eyes. Hiroshi closed his eyes and sighed at his touch. Machiavelli smiled, a tear breaking, beading down the soft crease twixt nose and cheek before settling between his lips. He sucked his bottom lip and the saltiness of the tear spread up the sides of his tongue and made him shudder. He retreated, placed his hands in his own lap, looked down.

'You're here to say goodbye, aren't you?'

'Why would you say that?'

'Don't think me dumb, Hiroshi. I hear more than most in this world behind that bar. I know the Brothers of The Messiah Caravan are joined with some hokey desert messiah and plan to follow him, even into death.'

'It is true.'

'Then you shouldn't have come. Why do you insist on hurting me so? Why must I mourn you again and again?'

'I meant it is true what you said… about the Brothers.

But Mac, darling, I am a Brother no longer.'

'What are you saying?'

'I'm saying that it is time, finally, for us to leave. Together.'

Machiavelli just sat there, thunderstruck. His mouth slightly open. The words clanging about his head. Then, slowly, as the words became less sonorous, comprehensible, his lips spread wide revealing his brilliantly white teeth. In the next moment, he had thrown himself atop his love and was kissing him wetly on the mouth. Pinned to the bed, Hiroshi could only laugh between kisses. Machiavelli sat up, astraddle Hiroshi.

'You better not be lying, Hiroshi, my love.'

'I'm not lying.'

'Hell, it doesn't matter. Even if you are, I'll not let you take it back.'

'I'm not lying.'

'Good.'

Machiavelli started hiking up Hiroshi's robe.

'I was so scared,' he said. 'When I heard the devil was sending his army after you all.'

'What?' said Hiroshi as Machiavelli pulled the robe off over his head.

'But it's okay now. You're here. You're safe.'

'Mac, what do you mean? What army?'

'Forget I said anything. I'm killing the mood,' he said, kissing his chest.

'Mac.'

Machiavelli sighed and sat back, placing his hands on his hips.

'Word is the devil's hired a bunch of mercenaries to track down this so-called messiah.'

'Mercenaries. How many? Mac. How Many?'

'Thousand.'

'A thousand!'

Machiavelli nodded. Hiroshi rose up and flipped Machiavelli under him.

'We must warn them!' said Hiroshi, standing and pulling the robe back over his head. 'Mac. Please.'

Machiavelli remained on his back with his eyes closed, rubbing his temples with his fingers.

'So you *were* lying,' he said.

'Mac, they're going to kill them.'

'Why do you care? Is it Peter, huh? You want to save that bastard? After all he's done.'

'No!'

'I don't get it. You're out, you're in. I am so fucking tired.'

'Mac, please, they're my family. Fuck Peter. I don't give spit about him. But the rest, Mac. There are kids there like my brothers. I don't mean "Brothers". I mean brothers as in actual brothers. Sisters. Kids I've known since they was born. Kids I've helped raise. I can't abandon them.'

Machiavelli opened his eyes and stared at Hiroshi from where he lay. His gaze was a little off, unfocused. He did look so desperately tired.

'They'll kill us. You know that, don't you?'

'They won't!'

'A deserter and his faggot friend. Yes they will.'

'We'll just have to be careful. I know who we can tell. She'll know what to do.'

Machiavelli dragged himself to a sitting position and hung his head in his hands.

'And after?' he said at the floor.

'What do you mean?'

Machiavelli looked up, his eyes bloodshot, raw.

'What next? After we tell them?'

'Then we are gone. I swear,' said Hiroshi, kneeling beside him and taking up his hand. 'We'll follow the Rivers of Paradise until we find somewhere that no-one will bother us ever again.'

'Until they next need your help.'

Hiroshi opened his mouth as if to speak but closed it again and rubbed his forehead with his hand. Machiavelli took a deep breath and gazed absentmindedly around the room. The gunmetal morning was growing brighter. Dust danced in the shaft of radiance spilling sidewards through the skylight. His eyes settled on the sunflower he owned which lay on the floor beside his desk amidst its broken terracotta potting.

'Did you do that?' he said.

'What?'

'That.'

'Of course not!'

Machiavelli shook his head and blinked the tears from his eyes.

'Mac, we need to go. Every second we waste is precious.'

But Machiavelli was still preoccupied with the sunflower.

'It was probably reaching for the sunlight. They do that you know.'

'Mac, please, I need you with me. I can't leave you again.'

'But you will.'

'Please, Mac. It is the right thing to do. You know it is.'

Machiavelli looked down at their entwined hands. Then, at long last, up into Hiroshi's eyes, which now too were inflamed with sorrow. He sighed and nodded.

'Fine,' he said.

'Really?'

'I said fine.'

'Thank you,' said Hiroshi, and made to kiss his lips, but Machiavelli turned away, so he kissed his cheek instead.

'Right then. Let us make haste,' said Hiroshi, heading for the door.

Machiavelli lingered on the bed. Hiroshi opened the door.

'There you are,' said the soldier of fortune.

He was leaning on the doorjamb, blocking the way, picking at something in his teeth with his thumb. The tricorn hat was pulled down low so Hiroshi could not see his eyes. He smelled as if he had been pickled in mescal. Hiroshi backed up and the soldier of fortune swaggered inside and kicked the door shut with his boot heel.

'Right, boy,' he said, tipping the tricorn hat up with his thumb, revealing his small, sharp eyes, in which resided nothing but violence, like the eyes of a grizzly bear. 'Wait a minute... Who the fuck are you? Oh, never mind. More the merrier, right lads?'

He pulled his leather belt taut and undid the clasp and then started to unbutton his fly. Hiroshi stepped between the soldier of fortune and his love. The mercenary leered at him, slavering.

'You want to go first, boy?' he said.

The soldier of fortune dropped his kegs and sidled towards Hiroshi. Behind him, Machiavelli reached for the pillow of his bunk and drew out the pepperbox derringer lying thereunder. He rose and pushed Hiroshi aside and levelled the tiny handgun at the soldier of fortune. There was a pop, like a cork leaving a champagne bottle, followed by a puff of cobalt-blue smoke. The mercenary stopped. Looked down. Watched the little hole in his chest. How curious it was. Then a thick bead of blood rolled out of it. He swiped the warm liquid with his hand, leaving a smear of claret across his belly. Looking from his bloody hand to Machiavelli, he saw him standing there pointing that miniature four-bore handgun at him. Then the soldier of fortune's insentient face flooded with rage; and with a terrible bellow, he launched himself at his assassin.

Machiavelli fired off another shot and the bullet passed through the soldier of fortune's neck but he would not stop. He grabbed Machiavelli by the throat and they both went down onto the boards, the derringer skittering across the floor. In a moment, the soldier of fortune was up and astraddle Machiavelli. Machiavelli's slender, spider-like fingers danced over the mercenary's ferocious clasp. It was unclear if he would live to die of suffocation or whether the soldier of fortune would snap his neck clean.

The blood was spurting from the soldier of fortune's neck out of both bullet holes, as though he were Frankenstein's monster with the bolts wrenched free. Machiavelli could feel the warm spray as it rained down upon him, could taste the metal of it in his gaping, breathless mouth.

Hiroshi went clambering across the floor to retrieve the derringer where it lay by the fallen sunflower. He fumbled with the size of it as he ran back to the fracas.

'Hey!' he shouted, but the soldier of fortune paid him no mind.

He fired.

Through the powder blue smoke, Hiroshi saw what he had done. The soldier of fortune's tongue writhed freely like some peculiar, worm-like alien. Then a torrent of blood began to waterfall out of the soldier of fortune's neck.

He had shot his lower jaw clean off.

The soldier of fortune relinquished Machiavelli, who rolled over gasping, each breath a raking effort. Rising, the soldier of fortune stumbled towards Hiroshi. He did not look real anymore. His whole body a prosthetic like an extra in an old-world zombie film.

Hiroshi fired once more and the bullet passed through the soldier of fortune's eye, blowing out his temple. The soldier of fortune stopped, dropped to one knee. Still he would not die. He just knelt there, his arms crossed over his thigh for support. The breath in his throat a gargling nightmare neither boy would forget.

'Mac. Mac, my love. Put your arm around me. That's it.'

Hiroshi raised Machiavelli from the floor and dragged him from the room, his eyes reeling in their sockets, his breath caustic, excruciating. Around his neck, the mark of the mercenary flared up like a purple halo that had slipped from the head to the throat.

THE RIVERS OF PARADISE

The caravan loitered on the outskirts of Hope another day, in which time it became all too apparent that Gargantua would be the only proselyte among the townspeople. Cherry made another public address; but when none of the town showed interest, he took to harassing citizens in the streets. Plum could only watch and shake her head as her father grew more and more desperate.

'Cowards!' he cried, his eyes skyward in his phony blindness. 'Today is the most important day of your lives. The day ordained by god for you to choose between the devil and he. And you choose to hide. Shame. Shame on you all. Do you not know that in hiding the devil has made your mind for you? Well?'

The town retreated inside itself like a tortoise and the mayor came out only once to appease them; but finding neither the bogus flattery, nor the empty promises he expected as a bureaucrat, he retreated before the hostility of these dour visitants.

When Hope awoke the next morning to find nothing but empty hardpan all about them, the town breathed a sigh of relief.

199

*

They were a day and a night on the hardpan, hampered once more by the pedestrians among their number. Then, as the furious afternoon heat rolled up off the hardpan in choking waves, an elderly gentleman with great big liver spots on his head collapsed of heatstroke and a group of fellow pedestrians ran to his aid. When they hollered out to the caravan, the driver of the rear schooner merely looked back once and pushed the horses on. The rest of the pedestrians gawked from the driver to their fellows, their mouths cracked and blistered, as slowly the little band retreated behind them and were lost to the desert.

After that, none stopped to help the sun-stricken.

Plum did not see this. She was once again riding at the head of the column beside her father's schooner. They barely spoke. Cherry had become taciturn upon leaving Hope. Then every now and again he would break out in angry grumbles, cursing those who would deny him his divinity.

As always, Peter was at her father's side, driving the schooner, whispering to him, and at times he would brazenly glare at Plum. When she returned his gaze, he spat and turned once more to face the road ahead.

The next day they passed through a long, narrow canyon that split two high mesas. Here, finally, they were rewarded with shade and a cool breeze moaned through the canyon. When they re-emerged into the white heat, they did so to eruptions of plains lovegrass and black grama and as they pressed on, by and by, the earth began to soften, and ahead of them they could see the ground rolled green.

In time, the smell of damp earth rose up to greet them like a fond memory and the low roar of water seemed to come from all about and was growing louder. Then, as the caravan crested the rise of a relentlessly gradual hill, below them they were treated to the glittering, turquoise waters of the River Vida, one of the Rivers of Paradise.

Three rivers made up the Rivers of Paradise. The Muerte started in the White Mountains of Santa Muerte and oozed down through that radioactive wasteland to the north; its waters lifeless, poisonous, polluted with great fatbergs that turned dumbly on the claggy current. Then there was the Vida, what the caravan now looked upon, its waters wide, ferocious and salmon rich—a magnet for gold eagles, grey wolves and brown bears—and along its banks great forests of red pine and hemlock-spruce grew to magnificent heights on the nitrogen rich soil. Between the Vida and the Muerte hid the Espíritu, a slim river of shimmering, crystalline water, which ran independently down out of the Toda Mountains, the same source as the Vida, straight as a cable, unto the sea.

On the banks of the Vida stood a solitary saloon and it was towards this the caravan migrated. Fixed to the river-facing side of the saloon was a hydroelectric turbine, which lit up the weathered sign atop the roof. A number of the bulbs had popped but you could still read it if you had the words: *The Rivers of Paradise Hotel & Casino*. The combination of the turbine—which was made of wood and very much like a paddlewheel—and the phosphorescent sign made it look as though some old-timey gambling riverboat had run ashore.

On Cherry's orders, they camped that night a mile upriver from the casino.

'Ours are dealings best done in daylight,' Cherry had told Plum.

All night the casino's sign shuddered red, green and gold out there in the blackness.

Plum woke as the first spears of sunlight pierced the trees on the far bank. She rose silently, leaving her pony hobbled in a standing sleep, and made for the mudlarks' schooner by foot. Holding a finger to her lips, she roused them one by one and bid them follow.

They walked downriver, away from the casino, the waters raging beside them. Once they were a ways from camp, the freckle-faced boy among their number jogged to Plum's side.

'Are we going to see the fishies?' he said.

Plum yawned, her jaw clicking and popping. Then she looked down at him, smiled and nodded.

'You hear that?' he said, turning to his comrades and jumping up and down. 'Told you so!'

'Calm down, Jinxie-boy,' said the mudlarks.

'Yeah, Jinx, it's only fish.'

'We don't want you getting all disappointed again like with those pit vipers.'

The joy in the boy's face faltered, but then he waved his hand and all was well again.

'*Pah*! That was different. That was boring desert stuff. This. This is… Look at it!'

He pointed to the rushing, grey-blue waters beside them.

'Okay,' they said, but they were unconvinced.

They walked on in silence, the boy known as Jinx skipping beside Plum. The sun came over the trees and the whole world glistened like it was built of precious stones. After some time, Jinx's buoyant skipping slowed to a saunter. Then he sighed and tugged on Plum's shirtsleeve. He looked imploringly up at her.

'Hey,' he whispered. 'What will it be like?'

'What do you mean?'

'Will it be exciting?'

'I don't know. It will be what it is, I guess.'

The boy did not seem happy with the ambiguity of Plum's answer. He swung a kick at a passing stick but he missed it. Looking back at where it lay undisturbed, he clocked his friends' eyes upon him. He turned back sharpish, his face and ears blooming up crimson behind his freckles.

'They're right,' he said, his eyes downcast. 'It's only dumb fish.'

'And what's wrong with that?'

'I dunno. I bet they're boring.'

Plum sighed.

'You're fucking boring,' she said, lighting a cigarette.

The boy looked up at her, mouth agape. Then he caught the twinkle in her eye and snorted like a piglet.

*

After an hour or so, Plum held up her hand for them to stop. As they crested the bank, sure enough, below them were those promised scarlet fishies funnelling over the shallows. Plum shared the view with them a moment. Then looking down at Jinx she saw he was surly-faced.

'You see them?' said Plum.

'I see them.'

'Well.'

'Well what.'

She nodded at the fishies.

'What do you think?'

He shrugged and kicked at the stony bank.

'I dunno,' he said. 'The way you talked about them... it was like they were the most important thing in the world. I thought it would be bigger somehow. Not bigger. What's the word? I heard a preacher-man say it once. *Mah... Mah-jist...*'

'Majestic?'

'Yeah. That's it. *Mah-jist-stick.* I'm sorry. I know you think they're special. It's just... I guess I thought I'd feel different when I saw it. Like I'd be changed... or something.'

'Why'd you think that?'

The boy shook his head.

'Ain't no fishies gonna change you. Only you can do that.'

The boy lingered a moment, cleared his throat, and then slouched down the bank to the water's edge. Plum and the rest of the mudlarks watched as he pulled off his rags and waded naked out among the fishies. He looked down as they slowly streamed about his legs. Their bodies

203

bold as a courtesan's rouge. Their murky faces narrow and mean and curved like a rhino beetle's. It was the start of the fall salmon run and the sockeyes were labouring up the rivers and streams, therefore to birth, therefore to die.

The boy reached in and quickly pulled back and shook his hands as though he had touched something icky. He resolved himself and then he dunked his hands once more and came splashing out of the river hauling forth a sockeye the length of his arm and twice the width. He swung the fish against the pebbled bank and the stones crunched beneath it as it tried to flail its way back to the river. The boy was quick with a rock and he knelt over the sockeye and brained it once, twice. On the third, it stopped moving. The whole head frothed up pink and then a dark, terminal red spilled forth from the trauma. The boy dropped the rock and just squatted by it, staring at it. Plum came up behind him.

'Why'd you do that?' she said.

'I wanted to see what was so special about it.'

The boy's lip started to wobble. When he blinked, tears streamed down from both eyes. Plum lit a cigarette and blew the smoke out of her nose. The little boy coughed into his hand.

'Ain't nothing special about a dead fish,' she said. 'Unless it's cooking over a fire, that is. Here, give me some space.'

The boy shuffled up and watched as Plum pulled out her knife and made an incision lengthwise along the fish's narrow belly. She then dredged out its quivering, purple and grey innards and slung them off the blade with a flick of her wrist. The boy watched stone-faced as they splattered against the pebbled shore.

Plum ran her sleeve across her forehead, the bloody knife glistening in the sun. She looked over her shoulder at the mudlarks standing up on the bank and then back at the fish.

'This won't be enough,' she said.

'Huh?'

'I said we need more fish, fisherman.'

The boy grinned and in a flash of pasty skin went charging back into the water. Plum rose and turned to the mudlarks.

'Come on,' she called. 'Y'all gotta work for your breakfast!'

At that, the vagabond children commenced howling like a pack of wild animals and together as one they went skidding down the pebbled bank on their backsides and in an eruption of spray went stampeding into the shallows.

The mudlarks went to work and it was not long before Plum was waving her hands and calling out, 'Whoa there, kiddies, that's enough! You've got eyes bigger than your bellies.'

With that, the mudlarks let the fish alone and fell about japing, splashing and dunking, the sockeyes zigzagging around the jamboree, their beady bug eyes manic in their skulls. Plum left them to it.

In time, the smell of barbequed salmon rolled down the bank and across the water, enveloping the children like a fragrant fog.

When the mudlarks came clambering up the pebble bank, naked and dripping, laughing and jabbing each other in the arm, Plum was waiting for them at the cook fire, cigarette in mouth, with no less than three sockeyes turning on improvised spits made from sticks. Beside her, another three sockeyes lay in the grass, their outsides burnt black as bibles, their insides a lustrous fuchsia pink.

The mudlarks plonked themselves down about the fire and the salmon was shared around, each child pinching a chunk of tender flesh off the vertebrae before passing it on. One boy took a bite and started yakking.

'Careful of the bones,' said Plum, tapping the ash from her cigarette, smiling at the scene before her. She was the only one among them who was dressed, the mudlarks' rags lying in the grass to dry, and she looked both a part of the group and separate, like an outsider, or leader.

The mudlarks sighed as they ate and looked wordlessly to their comrades with glittering eyes. They had never tasted nothing so delicious, so fresh. The boy known as Jinx looked to Plum and grinned, revealing the salmon flakes stuck between his teeth.

'Well?' said Plum.

Jinx finished what he held and sucked his fingers.

'I'm beginning to see what's so special about them,' he said.

'Nothing like a full belly to restore one's faith in the world,' said Plum. 'Here, pass me some of that one.'

They ate until nothing but bones and burnt scales remained. Then they idled, chewed grass, dozed, talked about everything and nothing. Eventually, Plum rose and kicked dirt over the fire.

'Come on,' she said. 'We best be getting back.'

*

A hazy contentedness settled over the group as they followed the river back to the caravan. All wore lotus-eater smiles. Some held hands. One girl was seeing how far she could walk with her eyes closed. The sun was hot but the river cool and a crisp breeze rolled up off it.

As they neared, a gang of adults stood in wait for them, Cherry out in front with Peter conspiring at his side.

'Where have you been?' said Cherry.

'Just down the way,' said Plum.

She looked from her father to the group behind him. They were not of the caravan. Pirates, the lot of them. A ragtag band of thieves lousy with rum. Ornate knives hung at their hips and they were carrying machine guns every one. The most impressive among their number stood a full head above the others and was naked but for boots and a pair of cargo shorts. His chest and arms bulged with muscle, painfully so, and from breast to waist two scars criss-crossed his upper body like gigantic white millipedes forming a crude X.

'What's going on?' said Plum.

'A deal. A deal which you very nearly ruined,' said Cherry.

'Is there a problem?' said the man marked with the X.

'No. No problem, Attila. Here they are, as promised. Pleasure doing business with you.'

Attila gave the nod and Plum watched in horror as the pirates sallied forth and snatched the mudlarks up by the scruffs of their raggedy shirts. There they dangled kicking and screaming. The boy known as Jinx spat in his captor's face who instinctively dropped him so as to wipe the gob from his eye. Jinx hightailed it across the grass but was quickly hunted down and dragged back by the ankle.

'Let go of them!' cried Plum, wringing her hands. 'Papa, what have you done?'

Cherry said nothing. Looked away.

'Why them? Why not the others? Why not the children of The Messiah Caravan?'

'Oh Plum, because they have parents who will not allow it.'

'You bastard.'

She turned to the mudlarks.

'Don't worry,' she said. 'It's going to be okay. I'm coming with you.'

'Oh no you're not,' said Cherry. 'I'll not allow it.'

One of the pirates grabbed Plum around the waist from behind and hoisted her into the air.

'No! Not her,' screamed Cherry. 'She was not part of the deal, Attila!'

Attila nodded to his man and Plum was released. She slumped to the ground.

'Papa, how could you!' she sobbed.

As they were jostled past, the children stared down at Plum with wide, terrified eyes. She looked up at them, her eyes wet. In a last burst of passion, she rose and ran to their aid, hopelessly trying to prize the nearest mudlark free, but was briskly knocked flat on her back by a great big dirty fist. Her senses yawed and then plunged like an aeroplane in freefall.

'We trusted you,' she heard Jinx call as he was dragged away, snatches of grass in both his clenched fists.

The pirates brought the children to their leader and iron slave collars were fixed about their necks and looped with chain so as to bind them together. Just as they were to be led away, there came that innocuous click of a hammer being thumbed back on a pistol. The pirates turned, weapons raised, to see Plum with both .38s drawn and trained on their leader, Attila.

She spat the blood from her mouth.

'Let them go,' she said in a low, defiant voice.

There came not a twitch from Attila's hairless face. He stared at her out of his keen, serpentine eyes.

'Plum. Please. Put the gun down,' pleaded Cherry. 'I'm sorry, Attila. She's just upset.'

Plum did not look away from Attila, nor he from her.

'Let them go,' she said again.

'Please, Attila, she doesn't know what she's doing. She's—' said Cherry.'

'Silence,' growled Attila, stepping forwards. 'She knows exactly what she's doing.'

Plum backed up a half step and rattled the pistols at him.

'I won't ask again,' she said.

Attila stopped before her. Knelt down. Both pistols now pointed square at his bulbous forehead.

'You are angry,' he said, nodding. 'I understand. I know this feeling. I *am* this feeling.'

'Please don't hurt her,' said Cherry.

Attila raised a finger for silence.

'Speak once more. See what happens,' he said.

Turning back to Plum, Attila took a deep breath through his nose.

'You see this?' he said, tracing his finger along the scar that zigged from left to right across his body. 'Like you, I was also betrayed. I too was young and believed in the goodness of people. Then one day my own brother tried to kill me. And for what? For gold, as you might expect, and the power it buys. I ask you, how is it we can weigh our brothers against a nugget of gold and find our brothers wanting?'

He shook his head. Sighed, long and low. Then he continued:

'My brother's machete, that is what this is. If I had not moved, it would have cut me in twain. But I was quick then. Swift like the wolf. Down came his blade. *Whoosh!*'

He clapped his hands together. Plum flinched.

'Yes it bled me. But it did not kill me. Then down came my blade.'

Attila sniffed as though he might be getting emotional. But then he closed one nostril with his thumb and fired a green glob of snot out of his nose.

'As my brother lay dying,' he said, wiping his hands on his shorts. 'You know what I did? I turned my machete upon myself.'

He pointed to the other scar, which zagged from right to left.

'This. This was I. A reminder to myself, yes, but I also wanted to prove to my brother that finally I understood… that there is no love greater than the love of power. Now throw down your pistols or I will have my men execute every last one of your friends.'

The muscle in Plum's jaw was working overtime and her hands started to shake. She lowered her eyes and dropped her pistols into the grass. Attila reached forward and claimed them.

'Good. Good. It is best you learn this now,' said Attila, rising.

He turned his back on her and started to walk away. Plum dropped to her knees and hung her head.

'What will you do with them?' she said.

Attila stopped and looked back over his shoulder.

'Ah, this,' he said. 'This you do not want to know.'

REVENANTS

In the days that followed, Plum was confined to the mudlarks' old prairie schooner. She lay in the space where the mudlarks had once sat, the children of The Messiah Caravan cowering against the other side of the wagon as though she were a substance volatile. As a final indecency, Peter had parleyed for one of Attila's iron slave collars and this she now wore about her neck, the chain looped through an eyelet in the beam above and sealed with a padlock.

'You should count yourself lucky,' Peter had said as the lock clicked shut against his palm. 'If anyone else had done what you did, they'd be dead. We are not all as privileged as you are, little Blossom.'

Plum could only imagine smacking the smug off his conniving face. Could only watch as he alighted, turned to her, held up the tiny padlock key so she could see it glinting in the sun, before pitching it into the Vida.

For days, she travelled blind, the schooner rocking her where she lay, the chains jangling above her. All the time, she barely moved. Each morning and evening Peter would come with food and water and she would not touch it.

'Dear, dear,' he would tut. 'How ungrateful you are.'

Her eyes began to hollow and her throat grew so dry that her breath screeched in and out like fingernails on slate. Late on the second day, she noticed white eyes watching her from the shadows.

'How long have you been there, Bo?'

'What makes you think I left?'

'You not mad no more?'

'Naw. What'd I expect, that you'd never kiss no one ever again? I'm sorry.'

'It's okay.'

'Death has made me jealous.'

'You were always jealous.'

'Maybe.'

'You know what the funny thing is?'

'What?'

'I only kissed him cause he was acting like you used to.'

'Oh yeah, how's that?'

'Like a goddamn lionhearted fool.'

The ghost of Bo grinned and Plum tried to laugh but broke into a rattling cough.

'Looks like I'll be joining you sooner than we thought,' she said.

'Don't say that, Plum. You gotta fight.'

'Why?'

'I dunno. You just gotta.'

A sigh rattled out of Plum's lungs.

'I'm tired, Bo. I'm gonna sleep now.'

'Plum,' he said, but as he said it her eyes flickered and rolled over white.

The children looked at each other, their mouths agape, their eyes wide.

'Who's she talking to?' they said.

'Ain't talking to no one.'

'Figures we have to share with the crazy.'

Plum woke on the third day to find beside her another water skin and a shallow bowl of cold grey gruel that had skinned over. She let out a rasping cough and closed her eyes once more.

'Oh no you don't, Plum,' said Bo. 'Someone's here to see you.'

'Huh?' said Plum, blinking her vacant, rheumy eyes that saw both this world and the next.

'My, my, what a sight ye are,' said her visitor.

It was the leader of the mudlarks, her spectre anyhow. She stepped forwards and squatted by Plum's head. Plum looked up at her, her eyes twitching in her skull; saw that familiar bald, blotchy head; the cigarette burn still on her cheek. She smelled of desert sage after the rains.

'I'm sorry,' croaked Plum.

'Mm-hmm. I can see that.'

'Please. Please forgive me.'

'Alright, alright. Now are ye done with the self-pity or ain't ye?'

'What?'

'Don't tell me yer forgotten all about my kin.'

'They're all I think about.'

'Think and do nothing?'

'There's nothing I can do.'

'Maybe not. But ye can try.'

'What's the point? It's over.'

'Who says?'

'I says.'

'Well, I'm sorry, but yer opinion ain't worth a hill of shit no more. Look, yer all those kiddies got now. If ye don't try to save'm, no one else else gonna… and they'll be lost forever.'

Plum looked blankly up at the little ghost.

'Ye hear me?'

'I hear you.'

The ghost sighed like the wind.

'Honestly, ye don't wanna be dead, Plum. Seeing everything go by without even a hand in it. It's torture.'

A tear broke out the corner of Plum's eye and rolled down her cheek.

'Okay,' she said.

'Okay, what?'

'Okay, I'll save them.'

'I never asked ye to save them. I asked ye to try. I don't expect results, only a proper effort.'

'Okay, I'll try.'

'Good. Then eat something for god sake.'

Plum started slapping her hand against the boards of the schooner until it fell upon the water skin. Raising it up, she upended it onto her face, coughing and spluttering, as though she were waterboarding herself. Then she rolled over and started spooning the gruel into her mouth with her fingers.

The children of The Messiah Caravan screamed and clambered over each other to get away from this woke beast before them. Plum regarded them with wild eyes, the oatmeal smeared about her chops and in her hair.

*

In the days that followed, Plum regained her strength, and when Peter came by, taunting, jibing—saying things like 'Oh how quick you are to forget your friends!' and 'How do you live with yourself?'—Plum just told him to stop being a little bitch and to bring more oatmeal.

The children of The Messiah Caravan started to warm to her and she would talk with them at great length, long into the night, and would laugh at the stories they had made up about her. For some had thought she was a werewolf and dreaded the next full moon. Others thought her a mermaid and considered her incarceration on dry land a downright violation of the natural order. When she told them she was in fact a were-maid, a force more terrible and beautiful yet, something in her hushed tones and furtive glances convinced them it must be so. In deference, they brought her purloined oranges and dates; and on the morning Plum awoke restored and asked them to fetch her Gargantua, they were more than willing.

When she came, Gargantua sidled up to schooner,

glancing warily over her shoulder, as though she might avoid being seen. Though, of course, prodigious as she was, all eyes were already upon her. Plum wasted no time.

'You need to get me out of here, G,' she whispered.

'Me. Why me?'

'Cause ain't nobody else got the means.'

'Plum, you know I can't.'

'You know what he's done, right?'

Gargantua was silent.

'Well?'

'Yes. I know.'

'Then how can you still stand by him?'

'Cause… I'm sure there must be some higher reasoning behind it.'

'Of course there is! But it ain't the reasoning you so crave. He don't give a fuck about you, G. He don't give a fuck about anyone but himself.'

'That's not true. He spared you. He loves you.'

'This,' said Plum, rattling her chains. 'This is not love.'

'I'm sorry, Plum. I still believe there is some higher purpose in all this. He knows what he's doing. You'll see. I must go.'

'G. Please.'

'I'm sorry.'

'G!'

But she was gone.

*

For the rest of the day and long into the night, Plum sat like Buddha, her legs crossed, her eyes closed. Straight of spine, shoulders back, breath steady. Her face soft, relaxed. An equanimity to her, as though here, chained, on the wrong side of fortune was right now precisely where she was meant to be. It was as though she knew perfectly the transience of things and through this perfect knowledge was herself the transience of things. Her lips moved quickly over breathy incantations. Negotiations with nothingness. Communion with everything before and after, now and never.

The children of The Messiah Caravan watched on, wonderstruck.

'What is she—' chanced one of them, but was shushed back to silence.

'Just watch.'

Dark hours passed and the moon rose waning crescent, hanging over the caravan like a silver scimitar. The night was complete with the shrill chirping of crickets in the long grass. It was not quite midnight when Plum sighed and opened her eyes. She shook her head.

'Martha,' she said. 'If you can hear me, I could really use your help.'

Then, as if the universe valued straight talk over all pomp and grandeur, her prayers were answered.

'*Pssst!* Plum, is that you?'

'Martha?'

'What? Who? No. It's me, Hiroshi.'

'Hiroshi... what are you doing here?'

'We're coming in.'

'We?'

Stealthily as spiders, the dark forms of Hiroshi and Machiavelli crawled up into the schooner. They crouched before her, their eyes aglitter.

'Plum, this is Mac. Mac, Plum.'

'Hiroshi, darling, this was a mistake. We need to leave.'

'Calm down. No one knows we're here.'

'How do you expect her to save your kin?'

'Mac, don't be a dick.'

'Hiroshi, she's what... ten summers?'

'So?'

'And in chains!'

Hiroshi looked at her and for the first time comprehended the slave iron glinting in the light of the cosmos.

'Plum, what happened?'

'My pappy, he's lost his mind. Mac's right. You two

need to get out of here. If he catches you…'

'Don't worry about that. Look, we're going to get you out. But first we need to tell you something.'

'What?'

Hiroshi looked to Machiavelli expectantly. Machiavelli gave a great heaving sigh.

'The devil. He's coming for you,' said Machiavelli, without looking at her.

'I know,' she said.

'No. You don't understand,' he said, meeting her gaze. 'I'm talking about all of you. The devil has a thousand cutthroats all bought and paid for. They mean to wipe you off the face of the earth.'

Plum nodded solemnly, cleared her throat.

'I suppose it was just a matter of time.'

'Oh, was it now? Well it's a good job we risked our necks to tell you.'

'Whatever his other faults, the devil's not a quitter. You must give him that.'

'Plum,' said Hiroshi, interjecting. 'We need to tell everyone.'

'What makes you think they'll believe you, or even care? You've missed a lot since you been gone, Hiroshi. They're not the people you knew. They're an army now. Every man, woman and child. Guns and all.'

'No! You're wrong.'

'I wish I was.'

'Still. They deserve to know.'

'You're right. They do.' She sucked her teeth. 'Get me out of here. Get me out of here and I'll think of something.'

'And how are we supposed to do that?' said Machiavelli.

'The master carpenter! She'll have bolt cutters or some such,' said Hiroshi, jumping down out of the schooner. Machiavelli followed grimly after.

'Hiroshi,' hissed Plum.

'What?'

'Be careful. Stay hidden. Don't trust anyone.'

'Don't worry,' he said. 'We'll be right back.'

But they weren't.

*

Plum waited and waited but they did not return.

The night stretched on forever.

'Don't worry, we'll find out what's happening,' said a child of The Messiah Caravan.

'No,' said Plum. 'I'll not let you risk yourselves for me.'

So they waited.

*

The day dawned a hellish orange-red, setting ablaze the blue-grey clouds rolling against the ceiling of the world like smoke in a house fire. It was then her fears were realised.

She heard his tutting through the awning of the schooner before he appeared at the opening.

'Well, well,' said Peter. 'What a predicament.'

He signalled to the children.

'Out,' he said. When they did not move, he clapped his hands together. 'Come on. Chop, chop.'

They looked to Plum and only once she had nodded her approval did they disembark.

'My!' said Peter to Plum, the children shooting him sharp looks as they passed. 'It's as though you enjoy exploiting impressionable beings.'

'Where's Hiroshi?' said Plum.

'You'll see,' said Peter, slapping the side of the schooner. At which the driver pushed the horses forward at a trot.

Peter jogged behind the schooner a moment, intent on getting in one more taunt.

'Regarding what is to come, you only have yourself to blame,' he said, panting.

Before he had time to duck, Plum leaned forward on her knees, snorted up all the gunk in her nose and gozzed it in his face and mouth. Peter fell to his knees, clawing at his face, screaming.

'You bitch!' he cried. 'You bitch!'

Plum wiped her mouth on her sleeve.

As the schooner rolled on, Plum saw members of the caravan walking in the same direction she was heading. They pointed at her, whispered, and shook their heads in disapproval. Before long, the schooner pulled into a clearing and turned around so that she faced outwards on the scene.

Before her, Hiroshi and Machiavelli stood back to back, lashed together against a stake driven into the ground. Machiavelli appeared unconscious, his chin in his chest, his legs buckled. Blood had dried down one side of his face from a gash on his forehead. Hiroshi, however, despite two black eyes and a bloody mouth, was alert.

'Plum,' he cried when he saw her. 'I'm sorry.'

Plum opened her mouth but no words came out.

Around the prisoners, the caravan had gathered in a great semi-circle. In front of the crowd were half a dozen prodigious cairns, built for the occasion. Clutching the awning, Plum leaned out the back of the schooner the better for to see. Across the way, Peter came shuffling into view, continuing to wipe his face with the sleeve of one arm. On his other arm was her father.

Her father let go of Peter's arm and took centre stage. He raised his hands, begging silence. But he did not get it.

'There he is!' howled Hiroshi. 'Our lord and charlatan.'

Some gasped at his audacity but none denounced him. For a moment, all were silent. Only the river spoke; the wind through the grass.

Hiroshi began to sob. No. Laugh. He was laughing. And then he was screaming, the outlines of his teeth coloured in with blood.

'He's a liar! For the love of god, how do you not see it? Look.'

He was trying to retrieve something from the pocket of his robe but his arms were bound to his chest. With his fingers, he hiked up his robe until he was able to fish out a fold of glossy paper. It was the dust jacket of *The Messiah Caravan*. He held it scissored between his fingers.

'Proof. I have proof of his lies!'

Plum looked to her father. If he was concerned, he did not show it.

'This is a page from *The Messiah Caravan*,' continued Hiroshi. 'The rest are now lost. I was there. I was there when this madman pitched our holy book on the fire.'

The crowd bristled at this news, looked uncertainly from one to the other.

'What an imagination you have, child,' derided Cherry. 'Alright. Let us see this *proof*.'

Peter scuttled to Hiroshi's side. Hiroshi clenched the fold of paper in his fist.

'No. Not him. He's—,' he said, but Peter socked him in the stomach, knocking the wind out of him. The dust jacket fluttered down into the grass. Peter snatched it up and returned it to Cherry.

'Ah! There was once a time when I would have read this to you, my disciples,' said Cherry, holding up the dust jacket. 'But as you all know, the devil took my eyes. Is there not one among you with the words to read it?'

Silence.

'Anyone?'

If any had, none said.

'How about you, Doctor? You have read for me before have you not?'

Doctor Onabanjo had been mid draw on his kazoo pipe and Cherry had caught him off guard. He tried to stifle a splutter, thick white smoke shooting from his mouth and nose.

'Me?' he choked around a mouthful of cloud.

'Yes you. Why didn't you volunteer just now?'

'I… I…' he stammered.

Cherry held up a hand.

'Just read it and all will be forgiven.'

Cherry was holding the paper out to no one in particular and Peter took this as his cue to pass it to Doctor Onabanjo, who received it as though being offered something out of a dream. Unfolding the glossy paper, he cast his scarlet, stoner eyes over the familiar dust jacket.

'Come on, shaman,' muttered Plum under her breath. 'This is your chance to end this.'

Doctor Onabanjo looked from Cherry to the dust jacket and back to Cherry.

'Well,' said Cherry.

The doctor coughed a rolling, phlegmy number into his fist. Then he spoke.

'It's nonsense,' he said. 'Gobbledygook. The boy is lying.'

He extended the dust jacket as though that was all he had to say on the matter.

'Liar!' screamed Plum. 'All of you. You're all a bunch of damned liars.'

The crowd woke up jeering. Cherry held his hands up for peace.

'Calm, my disciples. The time for your rage is at hand, but it is not yet. Come on, little one, out with your doubt so we might put it to bed.'

'What are you doing, papa? Let them go. End this. End this before it's too late!'

'Ah! Such a tender display. You love him dearly don't you?'

Snorts of laughter could be heard from the crowd. Mock sighs of love.

'Oh, damn you. Listen, all of you, I'm sorry, it was I who killed the devil, it was I who destroyed the Red Basilica.'

'Lies! Such desperate lies she tells to save the malcontent Hiroshi.'

'And now, a-cause of me, and a-cause of my father's folly, the devil comes to do away with you all.'

'Nonsense! The devil isn't after us. Even if he was,

we'd drive him back! Wouldn't we?'

The crowd roared their approval and punched the sky.

'You don't understand—' cried Plum, but her voice was lost beneath the triumphant crowd.

'Are you with me?' cried Cherry.

The crowd gave an almighty cheer.

'Then I turn Hiroshi and his little friend over to you, my disciples. Consider him excommunicated. Do with them what you will. Let their bodies be the earth to your electric rage. But leave the girl. I will deal with her.'

The crowd advanced in upon the prisoners where they stood tied to the stake. Stones were taken from the cairns and passed around. Hiroshi struggled against his bindings, glanced frantically about. It was then that Machiavelli came to.

'Hiroshi,' he breathed. 'What's happening?'

Hiroshi stopped thrashing, took a deep breath.

'Nothing, my love,' said Hiroshi, his voice gentle, calm. 'Go back to sleep.'

'You sure?'

'Yes, darling. It's not time to get up yet. I'll come get you when it's time.'

'Okay,' he sighed, closing his eyes. 'Love you.'

'I love you too,' said Hiroshi, but Machiavelli was already asleep, his breathing steady, peaceful.

Plum watched as the crowd closed in upon Hiroshi and Machiavelli, taunting, cursing, some passing their stone from hand to hand as though it were nothing but a ball. A terrible anger juddered through the crowd and those on the front row began feinting with their stones; though still they did not throw. Then a lone stone was lobbed by an anonymous caravanner at the back. It arced above, disappearing briefly into the sun, then dropped, missed, disappeared hissing through the long grass.

However, this was all it took.

The entire crowd loosed their stones, hundreds of them, blotting out the sun.

'Hiroshi!' cried Plum.

His doleful eyes met hers, briefly, and then he and Machiavelli disappeared behind the curtain of rock.

'No!' cried Plum, leaping from the schooner in her desperation; but the chain went taut before her feet could touch the ground, causing her to swing back against the rear of the schooner, there to dangle by the neck.

The sound of the many dull traumas inflicted upon the bodies of her friends rolled like a drum.

She thrashed, choking, her eyes bulging in their sockets, her hands searching frantically for a hold. Still she would not look away from the scene.

What emerged from the melee was not they, was not those beings she had known, only the evidence of their having been there. Their bodies, slick with blood, glittered in the sunlight. In death, they remained bound; and though limp, the way they had been tied together meant that still they stood.

Plum's eyes rolled up into her skull and the world wavered like a candle. Gargantua came bounding to her side, the earth shuddering beneath her, each mighty stride the length of a car. She caught the little girl up around the thighs and restored her to the schooner.

'I'm sorry,' said Gargantua. 'I should have listened.'

And the world winked out entirely.

*

Gargantua made sure Plum was breathing and then she turned away. She walked past the crowd who were idling awkwardly. Past the bodies still fixed to the stake; above which now circled a turkey vulture, its wretched, inside-out face pink as a dog's pecker. She was striding directly towards Cherry, her eyes wet, her jaw and fists clenched in anger. Cherry saw her coming and signalled to Peter. Peter stuck his fingers in his mouth and whistled and their guards sallied forth with their shiny new machine guns.

They raised their weapons and Gargantua stopped.

'Come, child,' said Cherry. 'I do not wish to quarrel

with you. You are so dear to me.'

Gargantua seemed not to hear. She was gazing over their heads.

'What is she looking at?' Cherry said to Peter out the corner of his mouth.

Peter turned.

'Dear god,' he said.

A great dust cloud was rolling in off the horizon almost a mile wide. The ground began to tremble beneath its terrible pandemonium.

'What is it?' said Cherry.

Peter gawked, shrugged.

'It is the devil,' said Gargantua. 'He is here.'

MASSACRE OF THE MESSIAH
CARAVAN

Hysteria broke over the caravan like a wave.
'What's going on?' each demanded of others just as ignorant as they.

Then the call came.

'The devil. The devil is here!'

Frenzy ensued. Pushing, shoving. All trying to break free of the crowd.

'What should we do?' said Peter, though Cherry seemed not to hear him. 'My lord?'

'Yes,' said Cherry.

In his passion, Peter grabbed him by the shoulders.

'My lord, what are we to do?'

'Ah, yes, that. We take up arms. Not us, of course. Them. Tell them to take up arms.'

'And then?'

'Then we get out of here.'

Peter nodded. Turning, hands raised, he addressed the crowd who were still frantically trying to disperse, but in doing so seemed to mesh themselves tighter together.

'Please, Brothers, hear me,' he said, though none did.

Cherry shook his head and grunted, his lip curling up into a snarl.

'Never mind, let me,' he said, stepping forward, pushing Peter aside. 'Control yourselves, my disciples! Control yourselves!' he proclaimed. The crowd ceased its bustling. 'Yes, the devil is come. But we are ready, are we not? We have the weapons. Arm yourselves and fight!'

Before he had even finished speaking, Peter was coaxing him towards the nearest schooner, which just so happened to be the one that contained his daughter.

'But, my lord, we don't know how to shoot. We haven't practiced,' begged a member of the crowd.

'What's to know? You just pull the trigger,' said Cherry, visibly frustrated.

The crowd looked on dumbfounded as Peter leant their lord a hand up into the rear of the schooner.

'Bravery, my disciples. I believe in you,' Cherry called as he stepped in.

Peter climbed aboard the driver's seat and took up the reins. He was just about to bring them cracking down when Cherry cried out once more.

'Wait! Gargantua, Doctor Onabanjo, get over here.'

The rest of the caravan continued to gawk as the two disciples he had beckoned came jogging past, their eyes downcast, embarrassed. Gargantua wormed sidewards into the schooner and had to lie flat on account of her size. Before Doctor Onabanjo could board, Cherry whispered something in his ear, at which the doctor scurried off. He returned clutching to his chest a brown leather medical bag. He threw it into the back of the schooner and then climbed in also. Once he was clear, Cherry beat the side of the schooner with the palm of his hand and Peter put the horses forwards.

'Make me proud!' called Cherry, standing and waving from the back of the schooner as it rolled away. Then he ducked back inside and disappeared behind the awning.

The abandoned caravanners looked one to the other,

still in the tableau of their struggle. Then all started to scream and to clamber over each other as before.

*

Inside the schooner, the juddering of the cart shook Plum from her unconsciousness. She shot bolt upright, sucking down great lungfuls of abrasive air.

'What's going on?' she said.

She looked at each of them in turn. None answered her. None returned her stare.

'Anyone? Shaman? G? For the love of god, somebody tell me what's going on!'

'It's the devil,' said Gargantua. She was lying on her side, facing away. 'Guess he caught up with us.'

Plum crawled to the rear of the schooner and looked out.

Chaos.

Schooners containing substantially fewer humans than they could carry were rollicking off in all directions, desperate left-behinds hanging off the rear, or hopelessly sprinting after them, or on all fours in the grass cursing the driver. Horses and ponies too were galloping off every which way, some with riders, some without. Old folks were wringing their hands. Mothers hummed frantically to their screaming babies. Plum watched as the children of The Messiah Caravan stared down into the Vida, looked back once at the approaching menace, and then one by one leapt into the rushing grey waters and were borne away.

Amidst the bedlam, a small detachment of caravanners were rallying and prizing open the crates containing the weapons Cherry had traded the mudlarks for. Plum watched as these ever-diminishing dots formed an enfilade, stacking the detritus of the caravan into a makeshift trench. At the banks of the Vida is where they made their stand. As the devil's army bore down upon them in a fury of stamping horses and pistol fire, they did not waver, and when the first wave was in range they opened fire.

227

Then a strange thing happened.

The enfilade lit up like a sparkler as they emptied their machine guns. But the devil's army just kept riding. Not a single one fell. It was as if they fired upon an army of the undead. The enfilade then scrambled about desperately trying to reload but before they could, the devil's army burst their ranks and made easy work of them, slashing at them from horseback with their scimitars, or otherwise letting their horses in on the sport and running down the caravanners and trampling them. Before a minute was out, the entire enfilade was laid waste and a fine red vapour hung on the air, drifting away on the wind, settling on the Vida.

Plum glared at her father, her open mouth downturned in disgust. He must have felt her eyes on him for he looked up at her and then quickly away.

'You bastard,' she said. 'You dirty fucking bastard.'

He could not look at her. He dug the knuckles of both fists into his forehead and rocked back and forth.

'You knew, didn't you?'

Still nothing.

'Knew what?' said Gargantua, rolling over.

'That the guns were useless,' said Plum.

Gargantua shook her head and hugged herself. Doctor Onabanjo was packing and lighting his kazoo pipe.

'It wasn't the guns that were useless, little Blossom,' said Doctor Onabanjo around a mouthful of smoke. He was mesmerised by the burning matchstick he pinched. 'It was the bullets that were useless.'

Plum was shaking her head.

'You mean you knew? You all knew, didn't you, even you, G?'

Tears were streaming out of Gargantua's eyes and she doubled over in great heaving sobs, barking like a seal. Plum could not bear to look at them. With nowhere else to look, she watched the destruction unfold behind.

The devil's army had set about hunting down the

stragglers. They were easy game. The cutthroats' despicable laughter was the harbinger of death for many that day. They smoked and passed round hipflasks containing cowboy whiskey and sailor rum and many took to placing wagers on how many they could kill in an allotted time or from how far they could shoot or skewer some unfortunate runaway. The last straggler to get it was hightailing it by foot across the meadowland more than half a mile away from the nearest mercenary. The cutthroats stood on a hillock taking pot shots with their rifles and everyone that missed threw a silver coin into a beat-up top hat. Then some lucky lush stepped up to the plate and swigging on his flask of bourbon he fired a single shot from his pistola at some shonky angle, real high and into the wind. All the other cutthroats commenced laughing and slapping their thighs but the lush just kept on watching that little mite scuttling away through flame red eyes. Then, after a full three seconds, that little mite just stopped scuttling and all the cutthroats threw up their hands and cried, *Hallelujah!*

Grimacing, the lush picked up the hat and bowed and dipped his head into it and erected himself, his winnings jangling on top of his head. There came a smattering of applause from his fellows and a round of *For He's a Jolly Good Fellow* and the lush tipped the peak of his raggedy top hat, puckered his lips, and performed a curtsy of all things.

*

All this time, the devil had been searching among the dead with the obsession of one who seeks a friend or family member. Empty handed he came striding among the fun and the games, limping from the knife wound in his waist on which he lay the flat of his hand as he walked. His head jerked this way and that as though expecting those he sought to pop up out of the blue.

'They're not here,' he said to no one, to everyone.

'Who's not here?' said the lush.

'They. They. The instigators of all this… havoc. Cherry

229

Blossom and his bastard.'

'You don't know that. They're probably face down in the grass somewhere. We'll find them,' said the lush, shrugging, the coins in his hat chinking as he shifted his gait.

The devil walked straight up to the lush and stared him full in the face. Each shared with the other their sour breath.

'They're not here. I *know* it.'

The lush stuck out his bottom lip and nodded.

'You're right,' he said. 'They're not here.'

'What about the wagons, are they all accounted for?'

The lush shrugged.

'Well?' said the devil turning to the rest of them.

'All but one, sir,' said a cutthroat in a long black trench coat, his black hair lank and greasy like an oil spill atop his head.

'All but one?'

'Yes sir. One was seen leaving whilst we were still a-ways out.'

'Then that's where they'll be.'

'Sir, it's more likely—'

'That's where they'll be.'

'Yes sir.'

'Where was it last seen heading?'

'Thattaway sir. Upriver.'

The devil was nodding as though of course, of course this was how things were meant to be.

'They'll look to cross,' he said. 'Santa Muerte. Yes. They'll make for Santa Muerte. Oh Cherry, you think we won't follow you into the land of the dead? But we will. Won't we? Won't we?'

'Yes sir.'

'Saddle up.'

'Yes sir.'

IODINE-86

'Take this,' said Doctor Onabanjo.
'What is it?' said Plum.
'Iodine-86.'
'That it?'

'What do you mean?'

'I mean it ain't no wolf's bane, rattlesnake oil, cocaine lozenge, or some such other nostrum.'

'Where'd you learn that word?'

'What word?'

'Nostrum.'

'Heard you say it once.'

'Oh! You are perceptive aren't you, little Blossom? If things had been different, you would have made a fantastic student. And no, this is no nostrum. This is an authentic old-world medicament for radiation sickness. I have no idea what's in it.'

'That fills me with a world of confidence.'

'Don't be sarcastic.'

'Who's being sarcastic?'

Plum pinched the small white pill out of the doctor's palm, stuck it on her dry tongue, and swallowed it. She kneaded her throat with her fingers, trying to work it down.'

'I'll get you some water,' said the doctor.

'In a minute.'

'Okay.'

Doctor Onabanjo made himself comfortable and started rummaging in his pockets for his pipe and herb.

'Why'd you go along with it?'

'With what?'

'You know what. The kiddies. The bogus guns. Hiroshi. Hell, all of it.'

'I don't know.'

'Yes you do.'

The doctor raised an eyebrow at the girl and she held his gaze. He began to nod his head.

'Survival,' he said.

'Survival?'

'Yes. I've always been rather… adaptable… to change… when it comes, that is.'

'Surely you can't value your life that much?'

'Perhaps I shouldn't, but I do.'

He took a long draw on his kazoo pipe and exhaled slowly through his nose.

'At least you're honest about your lies,' said Plum.

Doctor Onabanjo gave a dour smile and placed a hand over his heart as if to say, *You flatter me!*

Plum started picking at a splintered board which her thumbnail.

'I can't believe they're all gone. Dead,' she said. 'I saw it happen, yet still I can't believe it.'

'It is the way of the world. Things fall apart, slowly, and then all at once. And our senses are left to play catch up.'

'Is that why you're always trying to slow things down?' she said, nodding at the pipe.

'This. No. This helps me think.'

'Naw. You lie. That stuff only ever helps me laugh.'

'That's because you are still young. In spite of how much you've lived.'

'What do you think of when you've smoked yourself?'

'Anything. Everything. Why, just now it helped me remember that there is indeed a story behind iodine-86.'

'Of course there is.'

'Nope. I mean yep. You want to hear it?'

'I got nothing better to do.'

'Well, so far as my nana once told me—'

'Wait. Your granny span you this. Real scientific.'

'Fuck you. You don't know my nana. She could be Marie Curie for all you know.'

'Who?'

'Exactly.'

'Whatever. Carry on.'

'Naw, I don't much feel like it anymore.'

'Oh just fucking get on with it.'

Doctor Onabanjo blew out his lips.

'Fine,' he said. 'So, as my nana once told me, in the year of our lord—and when I say lord, I mean Jesus Christ, not your damn pappy—in the year of our lord nineteen-eighty-six, a special plant bloomed in the kingdom of Pripyat. Now this plant was beautiful beyond reckoning. And big. Big as... Big as the Red Basilica. Bigger! The people of Pripyat called this plant Chernobyl. Every day they would visit the plant and remark at how sublime it was. In fact, they took it upon themselves to feed the plant. For it was a pitcher plant. Carnivorous. And they thought that if they fed it, it would grow even more beautiful. Well they fed it anything they could get their hands on. Cows. Dogs. Even the odd criminal or two. And it grew. And it grew. Then after a time a single bud started to grow at the top of its stem. It bulged and bulged and the kingdom of Pripyat—no, the whole world, for news had spread, y'know—they all thought that the Chernobyl flower would be the most precious thing in the history of creation. But then, one night, while the kingdom of Pripyat slept, the bud exploded. For it was no flower at all. Rather a burgeoning mass of terrible, radioactive spores. And these spores floated away in the wind and when the kingdom of Pripyat awoke, they were many of them sick. And so they rushed to Chernobyl seeking help, for it was a holy site to them, but when they came into the clearing, they saw that their once illustrious plant was slimy and repugnant as a bad mushroom. Anyway, my nana went on a long, long time and I must admit I cannot remember it all. The kingdom eventually contained the spores, but at a terrible cost. Anyway, what was my point? That was it, iodine-86. Anyway, after all the drama, the scientists of the old world produced a drug that would better protect them should these spores return. In memory of the Chernobyl incident of nineteen-eighty-six, they called the drug iodine-86.'

'Okay. But what is iodine?'

'I don't know. Like I said, I have no idea what's in it.'

'Right.'

'Good story, huh?'

'Sounds like a fairy-tale.'

Doctor Onabanjo shrugged.

'Doesn't everything?' he said.

Out the back of the schooner, Plum saw her father and Peter returning, muttering to one another, Gargantua walking behind them like a bodyguard.

'You know, the second I am out of these chains. I'm going to kill you all,' said Plum.

'Well then, it's a good job we put you in those chains.'

'Sounds to me like you're taking the effect and making it the cause.'

'Ah, touché! You really would have made an excellent student, little Blossom. Truly excellent.'

'Don't patronise me.'

The doctor rose, a little unsteady. He was nicely stoned.

'I'll get you that water,' he said with a devilish grin, and alighted.

BALL LIGHTNING

They forded the Vida at the same shallow place Plum and the mudlarks had spent their final morning together. On the other side, Peter drove them down a corridor running between two rampant forests of spruce and hemlock. The vista initially started out wide, three widths of the schooner and then some; but as they drove on, the vista began to narrow until the branches of the trees started whipping against their vehicle and the wheels jumped over knots of roots in the forest floor.

Inside the schooner, all sat helplessly about, silent, gloomy. The air rank with sweat for the forest was hot and close. Atop the driver's seat, credit where it's due, Peter guided the horses through the ever-narrowing path quite masterfully. After a time he had to de-robe on account of the heat and he sat atop the box starkers, every muscle in his bald body twitching as he pulled the horses this way then that. A low branch loomed up ahead and he ducked it, the branch snagging the awning and tearing the length of it so that a fissure of sunlight illuminated the dust dancing inside the schooner. Erecting himself back atop the driver's seat, another branch caught him off guard, ripping his cheek like a fishhook. He squealed and put a hand to his face.

'Everything alright?' called Cherry from inside.

Peter took his hand away from his face and looked at it. It was slick with blood. He wiped his hand against himself, smearing the blood across his chest like warrior paint.

'Fine,' he said, the skin of his cheek flapping in the wind, garbling his speech.

'Come again?'

'Fine!'

'I guess it's fine,' mumbled Cherry, rolling his eyes.

Eventually the path widened out again and they left the forest behind. Before them, a valley of rolling grassland, on the other side of which could be seen the river Muerte weaving away in the distance like a piece of black thread.

They switchbacked down the valley and passed over the River Espíritu without even noticing, slim as it was and obscured by reeds. Darkness was falling as they ascended the other side and clouds were massing, thick and black and rolling like volcano ash.

'Looks like we're in for it,' said Doctor Onabanjo.

They crested the rise and hit a plateau and Peter made the most of the flatland and drove the horses onwards. It was not long before the grass started to give way in patches on that alopecia-earth. Soon the ground all about them was bare and rust-brown for it was scorched irreparably many years ago.

And so it was that they entered the radioactive wasteland of Santa Muerte.

A foreboding spread among the passengers and they grew restless. Cherry was tapping his fingernails against his teeth. Doctor Onabanjo took a hit from his pipe.

A thud made them all sit up.

'What was that?' said Cherry.

'Probably just the first of the hale,' said Doctor Onabanjo.

Then something small and black whizzed through the hole in the awning above and slammed against the boards.

Its spindly yellow legs twitched and then were still.

Birds. Birds were falling from the sky.

Plum shuffled on her backside to the rear of the schooner and looked out at the crimson dusk. Something caught her eye and she called for Peter to stop. He ignored her but Cherry insisted.

'What is it, Plum?' said Gargantua.

'Wolves.'

'What are they doing?'

'I don't know.'

A pack of wolves lay about whimpering like scolded housedogs. A little apart from them, a doe was lying on its side, its black eyes wide. Something was writhing within its swollen stomach.

'I hope those pills of yours work, shaman,' said Plum.

*

They rode on into the night, Peter navigating by the recurrent flare of sheet lightning, which battered the horizon and staggered the landscape in clattering blue-white frames. He kept up a tremendous pace and the horses were crazed and frothing at the mouth. They thrashed their necks and fought him something fierce but he just whipped them all the harder and cried, 'Onwards, wretched beasts! Onwards unto death!'

'We should stop,' called Cherry through the awning.

'No!' howled Peter against the onrushing wind. 'Either way, we'll not have horses by the morning. This place will have eaten them up.'

Cherry looked to the doctor. He nodded solemnly.

'Very well,' said Cherry.

*

And so they rode on.

When the horses started bleeding from their eyes and mouths, Peter did not say a word, just whipped them on. In time with the horses, Gargantua too started to sicken. As all but the driver rocked in a disturbed half-sleep, Gargantua sat bolt upright, her head and shoulders pressed against the awning overhead, and pulling her knees up to her chest she vomited over the boards. It was a deep, wine red.

'I'm sorry,' she said, wiping her mouth with the back of her hand.

'G?' said Plum.

'I don't feel well.'

'It's okay.'

Plum adjusted her chain and crawled to Gargantua's side. She rubbed her broad, muscular back with the flat of her palm.

'It hurts. It hurts.'

'It's okay.'

'No. Your hand. It hurts.'

Plum recoiled and clutched her hand as though to stay it from its terrible compassion.

'I'm sorry,' she said.

Lightning flashed and Plum could see that where she had rubbed was quickly flowering into a green-purple bruise. The skin atop it peeling, blistered.

'What's happening to me?' said Gargantua.

Cherry and Doctor Onabanjo shared a look of apprehension which did not go unmissed by Plum.

'What is it this time that you know and I do not?' said Plum.

Each waited for the other to answer.

'Well?' said Plum.

'We should tell them,' muttered Doctor Onabanjo.

Cherry shook his head.

'It's the right thing to do.'

Cherry shrugged and blinked his dramatic eyes. Doctor Onabanjo turned to regard Gargantua and Plum.

'We don't have enough iodine-86 for everybody. On account of her size, Gargantua requires triple the dose. So—'

'So you lied to her.'

'Yes.'

'But… you gave me the pills… three of them,' said Gargantua.

Doctor Onabanjo cleared his throat.

'Ah. That was not iodine-86,' he said.

'Then what was it?'

'A placebo.'

'What?'

'Nothing. A sugar pill.'

'What's going to happen to me?'

'It is hard to put nicely.'

'Just tell me.'

'Your body will unravel… like a ribbon.'

'Fuck you. Like a ribbon. Like a pretty ribbon?'

'I'm sorry.'

'When?'

'When what?'

'When will it happen?'

'But it is already happening. There is no stopping it.'

'That's not true,' interrupted Plum. 'What about Martha? She never come apart.'

'Martha Biobaku is… an anomaly.'

'Why?' said Gargantua, shaking her head. 'Why did you drag me along… here… to this place… knowing full well?'

Doctor Onabanjo looked to Cherry as if only he had the authority to answer this.

'My dear, because you might have proven useful to me.'

'But I wasn't.'

'True. But I did not know that at the time.'

'I don't believe it. Who are you? Who even are you?'

Cherry did not answer her. Eventually, Gargantua lay back down and rolled away from them.

*

The schooner rolled on into the night. Gargantua moaning from the jostling of her bones. Her skin dissolving in patches like sugar paper. The slow blood leaking over the boards.

'Have you nothing for the pain?' Plum said to the

doctor.

He shook his head.

'Nought that will work now. The passageways of her body are corrupted.'

'Then what can we do?'

'Sometimes, little Blossom, there is nothing one can do.'

'No. There is always something.'

Plum lay down next to Gargantua like they were children on a sleepover. For a while, neither said anything. Then:

'Plum?'

'Yeah.'

'You reckon we get to see our mamas again after all this madness?'

'I hope so.'

'Me too.'

'Certainly would make up for things.'

'Yeah. Plum?'

'Yeah?'

'I've always felt it, y'know. Her love. Even though I never knew her. It's always been there. I've never questioned it. Is that stupid?'

'Naw.'

'My daddy on the other hand, I never felt it. Is that strange?'

'Mothers command love. Fathers demand it.'

'Amen to that.'

'It's true. Both our daddies don't seem to realise love is not for the taking. It is only given.'

'Mm-hmm. Plum?'

'Yeah?'

'Come here.'

Plum shuffled forwards. She could feel Gargantua's blood, warm and sticky, seeping through her clothes.

'What is it, G?'

Gargantua sat up on her knees and, hooking a finger of

each hand into the iron collar about Plum's neck, she began to pull. The metal probed them both, drew blood from both. Plum could not breathe but she made no plea, only stared wide-eyed upwards at her friend, willed her on. The metal whined. Then the iron hinge popped and a piece of it skittered across the boards. Gargantua continued to prize and the collar began to open up like a metal flower. With the room this afforded her, she adjusted her grip and after that she made short work of it. Tenderly, she guided Plum's neck through the gap in the metal. The chain crunched as it coiled down upon itself and then the collar clanged against the boards. It was done.

Gargantua collapsed back down onto her side, the impact crunching the schooner and causing the back wheels to skid.

'What was that?' called Peter.

No one answered him.

Gargantua and Plum lay side by side as before.

'Thank you,' said Plum.

Gargantua nodded. Then she said:

'I don't want to die like this, Plum. Slowly coming apart.'

Plum furrowed her brow. Then, feeling in her pocket, she pulled out her little knife. Held it out as an offering. Gargantua looked down at the small black blade. It was edged with starlight. She looked back at her friend whose eyes were wet, glistening.

'I once had a cat, y'know,' said Gargantua. 'Useless, that's what my daddy called it. It never once caught a mouse y'see. Whenever the varmints had been at the stores he'd be all like, *You are useless.* Anyway, it sort of stuck. To the point I'd be like, *Here, Useless!* whenever we put food out for it. I loved that cat. When it got old, it would just sit around the house all day doing nothing. Just being Useless. Then one night we had a fire in the hearth and we was all sat around it. Me, daddy, and Useless. It was warm and comfortable. There seemed no reason at all to go anywhere. But Useless got up, its legs all jittery, and walked on over to the door. It sat there until my daddy told me to go open it. Then it walked out into the night and we never saw it again. When I asked my daddy where it was going, he said it was going off to die. I knew what death was but something in the way he said it made it seem like maybe cats died differently to humans. Humans died in front of everyone, in terrible pain, and we watched them turn ugly, pale and stiff. Useless, on the other hand, it was like he knew where to go. He just walked off into death easy as that. That night, I promised myself that I would die like a cat.'

They gazed at each other unspeaking for some time. Plum noticed Gargantua was smiling thinly and she smiled sadly back.

'I'll tell Peter to stop the schooner.'

'Yes. If you wouldn't mind.'

*

Peter kicked up a fuss when Plum told him to pull over. However, when he learnt the reason, he was an ardent accomplice.

'Yes. Good. Good,' he said. He was blathering like a mad man. 'The reduction in weight will speed us up dramatically.'

Plum ignored him. Moving to the rear of the schooner, she offered Gargantua a hand. Gargantua refused.

'No. It's okay,' she said.

The boards of the schooner creaked as she lowered herself down and the whole vehicle jumped up as her weight left it. She erected herself to her full height, pushing her hands into the small of her back to work out the cramp. She stood taller even than the schooner.

She stepped out of the robes she wore about her waist so that she was altogether naked. She regarded the last of The Messiah Caravan. Plum was the only one to meet her gaze. Cherry and Doctor Onabanjo just looked down into their laps. Peter remained on the driver's box in his rambling senility. Plum nodded at her. Gargantua opened her mouth as if to speak. Then she shrugged, turned, and disappeared into the night and the approaching storm.

'Is she gone?' called Peter.

'Aye,' said Doctor Onabanjo.

'Right. Good,' he said, whipping the horses onwards.

As they rolled out, Plum watched Gargantua diminish frame by frame before the strobing storm. She looked like something loosed from a fairy-tale, an ogre or golem, the last of its kind, cast out, itinerant.

*

The storm raged on behind them. Chased them. When lightning forked down, Plum could see monstrous dark columns of air twisting up to the sky. Thunder broke louder and louder and after the initial burst there would follow a great rolling wave of smaller explosions, like a cluster bomb. Then, all of a sudden, like turning on a shower, the rain came down in an unrelenting hiss.

Doctor Onabanjo beckoned to Plum and Cherry and they gathered around him.

'Here,' he said. 'It's time for another dose.'

He took a plastic pillbox from his leather satchel and shook out three pills into the palm of his hand.

'What about Peter?' said Cherry.

'He'll be okay for now.'

They each placed a pill on their tongue and swallowed.

Peter was shouting something but none of the passengers could discern him over the storm. The White Mountains of Santa Muerte loomed ahead, piercing the horizon like arrowheads whittled from bone. Still he drove them on. The wind battered the schooner, threatening to chuck it over sidewards. The awning was like a sail and at one point it caught the wind and shoved the schooner up onto two wheels. Everyone leapt to the side that was risen and managed to bring it down.

'Get that awning off,' cried Doctor Onabanjo.

They all set about undoing its lashings. But before they

could, something happened. Something altogether strange, unprecedented.

'What's that?' said Plum.

Cherry and the doctor could not hear her over the storm. Each continued fiddling with the ties. Out the rear of the schooner, what appeared to be a cannonball of white-blue fire had descended smoothly out of the heavens and was levitating towards them. It floated right up to the entrance of the schooner and Plum backed up against the awning to let it pass. It floated right over Cherry's back as he worked on the awning. It seemed drawn to the iron slave chains, which lay coiled at Doctor Onabanjo's feet.

'Doctor. Doctor!' said Plum.

Doctor Onabanjo stood and turned and found himself pinned against the far side of the wagon with the ball of fire between he and his compatriots.

'Get out,' said the doctor.

'But—'

'Get out!'

Plum and Cherry needed no third telling. They leapt from the schooner, hitting the hard ground feet-first and pitching into a roll. They looked up just in time to see the schooner explode in a supernova of platinum coloured electricity. They could only watch as the hysterical horses dragged the flaming wreckage off into the night.

GARGANTUA IN LATENCY

T he night was black as nothing at all and Gargantua wandered blind into the storm. The wind keening all about her, the rain stinging her face. With each flash of lightning, she was privy to the dancing of the clouds, terrific black vortexes that coiled up from ground to sky and swayed drunkenly like charmed snakes. And she walked between these titans with the utmost composure, as though this was indeed the fabled crossing she sought between the lands of the living and the dead.

A lightning bolt drew heavenly veins across the veiled firmament, illuminating a prodigious boulder ahead with an overhang that might provide a little cover. Gargantua nestled beneath it and listened to the rain, the rolling of thunder. Smelled the divine wetness of the earth. The night was warm, sultry. In time, she slept.

*

She awoke anew. The interminable anguish gnawing at every atom of her being, gone. She dozed, blinking her heavy eyelids at the resurrected morning, the leukaemia-white mountains in the distance before a wash of bubblegum sky. She crawled out from beneath the overhang like a lizard. The storm had passed over leaving behind great puddles on that impermeable wasteland which shimmered in the sun and made it look as though she were marooned on some silver sea.

'Maybe it wasn't as bad as all that,' she said, nodding in agreement with herself. 'Yes ma'am. I declare I feel rather fine indeed. And my, my, I sure do have an appetite!'

As she stretched in the golden heat of the sun, how was she to know she was in the latency of her illness, that her very DNA was irreparably compromised, decaying, that in only a few hours her cells would forget their function altogether and die outright, one by one?

Anyway, never mind that, for fate, or perhaps dumb luck—whichever you subscribe to, good reader—had fabricated her another death entire. For so continues the mortal pantomime. *It's behind you!*

There was a low rumbling that seemed to come from all about. She bellied it up onto the boulder to scan her surroundings and from her place of vantage she saw the devil. Three black 4x4s amidst a haze of rising rain. She must have stuck out like a sore thumb on that desolate waste for the automobiles shifted their trajectory and made straight for her.

She looked about for an egress but, of course, there was none to be had. The wasteland stretched flat and featureless all the way to the White Mountains, which were many miles away. She shimmied back down and crawled once more beneath the overhang, flattening herself against the furthest reaches of rock, so that she was completely banked in shadow.

*

'You're sure you saw someone?' said the devil.

'Yessir. Atop the boulder. They were there then gone, but I definitely sin'm.'

'So where are they?'

'I don't know.'

'Do you enjoy wasting my time?'

'No sir.'

'So you *are* wasting my time?'

'No sir! Like I said, I sin'm. I swear it.'

'Well then, get out there.'

'Yessir.'

The devil's man hesitated, his hand on the door handle.

'Well?' said the devil.

'Do I need go alone, sir? It's just… what I saw… it was big… real big… like a giant.'

'A giant?'

'Yessir?'

'A giant. Am I hearing you right?'

'Yessir.'

'There, there, now,' said the devil, leaning over and pawing the man's hair, whispering in his ear. 'Don't you be scared of giants. You just be scared of me and what I'm going to do to you if I find you are indeed wasting my time.'

'Yessir.'

The man alighted without further ado. The devil was shaking his head as he watched his man round the boulder and disappear. From his pocket, he drew his own pillbox of iodine-86 and tipped the whole thing against his pursed lips as though taking a drink. He caught the driver of the 4x4 watching him in the rear-view mirror. The driver quickly looked away.

'What the fuck are you looking at?' said the devil.

The driver did not answer.

'That's what I thought,' said the devil.

A full minute came and went, yet the man did not reappear.

'Curious,' said the devil.

'Sir? What should we do?' said the driver.

'I bet he's holed up back there wishing he'd never opened his idiotic mouth. Go get him. Tell him all is forgiven. Tell him all is forgiven and then kill him.'

'Yessir.'

The two remaining mercenaries alighted from the

devil's automobile and on their cue so did the eight split across the other two 4x4s. As a single mass, they approached the boulder.

That is when Gargantua came charging out to meet them.

In one hand she clutched the scout by the scruff, holding his limp body up as a shield, and in the other hand she held his machine gun. She opened fire, but she was a terrible shot. I guess you might call it spraying and praying. What is more, being so much taller than they, in many cases the bullets just whined over their heads. Still a few of those wayward slugs hit home. Three of the mercenaries crumpled. The rest returned fire, their comrade absorbing most of the barrage, twitching with each impact so that it looked like he was fitting.

She clattered among them like some drunken troll, swinging their comrade like a club, knocking over three of the devil's cronies in a single sweep. Dropping her weapons, she grabbed up two where they had fallen, one in each hand, and smashed them together and then dropped them and they remained pretzeled together in a crippled embrace. In the melee, a soldier discharged his shotgun, blowing a chunk out of her side and killing one of his comrades outright in the process. She rounded on him and seized his whole head in a single massive hand and shook him until he spasmed and died. Then one of the two remaining mercenaries closed in behind her and fired his shotgun into the small of her back and she was knocked onto her front where she lay snorting like a wounded rhino, the dust stuck to her bloodied lips. The soldier pumped his shotgun and stood astraddle her.

'Wait!' said the devil.

The man shouldered his shotgun. The devil crouched down to face Gargantua.

'Which way did they go?' he said.

She said nothing.

'Look. This storm has just about wiped out the trail.

You'd be doing me a favour.'

Still nothing.

'Fine. Be that way. Where did they go?'

With these words, the devil reached over and slotted his fingers into the shot holes in her back like she were a bowling ball. She rose up screaming and succeeded in grabbing him by the arm but the mercenary was quick with his shotgun and fired, making a cereal of her head. And that was that.

The devil rose, his arm swinging uselessly in its sleeve, his face quickly draining of all colour.

'Sir, sir, we must get you to a doctor,' said the mercenary.

'No,' said the devil. 'No. We carry on. We are close.'

THE GODKILLERS

P lum carved a way through the blackness and the
storm, dragging her hysterical father by the wrist
until they found themselves at the foot of the White
Mountains. Lightning flared and in that fleeting image
Plum distinguished a perfectly black disc situated against
the white of the rock. A cave. It was towards this she
made, feeling her way blindly, the rocks slick and jagged
against her hand. It was slow going on account of having
to test each perilous step before taking it. When finally
they reached the mountain face, waterfalls of rain fell upon
them in sheets as they sidled along it searching for the
opening. Then, all of a sudden, as she sidestepped and
pressed once more against the darkness, it consumed her.
She fell forwards into the cave, dragging her father in
along with her.

They lay panting in the perfect dark. The relentless rain
now a muffled drumming. Both of them were shivering,
freezing.

'Come here. We need to get warm,' said Cherry.

Plum ignored him and shimmied on her backside
further down the cave. She kicked off her waterlogged
boots. Peeling off her sodden clothes, she wrung them out

and spread them on the floor. Shuddering, she caught her legs up against her chest and tucked her head between her knees and rolled herself up tight as a hedgehog.

*

When she woke, the storm had passed and the sun was risen. The cave mouth hovered turquoise overhead. She tried to remember what had woke her. Then she heard it. Moaning, echoing up from deep within the cave. She retrieved the matches from her baccy tin and, sparking one, she proceeded down into the abyss.

'Hello,' she said.

'Help.'

'Hello.'

'Plum?'

The flame licked her fingers and she dropped the match. She struck another and a humanoid form swam into view, pallid as a cavefish.

It was Peter.

She knelt down beside him. He was lying on his back, naked, his head propped against his sodden robes. His breath weak, rasping. His chest swelling pronouncedly with each laboured intake. The skin above his heart fluttered. Terrible lesions had bubbled up all over his body, staining him a poisonous orange colour. He reeked of his own waste. He reeked of death.

'Plum, is that you?'

'Yes.'

'Praise be. Listen. Please listen. I had a vision last night. I know now who you really are. I know I have been wrong. So wrong. I am sorry. Help me, I beg you.'

'I can't help you.'

'Please.'

'There's no hope for any of us now.'

'Then kill me.'

Plum was silent.

'Please. I don't want to die like this.'

The flame grew hot and she blew it out and they were

dropped into blackness absolute.

'Kill me,' said Peter.

'No,' said Plum.

With that, she slunk away, back up towards the cave mouth. Peter's desperate voice followed her, echoing up out of the void.

'I'm sorry! I'm sorry!'

Her father was sitting by the opening.

'Whose down there?' he said as she appeared, clutching her clothes.

'Peter.'

'Ah. Is he… y'know?'

'Yes.'

'What should we do?'

'Nothing.'

Cherry was staring off into space. A tear rolled out the corner of his eye.

'He was my most trusted disciple,' he muttered to himself.

Though all was still, silent, he covered his ears with his hands and started to rock back and forth as though tormented by some incredible noise.

Plum spat and started pulling on her dungarees.

*

'Where are we going?' said Cherry.

'I don't know. Onwards. Upwards,' she said.

'Why. What's the point?'

Plum shrugged. Cherry stopped and leant against an outcrop of chalk.

'I'm sorry,' he said, panting, wafting his hand as though dismissing her. 'I'm not going any further. This is useless.'

'Fine,' said Plum, and without further ado she turned and walked off.

When first she looked back, he was still leant against the outcrop, his exhumed eyes fixed upon her. When next she looked back, he was clambering after her once more.

*

They muddled on through that labyrinth of white rock, disorientated, snow blind. The white sun directly overhead rebounding dizzily off the bleached mountainside. All of a sudden, Plum stopped.

'Listen,' she said.

They stood in silence.

'What is it?' said Cherry.

Plum held a finger to her lips. Her face had a gaunt nobility.

'Plum?'

'Water. It's water,' she said.

*

They meandered on through jutting pillars of chalk, which shot out of the ground at shonky angles like crooked teeth. At long last they rounded a bluff and discovered, rolling blackly off a chalk precipice, the beginnings of the river Muerte. The sound of the waterfall was thunderous. It cascaded down into a pool, which stretched outwards like a plate of obsidian before streaming over the lip of the pool and down the mountainside.

Plum and Cherry knelt beside it and in their desperate thirst they drank of that treacherous water which was itself the colour of ink. Slaked, they found shade beneath an overhang of chalk, the mountain hot against their backsides.

'What now?' said Cherry.

Plum got out her makings and built herself a cigarette. Her father gazed longingly as she struck a match and brought it to life. She then set about rolling another, which she placed on the rock beside her. She then rolled another. Then another. Each time placing it to the right of the last, like a tally.

'Plum.'

'What?'

'Can I get one?'

'No.'

'You can't expect to smoke all that toby before we die.'

'I might.'

'Please.'

'No.'

He reached over regardless and she slapped his hand away. He shrunk back against the rock, clutching his thin hand in the other, watching Plum with miserable eyes.

Once she had smoked her first cigarette all the way down, she placed a new one in her lips and lit it from the embers of the last. In this way, she idled away the afternoon.

*

As the hour grew late, the iodine-86 wore off and they were both of them plagued by terrible sickness. Cherry slunk off to empty his guts. Plum on the other hand just heaved it up there and then, whenever the nausea reared itself. Cherry returned to find his daughter covered in her own pink vomit. He said nothing. Just sat down beside her, a little apart. Plum leant her head against the rock and continued to draw on her chain of cigarettes.

'Can you see that, chaps? That.' came a voice from below.

'It looks like smoke,' said another.

'Come on, old sport. Give me a leg up.'

Cherry turned to Plum.

'Looks like we're rumbled.'

'Mm-hmm.'

'We should go.'

'You go. I'm alright here.'

Cherry nodded.

'Me too.'

A dark figure appeared over the crest of that white world. Then another who reached down and gave a hand up to a third. As they approached, their forms scintillated in the rising heat, blurred at the edges. They stopped before them. Plum found it hard to lift up her eyes. She rolled her head back against the rock.

'Huh?' she said.

The three visitants wore blue hazmat suits with black masks, black plastic tubes running from each mouthpiece round to equipment they carried on their backs.

'Who's the girl?' said one of them.

'You tell me, old sport,' said another.

It was impossible to know who was speaking for you could not see their mouths and their voices emerged crackling like a poorly tuned radio.

'Right, chaps, give me a hand.'

They all bent down and together they picked Cherry up off the floor. One opened his mouth and inserted a number of brightly coloured caplets. Another was on hand with a bottle of perfectly clear water, which Cherry sputtered on. Then they said, 'Right, let's go,' and they started dragging him away. Plum could only watch him go. She did not have the energy to move any more. She could not even raise the cigarette to her lips.

'No,' said Cherry. 'What about Plum? What about my daughter?'

'Daughter?'

The three figures exchanged glances behind their masks. Then one broke off, returned, and knelt before Plum.

'I am sorry, old sport,' came that same crackly, robotic voice. 'We are unable to provide you with transit.'

'Listen to me,' heaved Plum.

'Yes, old sport?'

'There are children… at the Rivers of Paradise… the casino there… they need your help.'

'Ah! I'm afraid there are children everywhere and all in dire need, old sport.'

'But—'

'No, I'm afraid we're of no help to you there.'

'I don't understand.'

'You see, we… we are the godkillers.'

'I don't understand.'

'Yes. Terribly la-di-da I know. Still.'

'I don't understand.'

'I see. You are thinking, *If you are the godkillers, why not leave him here to die?* You see, old sport, the man is not god. God is in the mind. We aim to use this man—your father—to rid the world of its malady.'

'I don't understand.'

'Well you see, old sport, your father has shown an unprecedented capacity to influence others. We will show him the truth. Then he will bring the truth to others.'

'I don't understand.'

'Yes. I appreciate it must be awfully confusing, old sport. Alas! I fear we owe you an apology. You see that funny old chap that called himself the devil of New Sodom was our first foray. Unfortunately, he was interrupted mid-regression. Terrible shame. That is what set this bizarre chain of events in motion.'

'I don't understand.'

'You see, old sport, we subject the patient to an extended course of Dimethyltryptamine. We include the essential vitamins and proteins in the solution of course to keep them nourished. We then tailor their surroundings to optimise an uninterrupted period of self-reflection where they will inevitably arrive at the truth.'

'I don't understand.'

'Yes I know. *Very* unfortunate we were interrupted first time around. The patient was proving rather receptive as well. More than we could have hoped.'

'I don't understand.'

'I'm not surprised, old sport. It must all be rather a big shock, mustn't it? Still we must be going now.'

The person in the hazmat suit rose and started backing away.

'I don't understand.'

'Yes. Hate to do this to you, old sport, but we really must be going.'

The godkiller addressing her was lowering her father

down to its comrades.

'Plum! Plum!' cried her father.

'You got him? I'm going to let go now. Well done, chaps.'

'I don't understand.'

'Yes, yes. Dreadful business,' said the godkiller over its shoulder. 'What a perfect mess indeed.'

Then he shimmied down off the lip of the ridge and disappeared from sight.

THE OUTSTANDING DEBT OF SOUL, REPAID

She walked abroad in that pale wasteland and by and by she came to an assembly of the dead… and she saw it was The Messiah Caravan… for there was Hiroshi… and there was Gargantua… and Doctor Onabanjo… and Peter… and they were all of them bent low before an acacia tree, begging forgiveness… and the tree was consumed by fire but was not affected by the fire for she could see its bright yellow blossoms through the flames… and the tree had a voice… and the tree was crying… and the tree was crying:

No! No! It was meant to be her. Not him. Her. She was mine. She was mine and I gave her to you. I gave her to you. I gave her to you and she was mine. Mine to hazard. Mine to hazard. I gambled her away! Forgive me. Forgive me, my love. Why? Why did you renounce her? How? How could you nominate him instead? Him. The charlatan. When it was not him. It was her. Always her. Are you blind? It was self-evident. She was the strength. The courage. The wisdom. The kindness. She was the storm. The calm before and after. It was her. Always her. What have you done?

And Plum stood before the flames and called out to the

acacia.

Don't cry, mama, she said.

Then she woke up.

*

When she came to, the red sun was setting on the White Mountains, colouring the chalk a flamingo pink. The latency of Plum's illness was swift, barely the length of a cigarette, but she used this fleeting improvement of health to drag herself out from under the overhang and bathe in the final swells of crimson sunlight. Toxic fissures lined her tender skin from her body's seismic revolt. As she lay on her back, the cigarette burned out between her fingers and she noticed the smell of her singed flesh before she discerned the pain as separate from the rest racking her body. She looked down at her hand, the thin wisp of smoke rising from between her fingers. Then she lay her head back against the mountain and exhaled, her whole interior rattling as though something vital within her was now detached.

It was in this wretched state the devil came to her.

She heard him cursing his way up the mountain. Then his squashed up little face appeared overhead, blocking out the rose-coloured sky. He wore his shirt tied about his neck as a sling for his crippled arm and his round, pale belly was piglet pink in the light of the dying day. He was alone. The last of his mercenaries having succumbed to the silent havoc of that place.

'So,' said the devil. 'Here we are. At long last.'

He crouched down on his haunches beside her.

'Look at you,' he said. 'You are no prize.' He sniffed the air. 'Have you shit yourself? Yes, it would appear you have.'

Plum just watched him, her eyes all pupil. She was shivering.

'This is not how I thought it would be. Still.'

He unsheathed the stonking great bowie knife that hung at his waist and dangled it above her. Her eyes twitched from the devil to the blade and back again.

'I just wish I understood… why my brother did what he done… why he left me. Can you tell me this? If you tell me this I promise I will make it quick.'

Plum opened her mouth but no words came out. The devil shook his head.

'Yes. Why would you know? And yet, this is why I am here. Of course it is. Why else would I follow you where none return?'

Something caught his attention. The waterfall.

'Surely not,' he said. 'Be this the place of Martha's retribution also? How fabulous. Another man might find meaning in that.'

He regarded her once more.

'I am going to take a look. Then… Then I will cut out your heart.'

He stood and walked away. Plum watched him climb a set of rocks that wound up perfectly like a staircase and disappear behind the black sheet of water. His lofty voice carried to her over the roar of the falls. He wanted her to hear.

'Why it is! This is indeed the place where Martha had her revenge. How fitting. And what is this? Oh Martha, you told me you went easy on them!'

The devil reappeared from behind the black curtain of water and stepped down the rocks. He was shaking his head and grinning, his green eyes wide, malevolent.

'Oh Martha, I feel inspired!' he cried.

Plum tried to move but her body did not work anymore. She could only watch the devil approach, his pale form growing until his reflection filled all her black eyes, the huge bowie knife in his hand coloured menstrual in the failing light. He knelt beside her and raised the knife as if it were a sacrificial rite.

'Brother, I do this for you,' he said to the indifferent sky.

He looked down at her. All teeth and eyes. Slavering.

Evil. Desperate.

'Lucien!'

The devil looked up.

'Martha. Wait—'

Two shots rang out, fired so close together that they could have been one, and the devil's head exploded in a spiral of brain and skull-bone, leaving only his tongue and lower jaw atop his neck, his bottom teeth jutting up all crooked against the sky. The body continued to kneel and a vaporous red drizzle hissed out of the stump, speckling Plum where she lay. She tried to blink away the blood but it fell relentlessly until it blotted out the world entire and then it was in her mouth and she could taste the devil's corrupt vitality. His cadaver then pitched over and lay next to her, his arm falling over her like they were intimates. The blood, dark and terminal, deluged out of the neck and Plum could feel it, warm and sticky, soaking into her clothes and hair.

Martha holstered her pistol and dragged the devil off her and then carried Plum to the edge of the pool where she rinsed the blood from her eyes with the black water of the River Muerte. Plum looked up at her, blinking, coughing.

'Where you been?' rasped Plum, but a coughing fit wiped the grin off her face.

'Hush now,' said Martha, placing her cool, leathery palm against Plum's forehead.

Plum looked up at Martha with black, glittering eyes, and steadied her grating breath. When she blinked, tears rolled down her face.

'Don't worry,' said Martha, 'It's nearly over.'

Plum gave a weak, faltering smile. Martha stroked her hair.

'Does it hurt?'

Plum nodded.

'I can end it, if that's what you want.'

Plum hesitated. Then she shook her head almost

imperceptibly.

'No.' she choked. 'Not yet.'

'Okay.'

'Martha.'

'Hush now, child.'

'No. Mar—' she broke off spluttering.

'Okay, Plum, if it must be said, calm yourself and say it.'

Plum steadied herself once more.

'Attila,' she gasped. 'Attila.'

'What's that palooka got to do with things?'

'Kiddies, Martha. My daddy sold him the kiddies.'

Martha sighed.

'What happened, Plum?' she said.

Plum shrugged and scrunched up her eyes and cried fresh tears. Martha placed a hand on her cheek.

'Hush now, little one. Don't worry. I'll see them free.'

'I'm sorry, Martha,' moaned Plum. 'I'm real sorry.'

'Don't you go apologising for your daddy's mistakes now.'

'I tried to do good. I swear I tried.'

'I know you did. I know you did.'

'Make it go away, Martha.'

Martha nodded and hugged that little ragdoll of a girl up in her arms and drew the revolver from its holster.

'I'm sorry,' whispered Martha, as she pressed the cold bore against her chest.

'Hey, Bo. Is it time?' said Plum. Her voice was like an echo of words uttered far, far away.

'What's that?' said Martha, looking at her, blinking in disbelief.

'Bo's here,' said Plum. 'Look.'

It was all Plum could do to lift a finger. Martha turned. There was nothing there but sky.

'You see him? Plum, you can see him?'

'Yeah, course I see him.'

'Then you tell him… You tell him his mama loves him.'

'He hears you.'

Martha enveloped the girl and squeezed her to her chest, half-moaning, half-laughing.

'You two play nice, you hear!' she cried, and she thumbed back the hammer and fired.

The shot rang out like thunder on that barren mountainside and a rose flowered sluggishly over the child's heart. Her blood was slow, cold, as though she was long dead. Looking down, Martha saw herself reflected in the marble eyes of the child. Then her likeness evanesced and there were two children running through an open door, a cornfield swaying before them. She placed her hand over the child's eyes for the image was too much to bear.

And like that, Plum was gone. The voyage of her transient mind now charted through space and fixed in time. Her body now an asset of the earth—like rock, like river—but also a temple of the human, in memory of a chance, a chance of something wonderful, a chance of something wonderful gone by.

THE END

ABOUT THE AUTHOR

Rick Hughes

Did you enjoy this book?

If you did, please leave an Amazon review.

If you'd like to discuss the book (or writing in general), I'd love to hear from you. You can contact me via Facebook or by email:

Facebook: www.facebook.com/RickHughesAuthor
Email: rickhughesauthor@gmail.com

ACKNOWLEDGMENT

The author would like to thank John Bowen, author of the bestselling *Where the Dead Walk*, for the fantastic book cover he designed and his invaluable guidance and support.

Cheers mate.

Printed in Great Britain
by Amazon